Praise for

# MARILYNN GRIFFITH

### and her novels

"With a voice that begs you to relax, sit down and put your feet up, Marilynn Griffith writes of the complexities of love, family, friendship and what it means to be the bride of Christ and does so with honesty, humor and grace."
—Lisa Samson, Christy Award–winning author

"The characters and their spiritual insights wrap around the soul like a comfortable blanket."
—*Romantic Times BOOKreviews* on
*If the Shoe Fits*

"Marilynn Griffith's voice just sings! Watch out, world, *Made of Honor* will make you laugh out loud and welcome you into the Sassy Sistahood."
—Kristin Billerbeck, bestselling author of
*Back to Life*

"With honesty and humor, Marilynn Griffith takes you on a poignant journey through the pages of life—yours or someone you know. *Made of Honor* is a spellbinding tale about the power of love between family and friends, with one's romantic soul mate, and from the Lover of our souls."
—Stacy Hawkins Adams, bestselling author of
*Speak to My Heart.*

## Books by Marilynn Griffith

Steeple Hill Single Title

*Made of Honor*
*If the Shoe Fits*
*Happily Even After*
*Mom's the Word*

# MARILYNN GRIFFITH

## Mom's the Word

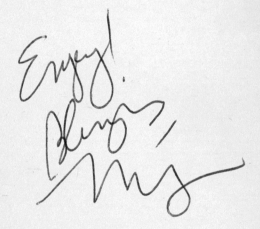

Steeple Hill®

Published by Steeple Hill Books™

STEEPLE HILL BOOKS

Steeple
Hill®

Recycling programs
for this product may
not exist in your area.

ISBN-13: 978-0-373-78641-1
ISBN-10:    0-373-78641-7

MOM'S THE WORD

www.SteepleHill.com

**Printed in U.S.A.**

For Joy and Melissa. Though you are now far away, your hearts are always with me. Thanks for everything you taught me about being a mom.

# Mom's the Word

# *They Come Softly*

They come softly, like the kiss of
newborn skin. Words, brushing my
Heels as I head for the kitchen, bruising my
Heart as life reaches for my hand.

Stirring the morning against my
Belly, I listen as they sift through my
Fingers, stories I've never heard,
Places I've never known.

Pouring into the pitcher of my
Day, they blow by. I open my
Hand, trying to catch a phrase,
To hold what cannot be held.

Love beckons, Purpose calls,
Drowning out the whisper words
Skating, out of place like fall leaves
Across the summer of my soul.

Truth swallows Hope, drowns the
Words. I squint against the glare
Of throaty screams and scarred
Earth, listening, wondering
If they'll ever come again.

—Karol
The morning the new neighbors moved in

## Chapter One

"They're ruining everything." The words tangled in Karol Simon's throat as she watched in horror as a backhoe bit into the tree house she and her family had constructed with their former neighbors and best friends Hope and Singh. The rest of the yard, including Hope's prize-winning roses and the strawberry bush the children had planted, lay in heaped mounds of roots and blooms.

To Karol, it looked a lot like her life.

Her tears, few at first, now streamed down her face as she watched butterflies and birds flee into her yard to escape the destruction of their homes and so many of Karol's memories. She wanted to run to her husband, to collapse into his arms… Instead, she pulled the curtain back farther, using it to wipe her tears. "It looks like a cemetery," she said without turning around, certain Rob wasn't listening.

He was. "Get away from the window, Kay. It's rude for one thing. It's depressing for another. Do you think I don't know how much you miss Hope? I miss Singh, too. But the Lord led them to another place, to another job, to other—"

She held up a hand. "Don't say it."

"I will say it. To other friends. Hope and Singh are going

to find new friends. A new church. A new life in North Carolina. That doesn't mean they'll forget us here in Tallahassee. It's just a chance to share them with someone else."

Rob laid aside his Linux Pocket Guide and stood. Four strides brought him to the window. His weekend work boots struck the floor with the same confidence she heard in his voice. Not so long ago, Karol had heard the same assurance in her own voice. Was she the same woman who'd once run Vacation Bible School and the women's ministry committee? These days the only running she did was from herself…and from God. She'd expected to miss Hope, to be sad for a little while, but this was more than that.

Karol needed her.

She hadn't realized how much her friend helped her be a good mom, a good wife. Hope had a houseful of children, seven in all, and taught her children at home. She'd taught Karol a lot about being a mother and being a friend.

Now that the crew next door had moved away, though, Karol couldn't just pick up the phone and call. Their busy schooling schedule had been easier to interrupt when it only meant walking next door and waiting for a break in the action. Now when Karol called, she got the answering machine indicating the family's school hours. In the evenings, Hope was tired with moving in at first and then Karol started to unravel and didn't want to call and detail her failures. She called her friend less and less these days and seemed to lose it more and more. And her husband was starting to notice.

That was the part that made her heart pound as Rob took her hand. Her pulse quickened, too, both in anticipation and fear. Things had grown awkward between them. Rusty. She wasn't ready to deal with him quite yet, though lemon Pledge and sawdust were a hard combination to ignore.

He knew it, too. Rob stood close behind her, running his hands over hers until she released the curtain. He brushed away her last tear with his thumb before lacing his arms around her waist. She closed her eyes as his stubbled face prickled against her smooth one, waiting for the kiss that was sure to come. It'd be a soft one, right in the curve of her neck most likely. Even after three kids, he still knew how to buckle her knees.

He kissed her ear instead, first with his lips and then with a whisper. "I know this is hard, honey. We all knew it would be. I get up every morning and reach for the phone to call Singh to pray or to borrow a tool from him, only to realize he's gone. I know it's even deeper with you and Hope, but maybe God has a purpose in this, for us as well as them.

"We'll see them soon enough. Charlotte isn't that far away. They mentioned coming down for Ryan's birthday, remember? And we're taking Mia over for hers and Eden's party next month. Until then, I figure we can work on some things between us—you and I. For starters, I was thinking that maybe I could be your best friend again."

Karol swallowed hard and closed her eyes, drinking in this closeness with her husband. There had been a time before, when Hope and Karol had been close, but she and Rob had been closer. He had been her world. Then storms came and shook their little marriage tree, blowing away some of the blossoms, shaking off much of the fruit.

Hope had helped her push things down in the soil again, prayer by prayer, day by day. Now Karol would have to do that alone. Rob wanted to help, to be friends, but there were things that she used to tell Hope that she just couldn't say to her husband. What would he do if he knew that sometimes she didn't like her life or herself? What would he think if he knew that sometimes she just wanted to run away?

*He'd think that you're human, Karol. He is, too.*

When women from church had come to Karol for advice about their marriages, she'd reminded them that they'd married sinners, broken people who continued to need forgiveness once the honeymoon was over. It had all made so much sense to her back then, until the stitches on her own marriage had loosened. Before then, she'd never understood those couples who disappeared and showed up with other spouses, the ones who lived in the same houses but drove to service in separate cars.

Those were the couples who had once been friends with Karol and Rob, part of the couples ministry that had met at Hope and Singh's. One by one, those couples had disappeared: divorced, separated, moved away. They had discovered, as Karol had, that family came at a cost, that love required effort.

Rob kissed the top of her ear again and tightened his hands around her. She rested back against him and wondered if he wasn't trying to get her to hear him. To really listen. Sometimes that was so hard to do, even though Karol tried.

She was blessed to be this man's wife, the mother of his children. And now here she was, coming undone over new neighbors. Once more, she lifted her hand to the curtains, a green gingham set Hope had taught her to make during the months after Mia was born, the summer of darkness. At the thought of those hard days, her worst postpartum depression ever, Karol let the fabric fall from her fingers. Nothing was worth going back there.

Her husband ran a hand through her hair. "I mean it. I want to be your best friend."

She turned to face Rob, trying to ignore the creaking sound as the tree house toppled to the ground next door. Would these strangers burn the wood they'd all signed and decorated, or should she go over and beg for it? No, it was their house now. She had to let it go. All of it.

Karol tried to laugh but it came out more like a groan. She punched Rob's shoulder lightly, then squeezed it.

"You are my best friend, silly. You're just not acting like it. Hope wouldn't take their side against me."

Rob's dimples appeared, but his eyes went dull. She'd chosen to stay on the surface of things, skimming across the hurt he wanted to dive into. He joined her in the chitchat with a reluctant smile. "Whose side? The new neighbors'? Or the kids'?"

"Both." Karol stared at him, once again wondering how he'd ended up with her. He had a careless beauty about him, a bearing that made him look like a king in a pair of jeans. Three kids had moved her body parts to new zip codes and left her face looking more like her mother's than she wanted to admit. Except for the sprinkles of gray in Rob's beard, he looked the same as the day they'd wed. Unless you looked closely at the years in his eyes, he didn't look much different from the husband of the young couple who'd moved in next door. Was this how the two of them had seemed to Hope and Singh? She peered through the window again, trying to convince herself otherwise.

The woman, "Dianne with a y" as Hope called her, shouted over the noise for the men to dig up a shrub they'd missed. No, she and Rob hadn't been quite like this. This was a new kind of crazy. And from the way things were going in her own house, it must be contagious. "The kids are definitely out of control. It seems like they're screaming at me every minute now. Like they've totally forgotten how to communicate."

Rob's look conveyed his thoughts but he voiced them anyway. "Maybe *we've* forgotten how to communicate, hon. Things have been hard lately. They lost their best friends, too. There's no one to play with. Naturally they're going to be a little out of sync."

Out of sync? "Judah tried to put Mia in the dryer yesterday, Rob. Ryan hid in the closet reading a book so that he didn't have to deal with them during the whole ordeal. When they found him, he shut them in there!

"They are more than out of sync. And don't start with that 'we've forgotten how to communicate' stuff. I know what you really mean. You mean I've forgotten how to communicate."

Rob scratched his head. "I didn't mean that, but since you mentioned it—you have been screaming quite a bit lately. It seems like we're going back in time. I have to catch myself. Yesterday, I almost started screaming, too."

Karol rolled her eyes. *As if.* "You did not."

More dimples. "Okay, so I didn't, but I thought about it. Anyway, I am on your side, both with the kids and with the neighbors. I just don't think you're seeing the big picture right now because you're hurting over losing Hope. Singh got a good opportunity there. He prayed about it and chose, with Hope, to make this move. Don't forget that. We will get through this. I'd rather come out of it with a good relationship with our kids…and our neighbors."

Karol couldn't help being stung by the truth in Rob's words. The move had been unexpected, a near-parallel offer for Singh with a possibility of advancement. A slim possibility. And yet, Hope hadn't thought twice about leaving her behind. It was right, of course. Singh was her husband. Hope's only hesitation had been the house. None of them had believed that it would sell—for so much and so quickly. It was a deal they couldn't refuse. A God thing. And yet, Karol couldn't help feeling as though someone had ripped the rug out from under her.

*More like the security blanket.*

"You want to have a good relationship with those two? Even if they're insane? I mean look at them." She pointed out the window. "They're so…so…"

Rob planted his chin on her shoulder. "What? Young?"

"Skinny!" Karol said, louder than she'd meant to. Was the window still cracked from airing out the living room after Mia's pull-up explosion this morning? Surely not. Her husband chuckled and she laughed, too, in spite of her efforts not to. "I'm serious. They're skinny and young and weird and they have no kids."

"We were skinny and young and weird and when we moved in next to Hope and Singh, Kay."

"I was never skinny," Karol said, taking a deep breath.

"Thank God," her husband whispered, slipping a hand in her back pocket. "But I was definitely weird. Remember how I slammed the door on Singh that first time he came over?"

"Well, in your defense, not many people serenade their new neighbors…especially people who are tone-deaf. If he'd just handed you the pie, things would have gone much smoother." Her words slowed as her new neighbor, dressed in a celery-colored suit and tangerine pumps, tripped over the woodpile Singh had kindly left behind. "Dianne with a y" stared down at the timber in confusion and shook her head before motioning for someone to cart it away.

Karol shook her head, too. "Okay, so we were a little goofy at first, but these people are unbelievable. She looked at that woodpile like it was going to come alive and eat her. Surely she saw the woodstove when they bought the house. It's one of the best features."

Rob stroked her hair. "It's not Hope's house anymore. Let it go, Mom."

Mom. It'd been funny when Rob first started calling her that, but now it'd worn thin. She'd started it first of course by calling Rob *Dad,* only to abandon it when he returned the favor. Where had she gotten that from anyway? She closed her eyes.

Hope and Singh.

It fit them. It didn't fit Karol. She wanted, needed, a name again. "I'm trying, Rob." His name rolled off her tongue before she could call it back, say it better. Say it the way she used to, in the sweet, husky tone he loved. Instead, it came out nasal and high pitched, almost as piercing as the cry from upstairs.

He gave her a funny look and lifted his head as if he were going to ask her something before their youngest child and only girl, Mia, let out one of her signature siren screams.

"Moooooooooooooom!"

Karol pinched her eyes shut. Her four-going-on-fifty-year old was either going to be an opera singer or a very good referee. Either way, naptime was over. Not that it had ever started really, but after little Mia's poopy finger painting incident this morning and five-year-old Judah's egg juggling at lunch "—I thought they were boiled!—" her three children, especially the oldest, who only liked to encounter body fluids on the page, had gladly escaped to their rooms.

Now they were up and ready to roll and she'd been too busy staring at the mess next door to get together an activity for them. After a morning of Saturday cartoons, Karol liked to keep the TV off in the afternoons. Until lately, anyway.

Her oldest son, Ryan, must have been thinking the same thing because he switched off the TV and started reading his younger brother and sister a story. Though only a few weeks shy of his eleventh birthday, Ryan had an old soul. His younger brother and sister drove him crazy and often interrupted the book he always seemed to be reading, but Ryan always knew what everyone needed—especially Karol. She mouthed a thank-you to him. He replied with a curt nod, which meant she'd probably have to make it up to him with brownies.

Karol wrapped an arm around her husband's, bare to the elbow and hairy as ever. Her mother called him Sasquatch. To his face. She was not always a kind woman. Karol thanked God that Rob was a kind man. Too kind sometimes. She pinched her eyes tight, shutting out her new neighbors, her old memories and the sound of her two youngest children tumbling down the stairs.

"I've got it, Mom," Ryan said quietly, still holding the book as he collected the two gymnasts. "Keep talking. Nobody's hurt."

Karol was headed to check anyway, but Rob pulled her back. "Ryan wants to grow up a little. Let him. Besides, you need a break. I'll go and take them all out in a few minutes."

"I don't deserve you," she whispered into Rob's shoulder.

He lifted her chin and leaned in, finding Karol's lips this time. The brevity and passion of the kiss took her by surprise. Rob's love was like that: quiet, but powerful, coming alive when she least expected it. When she most needed it. "You *don't* deserve me, Kay. You deserve better."

She slumped against him, never knowing what to say when he was like this. When life was like this. Paint rubbed off on her arm as she twined her hands behind his neck. Her eyes narrowed, first at her husband and then at the window. She'd repainted enough kid-dingy walls to know white washable paint when she saw it. This wasn't it. It was ecru or eggshell or some other froufrou color. A color for city people who bull-dozed yards and ran off friends… "Are you helping them?"

Rob didn't answer. He shrugged instead. Inwardly, Karol did, too. He could only be who he was, her husband. He didn't know how to be anything but giving and kind.

*I wish I could say the same for myself.*

Right now, Karol wasn't sure who she was. Her middle son was glad to clear that up for her.

"Mom!" A pair of hands slipped between the two of them, adhering to the front of Karol's shirt. The very front. Though she'd weaned her son Judah years before, he still seemed to find a use for the parts which had once fed him. The current choice? Doorknobs into Mommy world. Very effective, Karol had to admit. She worried, though, that he didn't pay attention to where his hands went sometimes.

Rob peeled his son from Karol's shirt and lifted him into his arms. "Judah, don't touch your mother there, okay? And go wash your hands—"

"But, Dad—"

"No buts, son. Mom and I were talking. Use your manners." He winked at Karol and took one step before the next child, little Mia, barreled into the room, wearing her bathing suit from last summer. Hadn't they given that to Eden, Hope's youngest girl, before they moved away?

"Moooooom! Judah 'it me!"

Both adults stared at the oldest brother, Ryan, who'd just entered the room, hoping for a translation of their only daughter's language. Only he knew this latest version of Mia-latin. She removed the first consonant of all incriminating words. In this case, the first sound meant a big difference. While hitting his little sister was enough to get Judah into a mess, biting her would be even worse.

Karol rubbed her arm thinking of how bad his biting had been when he was a toddler. Hope had helped her through that, too. Her middle child hadn't bit anyone in three full years now, and she prayed that losing his friends wouldn't start him up again.

Ryan's translation skills didn't disappoint, but their budding young man looked plenty frustrated. Sharing a room with his little brother was "stagnating" or at least that was the latest update he'd given Karol and Rob before putting his little brother's things into the hall to make room for his books. Puberty came a lot earlier these days, evidently.

"She said hit not bit. But, Mom—"

A banging sound echoed from down the hall. Karol and Rob looked at each other and at Ryan with panic in their eyes. Judah unattended usually meant disaster.

Rob moved first. "Where did he go to wash his hands? Bathroom?"

Karol screamed. "Kitchen!"

If there was ever a sure way to catch up with the plumber, it was Judah alone in the kitchen. Karol picked up Mia, taking a wide step to leave room for Rob, who ran to check the bathrooms just in case Judah was clogging some fixture instead of scrambling eggs on the kitchen floor.

Just the thought of what might be happening made Karol's heart pound. She wanted to scream at him so loudly that the people next door would hear and run away screaming, too. But inside her head, Hope was there, as sure as if she was sitting on that battered couch in the corner.

*Man's anger doesn't achieve the righteousness of God, Kay. A mother's anger doesn't accomplish much, either. You have the authority. Use it wisely. Don't waste it screaming.*

Another tear salted the corner of Karol's eye and she rounded the corner in time to catch a glimpse of Judah's superhero cape fluttering away from the scene of the crime. Karol tucked her daughter under one arm like a football and headed for the kitchen. Her socks glided across the laminate and into a pile of…hamburger, the meat for the church potluck. Rob ran into Judah in the hall and grabbed him up just as he was about to take a bite of meat that he'd taken as a souvenir.

Karol froze, unable to do anything but stare as she calculated the cost of the food her son had fed to the floor.

*And just when I'd splurged on the grain fed beef too.*

The perpetrator returned. "Mom! See my burger? My burger!" Judah cried, wiggling in his father's arms and pointing to the bloody mound on the floor.

Karol paused, looking into Rob's eyes, the same eyes she'd looked into on her wedding day and she could swim in their chocolate depths forever. Back then, love meant flowers and candy. Now it meant capture and cleanup. Lines etched those eyes now and a frost of wisdom sprinkled Rob's beard, but he'd never looked better to her.

"Do you want to deal with meat or munchkins?" he asked.

*Neither. Today, I just want to sit down in the corner and have a quiet talk with my friend.*

Karol smiled. Outwardly, anyway. The never-ending discipline that Judah seemed to require wore her out. She'd let Rob be the bad guy today. "I'll take hamburger. And let's blow up the pool. I know they're used to being outside all summer. I have to go outside some time."

Something like sunshine spread over Rob's face. He slapped the back of her jeans. "That's my girl."

Judah made a gagging sound and ran ahead of his dad up the stairs. "Cover your eyes, Mia, they're gonna kiss!"

"Ewwww!" Mia said before shielding his face from such horror.

Ryan pulled a book from the pocket of his cargo shorts and walked away from all of them. He probably wouldn't surface until dinner, when he'd have started another book with a similar cover—dragons and swords—but a different name. Every now and then he showed up with a book of theology or philosophy, which probably worried Karol more than the dragons. Ryan was growing up too fast. They all were. And she wasn't keeping pace with them.

As Rob's lips met hers in a fake kiss just to freak out the kids, Karol laughed softly. Laughing was definitely better than crying.

Rob gave her a wink that meant the real kisses would come later. She watched as he left the kitchen and started toward the stairs. He stopped halfway and turned back. "I know this is hard, Kay. But it's going to be all right. Really. I just feel it in my gut."

What gut? Any knowledge held in Rob's six-pack was less than reassuring. If there'd been a feeling in Karol's nonexistent abs, that might really be something. It'd be hard to locate, but it'd be something. Still, she knew he meant well and was probably right. He usually was.

"You're right, honey," she said, reaching for a trash bag and hoping that what he'd said was true. Anything could happen. The new neighbors might even turn out okay.

Probably not.

Not for Karol anyway. For Rob, well, everything would be fine. He'd already gotten over losing Singh as though he'd barely known the man. Sure the two of them were better about e-mail—Hope wasn't much of a computer person—but still the two men didn't talk anywhere near as much as they once had. The kids still asked for Heidi-Katie-Lizzie-Tony-Aaron-Annie-Eden-and-Bone-the-dog at least once a day, but their pleas were much less urgent. They'd be fine, too.

Karol might not be fine, she was starting to realize as the manic mama feelings tumbled in her stomach. There was none of Rob's confidence to settle it. The clump of ground beef slid easily into the bag, but scrubbing the floor proved harder. Everything seemed harder. Had the past ten years been a dream? Had she ever had Hope's consistency or Rob's calmness? She'd thought so until the moving van took her best friend away. Could she be a good mom without Hope?

The question that sprang from her heart in response took Karol's breath away:

*The question is, can you be a good mom without Me?*

The ceiling fan whirred above Rob slowly, breathing the first breath of summer into his upstairs bedroom. Though it was only April by the calendar, summer was always a breath away in Tallahassee, drowned only by the rains that began in October and trickled through spring. The bright, hot victory of summer retaking her throne usually happened on a May morning, but on this night in late April, Rob felt the humidity that signaled the rise of the order of the sun.

Usually, he welcomed summer. It meant more time outdoors with fresh earth and the soft, brown skin of his wife and children. In the northern Florida sun—which often seemed to have the red, patient glow of the peachy rays of southern Georgia—nothing could be hidden or covered up. In the end, sweat and sweet tea trickled into everything, seeping between the finest fabrics, the best of plans. By summer's end, there was never anything left unknown.

Not without a price.

As Rob slipped from his king-size bed and stepped onto the still-cool cherrywood floor that he'd installed with his own hands, he wondered if the price would not turn out to be higher than his marriage could afford to pay.

He took the phone into the bathroom, thankful that Karol slept like a log, especially on hot nights like this with the smell of crepe myrtle syrupy and sweet in the air. For once, though, he almost wished she'd wake up and overhear his conversation, saving him from being torn between his best friend…and the love of his life.

Rob's fingers eased quickly over the phone's keypad. Though his friend had been gone for weeks now, Singh's cell phone number still stuck in Rob's head like a familiar song.

Singh picked up on the first ring, probably in his bathroom, too. "Hello? Rob?"

A sigh. "It's me. Did you tell her yet? Hope, I mean?"

His friend didn't answer which was an answer in itself.

"You're killing me here, man. Kaye is going crazy. Today was really rough. On the kids, too. Weekends are the worst. At least they have school now, but that's only for another month and Mia's here all the time—"

"Forgive me."

The words made Rob swallow hard. How many times had he called this number and said the same phrase in the past ten years? He and Singh were prayer partners, accountable to one another in their walk with God, their actions as fathers and husbands. So many times they'd both fallen short of being the men they wanted to be, but one of them had always been there to hear, to believe, to pray.

When the tables turned a few years ago and Singh was the one calling Rob asking for prayer, it had been strange at first. Though theirs had been a great friendship, Rob had always felt himself to be the student and Singh the teacher. He'd had to address his own sin of holding Singh up to a standard of perfection no man could meet. It hadn't been easy to get over, though, and sometimes Rob still wondered if he wasn't harder on Singh than he might have been toward some stranger who'd walked into the men's ministry group asking for prayer. And yet, those two words—forgive me—reminded Rob of his own humanity and weakness. He was no better than his friend. No better at all.

*Forgive me, Lord,* Rob whispered in his heart. *Forgive us all.*

"All is forgiven, brother. I love you. I'm just worried that this is going to turn bad for both of us if we don't do what we agreed upon. We were both supposed to tell our wives by now. True enough, you have more to tell and it won't be easy, but we both know it has to be done."

"Yes."

More than a minute went by without speaking, but Rob wasn't worried. He knew that Singh was praying. He was, too.

Karol stirred in the next room.

"I'm going to have to go, man."

"Yes. Me, too. Quickly, though. How is it with the neighbors? The man, Neal? I know that the girls are worried about the wife, but I had a good feeling about him. Both of them. The same feeling I had when the two of you came."

In the dark of the bathroom, Rob nodded to himself. Though the new neighbors weren't very friendly, and his wife wasn't very fond of them, he had a feeling that somehow they would all end up as friends. What worried him was the future of their relationship with Hope and Singh.

"I hope we did the right thing."

Singh grunted in agreement. "As do I."

## *To-Do*

- Map a jog route

- Consult with landscapers about new yard design

- Order new stove

- Find a hairstylist

- E-mail author press kits to Julie for the Fall tours

- Find another person to travel with us on the Fallon Gray tour (in case I'm pregnant) ☺

- Check with *Publishers Weekly* on faith fiction showcase

- Get PDA repaired and order a backup

- Order Neal's supplements online—look for local supplier—not budgeted!

- Call sorority regional office to see about getting Fallon a table at national conference

- Talk to neighbors about toys in their backyard—fence options

- Get pregnant!

—Dyanne, Move-in day

# Chapter Two

"I still can't believe he came over to help." Dyanne stared out her side window, watching her new neighbor, Rob, amble back to his house, head high and smiling after helping them paint for the second day. Was he whistling?

*Gimme a break.*

"Look at him, Neal. I'm expecting him to start skipping any minute. He's like the black version of Pa from *Little House on the Prairie.*" She shook her head and moved away from the window. Moving back to Tallahassee, Florida, where the two of them had attended the prestigious business school at Florida A & M University, had been Dyanne's idea. Buying this house had been her husband Neal's thing. She'd gone along, even getting excited as the plans came together, but those people next door had her worried. All those kids of theirs were going to scare her husband right off her pregnancy timetable.

Neal passed Dyanne, heaving a footlocker full of her shoes into their bedroom. He brushed past her, muscles tight against his T-shirt. Her heart fluttered a little, but her head gently reminded her that ovulation was a few days away. Best to build up to that.

His arms enveloped her. She closed her eyes and took a deep breath. Who knew sweat could be so sexy? Maybe that ovulation stuff was overrated. Hadn't she read something about getting pregnant if you ovulated after an "event"? Anyway, there was always tomorrow....

"Rob's cool. He's different, sure, but that's what I like about him. The guy seems real somehow. He reminds me of your dad, actually."

Dyanne froze. Her husband's embrace suddenly seemed like a prison. Her father had the same demeanor as Rob, but beneath it there was nothing but deceit. "I knew there was something about him I didn't like," she said, tugging off her pumps one at a time before placing them carefully in one of the shoe boxes in the corner. There were matching boxes lining the wall of the living room and in the closet...and on the stairs. "I have a lot of shoes, don't I?"

Neal smiled. "Enough to make Imelda Marcos jealous, but you're not getting off that easy. Your dad is a good guy. Just because things didn't work out between your parents doesn't mean you have to hate him forever. You're grown now. To love him doesn't mean you love your mother any less."

She tugged at her skirt zipper while walking toward the kitchen. She heard Neal padding behind, pausing to grab a banana on the way. Leg cramps probably. Good enough for him, talking to her about her father that way. What would Neal know about it, with his *Leave it to Beaver* family? She swallowed her anger, wondering instead how many e-mails she'd missed since coming here. She had to get that PDA fixed immediately.

Her husband caught up to her, kissing her cheek, then her nose.

She turned away, still fumbling with her skirt clasp. "Can you send my PDA in for repair by FedEx tomorrow?"

His hands circled her waist, unsnapping the metal fitting.

Her skirt fell to the floor. He lifted her onto the counter. "You're officially unplugged, Dee, at least for this week. You've been touring with authors for the past six months. This will be the first month we've been in the same city for more than a few days since Christmas.

"Heather is taking care of things. If she needs you, she'll call. You need to be reading that stack of books for the new imprint and devising a marketing plan. I'll be your pool boy and bring you latte, but for now, the PDA is out of bounds."

*So is talking about my father.*

Dyanne looked up her husband, running the tip of her nail over his shoulders, staring into the honey that was his eyes. Those eyes had been with her since sixth grade, when Neal moved into the house next door. "Four boys," her father had said at breakfast. "Can you imagine?"

She couldn't imagine. Thoughts of blaring music and a street full of junk cars kept Dyanne and her mother from sleeping until a boy showed up at the door with a basket of scones and a pitcher of tea. Wearing a tie and khakis fresh from St. Mary's Academy for Boys, Neal had leaned over and kissed her cheek, saying he'd be back the next day for the pitcher. That night, Dyanne had added Neal's last name to hers in her journal, despite her mother's warnings against such things.

Tonight, looking into those eyes, everything she'd ever wanted stared back at her. Well, almost everything. She clasped her hands around his neck.

He kissed her fingers. "I'm glad we bought this house. And I'm glad you were assigned to the GracePages imprint. I started one of those books this morning. A reissue. Your dad gave me the original version when we were dating. I wasn't ready for it then, but it seems right this time." He kissed her cheek, then her mouth… He stopped. "That's what I forgot. I meant to ask Rob about their church."

Dyanne looked around her kitchen, subdued with blues and

grays instead of overwhelmed by the life-size family tree
covered with children's names and handprints left by the
previous owners. Though most everything had been torn down
or covered over, the wacky Christian couple who'd owned the
house somehow lingered, as evidenced by Neal's strange talk
about church and her father.

Sure, Dyanne was excited about the new line. Who wouldn't
be? Christian books were selling like crazy. She'd suggested
for years that her publishing house get into the game. She
hadn't counted on becoming the line's publicist as a result, in
addition to dealing with bestselling author Fallon Gray.

Her boss promised the double duty wouldn't last long, but
Dyanne knew better. Fallon had gone through everyone in the
company. She wouldn't take anyone else. Having hit the *New
York Times* Bestseller list for the first time under Dyanne's
watch, Fallon took her publicist for some kind of genius.

It didn't matter anyway. Dyanne had the month off for this
move. By the time she went back to work, she'd be pregnant,
Neal's objections aside. Maybe church was just the thing to
help make that happen. "Didn't he say their church was small?
Five hundred people?"

Neal's hands slid under her blouse as he lifted her into his
arms and started out of the kitchen. "Four hundred I think he
said. Like the church I grew up in. Maybe we could actually
make some friends. Get to know some people for real."

Maybe not. Dyanne stared at the hardwood beneath her
dangling legs as though it were a raging sea. What was happening to her husband? Reading the books she was working
on? Wanting to go to some rinky-dink church and make
friends? While they were dating, Dyanne had begged Neal to
attend services with her, but Neal made it clear that while he
believed in God, he wasn't going to become some fanatic like
her father.

Instead of sharing their faith, Neal and Dyanne had bonded

over their lack of it. Dyanne had missed her church involvement at first, but when she and Neal shared their first raised eyebrow at her father's rantings, she'd been hooked.

Everything from there had been about goal setting, hard work and becoming a better person. Becoming the publicity director had taken much of her time, but Dyanne had squeezed in all the seminars and yoga classes Neal thought they should attend. After a while, life had boiled down to getting ahead, though Neal still insisted on recycling and had fought her to the end about the woodstove and the yard. In the end, though, Dyanne always won.

Until now. Something new was happening with Neal and it wasn't on her to-do list. She could almost hear her father in her head, trying not to laugh. "Maybe this is a God thing, sugar."

*Whatever.*

It took longer than usual to rally her anger against the thought of her father. She couldn't muster her usual rift with God very easily, either. Still, she wasn't going to end up like her mother, watching while her husband turned and walked away, then later forgiving him when he changed into some Jesus freak. Dyanne had her own thing going now and no matter how weird Neal was acting, she'd find a way to make all of this work—for her and not against her.

That evening in bed, Neal leaned on one elbow, running a hand through his wife's hair, which was as straight as the woman next door's hair was nappy. In the back of her head, though, just above Dyanne's neck, there was a thatch of curls as thick as his own. He thrust his fingers in deep and made wide circles, knowing it would disappear as soon as Dyanne found a hairdresser that met with her standards. Coordinating the move and flying in to direct the landscapers had made her miss an appointment with her first choice of stylists back in New York.

She'd looked worried when he reminded her about it, but Neal didn't care. In fact, Neal thought his wife would be beautiful with a short natural style like the way she'd worn her hair in college, but he knew better than to say so. Dyanne's hair was a part of her image—pretty and powerful. She admitted to maintaining it for him, too, fearing his head might be turned by some weave-wearing temptress.

That was college.

Things had changed. Returning to Tallahassee made Neal realize just how much. Sure he was excited about being around for the annual homecoming game and the alumni events, but the canopy oaks and love bugs reminded him of something else, too: the faith he'd brought from Ohio and easily discarded in his first year on campus.

He'd talked Dyanne out of church back then, but now he regretted it. His parents were active leaders in the community by the age he was now and all he and Dyanne had been doing was building their own kingdom. The trees that bowed gracefully over his house with open arms reminded Neal of his need for roots and his desire to grow something more than a business. Dyanne wanted to grow something, too, only in her belly instead of her heart.

A baby.

Neal wasn't so sure that either of them was ready for that. According to Dyanne, they'd done everything right to prepare for being parents: undergrad together and grad school for him, great jobs, traveling all over the world…. Neal wondered if after conquering him and her job, Dyanne wasn't just looking for some other box to check off her list. If that was it, as much as he loved his wife, Neal just couldn't play along. This wasn't a cappuccino machine or a plasma TV they were talking about but a person. And people needed parents who did more than get on planes and close deals.

He kissed Dyanne's hair and rolled over onto his side,

reaching under the bed for *Living a Life that Counts*, the book from the new line he'd been reading. After reading another short but deep chapter, Neal gripped the book's pages tightly before shoving it under their bed. He laced his fingers behind his head and closed his eyes for prayer, a habit that had come back to him with an awkward ease.

*God, what am I missing? I have everything I need and most of what I want. But something just isn't adding up. Not for Dyanne, either. She thinks a baby will fix that. I think only You can fix it. If we're supposed to have a baby, show us. Get us ready...*

As his wife turned and rolled onto her back, Neal thought about the question that his father-in-law had raised to him a few days before they'd left New York. "If you had unlimited money, resources and time, what would you do? What is your passion? What do you believe?" The question haunted Neal as much now as it did then, when the only answer he could come up with was himself.

He believed *in* a lot things: taking care of his wife, working hard, getting plenty of exercise, eating healthy, making money, doing good in the world. But he didn't believe a lot of people. Everybody he met seemed to be out for some kind of con, including his wife. His own parents were the picture of perfection, but underneath that beauty ran a subtle cruelty, waiting to crush anyone who stepped out of line. He'd seen that same thing in his wife as she destroyed a beautiful yard to create her own idea of a fantasy landscape.

And now she wanted to create a baby for the same purpose. His plan to stay away from Dyanne had dissolved at the first sight...and first scent of her. Except for a few stolen lunches and a layover in Atlanta, they hadn't been together for weeks. As though she were thinking the same, Dyanne's hand moved along his spine, pausing at his neck before rubbing his head.

Neal closed his eyes, remembering how many times she'd

touched him this way, only to have one of them whisk out the door for a trip or take a late-night call. Could his wife want a baby because she was lonely? Or could God be using this to get to her, too?

He turned over slowly, throwing his thigh over his wife's smaller, but just as solid leg. He didn't know what God was doing or how it would all work out. Head rubbing, however, he understood perfectly.

## *The Once-Was*

I once was a star,
Shooting to the moon
On mile-high heels.
My hips spanned the
Galaxy, curving at the speed
of light. My light is gone now,
My wonder moved
On, taken residence in your
Eyes. In your laughter, I
Hear echoes of my reign,
Top notes of the once-was.
For you, I'd gladly give it
All again, flinging my hopes
Into outer space, tossing my words into
The black silence, once and for all.

—Karol
Upon waking, first Sunday after Hope's move

# Chapter Three

Karol Simon once stood in the foyer at church with Hope, looking for new moms to encourage.

This morning, weary and alone, she'd hidden from them.

They found her anyway.

One of the newest moms thrust a chubby baby in Karol's face. "I think he has thrush. His mouth is all white. I remember Miss Hope telling me something to use? Vinegar maybe? Someone said you might know…"

She took a deep breath and the baby. He returned her smile, just wide enough for her to see his coated tongue. "Yes, vinegar. Swab his mouth with it. You'll have to do yourself, too. Call the doctor. Maybe some gentian violet. It's messy, though. They have quick pills now. Antifungals. Limit your sugar—"

A three-year-old biter was pushed forward next. His mother, almost in tears and afraid to check him into the nursery—he'd bitten half the class the week before—hugged Karol after she finished dispensing more of Hope's second-hand advice.

"Thank you," she said softly. "He's really a good boy. I don't know why he does it."

Karol nodded and gave the young mom a squeeze. Having

a child do things that other people didn't understand could be embarrassing and even hurtful. Though church was supposed to be a place of grace and healing, people were still people and nobody wanted to see teeth marks on their kid—Karol included.

"If it doesn't get better right away, you may have to keep him with you in the overflow room for a few weeks. I had to do that with Judah and he still has his moments now and then, but for the most part, he's over it." She left out the fact that Judah still took a bite out of Mia now and then. No sense putting the woman over the edge, right?

As time wound down before service started, Karol hugged and helped all the women she could, all the time feeling like the biggest hypocrite on earth. On the way to church, Mia had thrown her shoe out of the window and Karol had nearly been run over when she pulled off the shoulder to get it.

And now she was standing in the foyer like some sort of Supermom, giving out advice when she really wanted to run to the bathroom and cry. Though she loved Hope and appreciated all her friend had taught her, she couldn't imagine how Hope managed to help all these women and run her own houseful. Karol had been hard pressed to stuff Mia into a dress and get her to church with both shoes. And yet, these women thought she had all the answers.

It was funny, but scary, too. Karol couldn't have been more relieved when she finally made her way into the sanctuary. The service flew by on mandolin strings and beats from the drums the last visiting missionaries had brought from Kenya. It was a unique and soothing sound.

Pastor Newton's sermon had been moving and informative as usual, but Karol found her mind wandering toward grocery lists and her mothering goals for the week: working with Mia on writing her name for kindergarten, getting Judah to help her in the kitchen with dinner and trying to get Ryan to make friends with someone who wasn't a fictional character or historical figure. She had her work cut out for her, especially on the last count. Ryan was now old enough to join the youth group, but after two Sundays there without Hope's sons, Aaron and Anthony, Ryan had slid into the pew beside Rob and Karol this morning without offering any explanations. Though she wanted to question him, a sharp nod from Rob kept Karol from dong so.

On the one hand, Karol was relieved. Some of the boys in the youth group were much older and more experienced than Ryan. She'd thought he might do better in joining the group after the eighth grade when he'd had a little more time to grow up. At the same time, though, each week that went by without him making any new friends, drew him further and further into the world of books, a place even Karol had a hard time pulling him out of sometimes. Rob didn't seem too worried. "There are a lot worse things the boy could get into besides reading. And think about it, Karol, he gets it from you."

That was exactly what worried her. Karol's love for books had led her down many roads, including a crazy attempt to be published when Ryan was young. Hope had helped her see the sense in focusing on raising her children instead of trying to fulfill some impossible dream. Somehow, though, that dream, or some part of it, had been passed on to Ryan. There were still boxes under her bed full of writing no one had ever seen—and never would see. Even this morning, she'd climbed into her window seat and scribbled out a poem. It was a madness of sorts, one she didn't want Ryan afflicted with, though in her heart, she knew it was too late.

And yet, the pastor's words rang true in her mind.

*Trust God.*

She didn't take the best notes or hear every word of the sermon, but the gist of it was, as always, applicable and true: God is faithful. He knows what He's doing, even when we don't. As the final amen was said, Karol directed that thought to her friendship with Hope, her marriage to Rob, her worries over her children and even her relationship—or lack thereof—with her new neighbors. Somehow, God would work it all out. She certainly couldn't.

When church let out and the women began to cluster around her again, Karol repeated the pastor's words and told them all to go home and trust God with the babies He'd given them. He'd tell them what to do with their children much better than she ever could. Some of the women seemed disappointed, but others were strengthened and thankful for Karol's confidence.

She was just happy to take Rob's hand and escape to the car.

Though Karol's two youngest children had been acting up lately, there were no incidents at the restaurant after church. Though they'd usually gone to buffets with copious amounts of family fare with Hope and Singh, today Karol had asked Rob to head to historic Frenchtown for some soul food: ribs, macaroni and cheese, greens seasoned with smoked turkey, tea as sweet as the morning had been sour and sweet potato pie that reminded Karol of the mother she sometimes imagined she would one day have or become.

Today, she doubted either.

Judah and Mia were so mesmerized by the sweet potato pie that they seemed back to their old, compliant selves, eating quietly with their best manners. As the family rose to leave, an elderly couple had complimented the children's behavior.

The woman, who all of Karol's children had greeted without the usual urgings, shook her wrinkled finger in the air and waved them over.

"Now see, you are a good mama. Children now days won't half speak to nobody and then they come in the restaurant and run all over and act a fool. Y'all are doing a good job. Just keep on like you doing. They are gonna turn out all right, you'll see. God bless y'all."

Though she accepted the compliment and gave the older woman a careful hug, Karol knew something for sure—she was a failure at motherhood. Rob cradled her head into his lap and tried to convince her otherwise that afternoon while their children watched *Finding Nemo* for the millionth time.

"You're a great mom, Karol."

She rolled her eyes before looking up at her husband. "Mia threw her shoe out of the van this morning."

Her husband had to be at service early to greet visitors and clean the windows. It wasn't a position exactly, just something Singh had always done. Rob had joined him a few years ago. Now their sons went, too, leaving Karol and Mia alone to fight over hair and dresses.

This morning, Mia had settled on a pair of Mary Janes a size too small. Karol had tried to explain that she was sending them to Hope for one of her daughters, but Mia had really lost it then. "Can I go with my shoes? It's no fun here!" she'd wailed, throwing herself onto her canopy bed. Being the only girl had its privileges…and its problems.

Rob stifled a laugh. "She threw them totally out of the car? But you two made it to church on time and she had both shoes on—"

Karol clenched her teeth. "I pulled off the shoulder and ran across the highway to get it. No one had run over it yet, thank God. They almost hit me, though."

Her husband's jaw tightened then. "I don't like that at all. There was an accident on that shoulder last week. The exits near the church are pretty close together as it is. Next time, leave the shoe."

She flipped onto her stomach, fluffing her afro from where it flattened in the back. "Now you know I couldn't bring that child to church with one shoe. That's just—just—"

"Life? Seriously, I don't know why you insist the kids dress up on Sunday, anyway. None of the other kids do now that Hope and Singh's kids aren't here."

Karol sat back on the couch beside her husband. "I know you think it's silly, but it's just important to me. I was raised to dress up for church. It was a sign of respect for God's house. I know everything is modern now, and I'm glad that I don't have to be dressed to the nines every time I go, but I just like for the kids to look nice."

"Mom! He's kicking me and I'm sick of it. He's trying my patience." Ryan raised a hand over his brother's head prepared to give it a sound whack in front of his parents as he'd done so many times before when they weren't watching.

Rob responded before she could. "Knock it off, Judah. And you, too, Ryan. Neither of you are allowed to put your hands on each other. Behave or the movie goes off."

Ryan jumped up and stood in front of the television before clicking it off. "Fine. I don't like this movie anyway. You always pick little kid stuff for them. What about me?"

Judah started to cry. "See what you did? Now we have go take a nap like babies—"

"I'm not a baby!" Mia burst into tears. "Mom-eeeeee!" She dived onto the couch and into her mother's arms, knocking her head against Karol's chin as she went.

"Humph. Yes you are. You're both babies," Ryan said before starting out of the room. He was in rare form today. Or maybe it was just the hormones that Karol kept forgetting he was getting to the age for.

"Okay, enough!" Karol sat Mia on the cushion next to her and swung her arms like an umpire. "You can watch the movie or not, but the fighting has to stop. And the yelling. I've tried very hard not to raise my voice at you the past few days, now I need you to do the same."

A tear wet the corner of Karol's eye as Ryan shrugged and

stormed upstairs. Having to leave Mia in the van alone this morning and dash through the traffic and now this—all simple things, but difficult, too—had taken Karol to the breaking point. And the thought of the same group of young mothers who used to cluster around Hope waiting for her had really taken her past the point of no return.

*Wonder what they'd think of me if they could see this scene?*

Rob stood and started helping the smaller children up the stairs. "Okay, you all have upset your mother. Time for a nap. Mom and I might take one, too. You all did so well at lunch today. I need you to act that way at home, too. Ryan, I'll deal with you later, okay, son?"

"Yes, sir."

Karol wiped her eyes, and helped her husband lead the kids upstairs and into their beds despite their pouting and complaining. Could they take a Sunday-afternoon nap without their friends next door to keep an eye out in case the children woke up?

Mia and Judah had always known that if they woke up before their parents, they could wander over to Miss Hope's for a hug and an afternoon snack. She and Hope had even staggered their naptimes to look out for one another. After the monster truck showed up next door to remove every kid-related thing in the yard, Karol was fairly sure their new neighbors wouldn't be any good for nap coverage. Still, she only had time to blow Rob a kiss before sleep overtook her.

"We've got company," Neal said as he entered the house with a little girl in a pink bathing suit a size too small. Despite her ill-fitting outfit, she held her head as if balancing a crown. The little girl's hair, two long braids in front and a giant afro puff in back, made Dyanne long to dig her fingers into it.

On another day, she might have done just that, but it was

Sunday, her catching-up day. Even if she was out of the office, she still needed to stay on top of things. With authors like Fallon on her list, she had to. Not to mention that ton of books for the new line. There was just too much to do to be dealing with someone else's kids.

"You run along now, okay, sweetie?" Dyanne said, before shooting her husband a glare. He knew what she was up against. Why had he brought the child inside?

*Watch it. He might be warming up to the baby thing. Be nice.*

She was about to tell the little girl how cute she was when the wild thing ran and flung herself against the wall. "The tree! You took the treeeeeeee...."

Neal wiped his brow on the towel around his neck. He was ahead of her on scouting out a jog trail, it seemed. "Calm down, honey. Your friends' tree was beautiful, but we live here now so we have to start over." He walked toward her and crouched down to eye level.

The little girl paused, bringing a finger to her chin. "So you're gonna make your own tree? With her?"

Dyanne, who hadn't moved since the girl attacked her new wallpaper, almost leaped across the room and hugged her. She was starting to love this kid more by the minute.

Neal's eyes told her to wait. He gave the girl one of his best smiles. "I don't know if we'll have a tree exactly, but yes, that's my wife, Miss Dyanne and we are...thinking about starting a family."

The child looked confused for a moment.

He rebalanced his weight on his heels before simplifying his words. "We might have a baby. Maybe."

Joy flooded out of the girl as if they'd unstopped a dam. "A baby! Girl or boy? Oh, I hope it's a girl. I'll show her stuff and make her a dress and give her my doll and—"

She stopped, eyeing Dyanne carefully. "Are you sure she can have a baby? She's awful skinny. Don't look like a

Mommy at all. No booty." She patted the back of her bathing suit, more filled out than Dyanne's would ever be.

Neal laughed so hard that he fell back on his own rear. He recovered quickly, hoping he hadn't hurt his wife's feelings too much. The child had caught him off guard. "I think we've got, um, all the equipment we need, sweetie. There are all different kinds of mommies."

Dyanne wasn't laughing. She took her neighbor's daughter by the hand and stepped around her husband, collapsed in a fit of chuckles at her expense. She had a lot on her list for today but being humiliated wasn't among the choices. "What's your name, honey?"

"Mia. You can call me Mi-Mi, though. Everybody over here used to. Now nobody does," the little girl said, looking at Dyanne's hand as if it were poison.

"I don't like nicknames." Having to endure her father calling her Dee Dee was enough to make Dyanne not want to call the little girl anything other than her name. Worse yet, Neal had picked up the habit of calling her that, too. It seemed a lot nicer when he said it, but she still didn't like nicknames.

At any rate, little Mia had come along just in time. Today's run-in would serve as a bridge to discuss the toy explosion in their neighbors' backyard and ways for the couple next door to keep their kids at home. What were they doing anyway?

Dyanne mused over the possibilities as she covered the distance between the two houses. As she and Mia stepped up onto the porch, she looked through the open window and knew exactly why no one had come looking for little girl. John Boy and Chaka Khan were on opposite ends of the couch… fast asleep.

For now anyway.

Dyanne was about to give them a wake-up call.

## *Jesus, Be a Fence*

Once pressed flat under
My feet, the land grows
sharp and steep, cutting
through all pretense.
Fences break through my
cool-soiled dreams,
a haven for my sorrow.
Providence makes no allowance
For rough-timbered tears.
Inquisition mocks from frosted,
Lips. A mouth fresh like new
Money and untried love.
One day, her flint will come,
Carrying a fun house mirror. Until then,
Some angel, soul aflame and wings
Outstretched must walk the line
Between us, whispering love songs
Long into the night.


—Karol
After the neighbors brought Mia home

# Chapter Four

"Lose something?"

Dyanne's city voice grated against Karol's ears, though she was still half-asleep.

"Pardon me?" she said, rubbing the corners of her eyes to see her neighbor clearly. "Can I help you with something?"

Dyanne stepped through the unlocked screen door. Mia was holding her hand.

Karol's breath caught in her throat. "Mia?"

Rob, now quite awake, gave his wife a weary look. "Did she come over to your place? We're so sorry."

Karol nodded in agreement but she was more embarrassed than sorry. Mia had on a swimsuit from the giveaway bag and her hair was tumbling down from the braids Karol had secured so well this morning.

Neal, Dyanne's husband, made a quiet entrance and shook Rob's hand. "I found her on the porch, so I brought her inside. She was fine with that until she realized we'd gotten rid of the tree your neighbors had painted on the wall. You all were really close, weren't you?"

"You have no idea how close," Rob said as he stood and walked to the front porch with Neal.

The two women stayed where they were, with Karol keeping one hand—and both eyes—on Mia. "Again, we are very, very sorry. When the people before you lived there—"

"You know what? I am so sick of this 'when the people before you lived here' business. You need to get a handle on your kids. This is ridiculous. I don't know what kind of skinny-dipping kid co-op you all had going, but could you have some respect for other people? I'm supposed to be working today. I don't have time for this," Dyanne fumed.

A look came over Karol's face that both surprised and annoyed Dyanne. Was that anger? It couldn't be. What did Karol have to be mad about? It wasn't as if she and Neal had done anything to the Simons.

"Look, I apologize for what has been going on. I admit it's been a lot to take. I can only hope that if and when you have children the people around you will be just as understanding when your little ones go through challenging stages."

*Touché,* Dyanne thought.

Still, she couldn't bring herself to excuse it. "I hear you, okay? But the key word there was 'stages'. Stages have to end sometime, right? I'm really hoping that whatever stage your daughter is in will be over soon. And for the record, trust me, I will have my children under control."

Karol whispered something in Mia's ear. The little girl ran up the stairs, sniffling as she went. When Karol heard the door close above them, she turned back to her neighbor and smiled her best smile.

"Got the perfect child planned, have you? Those are always the best, you know. I hope you stick around long enough for all of us to see how that experiment turns out. In the meantime, I assure you that my children will be instructed to stay as far away from you and your property as possible."

Neal, who had been laughing at something Rob said on the porch, changed his demeanor upon reentering the room. He'd caught the last of the ladies' exchange and wasn't at all happy with what he'd heard.

"Dee? Is everything all right? You and Karol don't sound too happy in here. Maybe you should have come out onto the porch with me and Rob. We had a great talk."

Dyanne looked at her husband and sighed. He was such a goody-goody sometimes. Sure, Dyanne did her share of brown-nosing, too, but only when the object of her attention deserved it. What was the point of him trying to be pals with Rob Simon? They were nothing alike. It was a waste of time. And that was something Dyanne couldn't afford. "We had a great talk, too. Or at least I hope so. We're clear, right, Karol?"

Oh, yeah. They were clear. "Crystal." The lady of the house didn't crack a smile.

Both husbands looked a little embarrassed, but the women seemed comfortable behind the lines they'd drawn in the sand, even if it meant they were losing ground by staying behind them.

The men shared a short goodbye before the wives turned their backs to one another. Dyanne's mind was turning in every direction as she stormed down the porch stairs. So much so that she almost missed the older woman walking up Karol's steps.

"Hello," the lady said. "Who are you?"

"Dyanne, the new neighbor," she answered, taking in the older woman's appearance. Couture clothes, quality jewelry, but nothing flashy, handcrafted shoes, a great haircut and manicured but natural nails rounded out the lady's package. She was, as Dyanne's mother would say, *un punto*. On point.

And she seemed very pleased by Dyanne's news. "How wonderful! I'm so glad someone new has moved in."

Dyanne wasn't sure if the woman should get too happy. The way things had been going lately, she might not be Karol's neighbor for long. "And you are?"

The woman shrugged as if there was no way to explain what she was about to say. "I'm Faith, Karol's…" She paused as if looking for another suitable answer. Evidently she could find none. "Mother. I'm Karol's mother."

Dyanne stared at the woman so long that Neal gave her elbow a nudge. She moved on, but only down the next step on the stairs. Maybe Karol was right. Maybe you really couldn't control how your children turned out. For a moment, Dyanne allowed the thought to form in her mind, before ruthlessly forcing it away.

"I know," the woman said. "I know. We're quite different, Karol and I, but if you get to know her, you'll find she's an amazing woman. My daughter just takes great effort to hide that fact. Don't give up on her."

"Right," Dyanne said before finally following Neal, who'd given a friendly bow, introduced himself and proceeded down the stairs. She didn't mean it, though, what she'd told Karol's mother about getting to know her neighbor. She had a lot to do and trying to figure out the housewife next door wasn't high on her list of priorities.

"I think you could have handled that a little better, don't you?" Neal asked, as their own screen door slapped shut.

"Maybe," Dyanne said, recounting her conversation with Karol. She'd expected for the woman to fold and retreat as most people did when she called them on the carpet about their behavior. Instead, Karol had insinuated that Dyanne might end up with a disobedient child, too. That wasn't what she or Neal needed to hear right now.

"I just hope she keeps her word and tells her kids to stay away from here."

Neal scratched his head. "That could be a problem. I told Rob the kids were welcome to come over whenever they wanted. During daylight hours, anyway."

"She was sunning herself on the neighbors' porch. Like some kind of animal. Yes, my thoughts exactly. I'll have to schedule another flight. Karol must be having some kind of breakdown—I will not quiet down. Someone has to say it. I like the girl next door. Just the thing for Karol. Spunky. No, no need for that. You stay there, Pops. I'll whip her into shape."

Karol didn't even look up or bother to say what she was thinking—there was no need for that. She was as whipped as she could be. Between her mother banging on the door with a handful of suitcases unannounced as always and the neighbors bringing home the child she'd left sleeping upstairs, things just couldn't get much worse.

"Now, how far is it from here to the mall, again, sweetie? You know I can't abide all these trees for long. Rob likes to chop wood so much, you should get him to cut down some of them." Karol's mother, Faith Antonia Ware the Second— long story—flipped through the Tallahassee Yellow Pages with a troubled look. "What happened to the beauty salon I went to last time I was here? I don't see it listed."

With a shrug, Karol shook her head. "I don't know, Mom." She trimmed her own hair and usually wore it tied back with a bright scarf or picked out in its full glory. Today it was blown out and braided down the center of her head with a ribbon that provided an annoying tickle.

Karol pretended not to feel it. She didn't want to feel anything but the warmth of Mia's back resting against her knees. The little girl had cried at first from all the scolding and Faith the Second's fierce looks, but Karol's only daughter had eventually taken refuge in her mother's arms and fallen asleep.

If only she could do the same. Karol knew better than to even try. Faith would likely hit her upside the head with the phone book. Some people had mamas. Others had mothers. Karol had Faith.

*If only Daddy had come.*

But Karol's father hadn't come, nor would he ever come without calling first. He'd probably never come without being invited. Though his house was always open to Karol and her family, her dad was never one for imposing. Unlike his wife.

"I'm going to ask the girl next door where she goes to get her hair done. Her perm was going, but well-done. High-end. She'll know where to go. I'm so glad she moved in over there. Better than what's her name?"

"Hope."

Karol's mother gritted her teeth, giving a sharp nod to a snapshot on the wall of herself, Karol and Hope taken at Ryan's birthday party the previous summer. Faith, Hope and Love the three of them were not. Nor would they ever be. Extreme dislike was the only word she could think of to describe her mother's feelings for her old friends. The thought of them twisted her mouth in ways Karol hadn't seen since… her mother's last visit. The funny thing was that Hope's mother felt the same way about Karol and Rob. Karol never told Faith that, though. She had enough ammunition.

"All those children! And that big ole dog. Oh, it was just crazy over there. I don't know how you stood it as long as you did. You always say that God answers prayers. Well, He must have answered some of mine, 'cause, honey—"

"Mom. Please. Don't, okay?"

It was Faith's turn to shrug, with an added warning look to remind Karol that she'd called her Mom. More than once. "Suit yourself, but I say that young couple is going to bring some life back into you. No hard feelings against the Waltons or anything. They treated the kids real good and God knows you needed a friend out in this godforsaken—"

"Mom!" Karol was crying now, only she didn't realize it until she tasted the salt on her tongue and felt Rob's thumb trail the tears across her cheeks. He would have kissed her if they'd been alone, but she doubted he'd do it with Faith looking on. Outside of their wedding kiss thirteen years before, he never did.

Until now.

And not just on the cheek, either.

Faith let out a disgusted sigh, but amusement danced in her eyes. "Go upstairs, for God's sake, you two. So crass, I tell you."

Karol bit her lip, trying hard not to say all the things that came to mind. Rob saved her by reaching over and taking Faith's face in his hands and kissing her on the cheek.

She dropped the phone book.

On Mia's head. The little girl shrieked in response.

"See what you've done!" Faith swept back her bottle-blond pageboy with one hand and reached for Mia with the other. "Come on to Number Two. Come on, sweetie."

Mia rubbed her head, then she rubbed her eyes, which widened quite a bit at the sight of Faith and her extended fingers, a French manicure half an inch from her eye.

All Karol could do was gather Mia up and wonder if her mother's madness was hereditary. She was beginning to fear that it was. All her life, she'd thought it insane that her mother insisted on being called Faith instead of Mom and Number Two instead of Grandma—especially when they'd called her father Pops forever. And yet, when she thought about it, her mother had remained Faith somehow, a person, something beyond a mother or grandmother, someone who people know better than to call to make cupcakes or drive in the car pool. Someone who mattered.

Before Karol could get the thought out of her mind, her middle child came thundering down the stairs, sporting the paint he wasn't supposed to use in the house. Rob stood quickly to take the situation in hand, but Karol waved him off, taking Judah upstairs to face his mess, while she was drowning in her own tangled thoughts.

When she emerged again, her mother had made a hair appointment—with the help of Dianne with a y, no doubt—and Mia was dressed in an outfit that Karol had never seen. The surprise was that her daughter looked happy about it. She enjoyed nautical looks, and Faith the Second had just happened to pick the right sailor suit. Where Mia would ever wear it again, Karol had no idea but she was thankful for the gesture, especially after the day she'd had.

"Thanks, M—" A sharp look from her mother made Karol swallow the word that she heard hurled at her so many times a day. Mom. "Faith. Thanks, Faith. I really appreciate it."

She produced similar outfits for the boys in varied sizes. Judah had a fit over it. Ryan stared at it for a full minute proclaiming it "nice," tugging on the shirt over the one he already wore and retreating to the corner with a book. With the way he was acting lately, that was a relative success. "Pops picked them. I thought it'd be a bust, but I guess he does know something after all."

Karol cringed at the way her mother talked about her father, knowing that her dad wouldn't have said a word in his own defense if he'd been there. The way she called him Pops was bad enough. Faith was the older one actually, by two years. "Mom, please don't call him Pops. He has a name you know. Eric. Do you ever call him that?"

Her mother shouted for the boys to clean up and come downstairs. She held one of the shirts up in the air and waved at Rob, in the front yard, smoothing things over even further with the husband next door. The way they were laughing, maybe it was a little too smooth, but Faith didn't seem to notice.

"Eric? Oh, I don't know. I guess I still call him Pops even though you left the house long ago. He likes it."

He didn't like it. Karol knew that from the face that he'd made when she started saying it. She was eight years old and her friend Tonya's mother was going on and on about "Daddy this" and "Daddy that."

It turned out that she was talking about her husband. They had a son who was a junior and to keep them separate, she just called her husband Daddy. He loved it. Pops, Karol's father, did not. He stated this a few times, but as always with Faith, she didn't listen. And now, decades later, he still tightened his jaw before he answered to it.

"You like it, Mom. He doesn't. I think it's a little strange that you insist on being Faith, but he just gets to be Pops. But then, you always did get to decide which part we all got to play." Karol regretted the words as soon as she'd said them, but it was too late to get them back.

The boys ran off to change without being bidden. Even cauliflower-eared-always-listening-to-see-what's-going-on Mia followed behind her brothers. She must have seen the look in their grandmother's eyes. If Karol had seen it sooner, she might have joined her husband on the front lawn. When she did see it, it was too late to escape.

Faith had frozen in place at the close of her daughter's words. She kept her pose and pivoted slowly, reminiscent of the best supermodels. Her words scratched from deep in her throat, somewhere raw and painful.

"Do you think you know what it takes to keep a marriage together? Do you think you know how to raise decent children, work a job and keep your man in your bed? How to stay whole even when your world is in pieces? Well, baby, you don't know. Not yet. So don't judge Faith so quickly. You don't know…Eric as well as you think you do. To be honest, you don't know that husband of yours too well, either."

Karol took a deep breath and tried to apologize, but her mother was already up and gathering the children into the car. She planned to take them to the Mary Brogan Museum to the latest exhibit, one she'd read about in the *Tallahassee Democrat*. Convinced the children were already ruined from the dearth of artistic freedom in their lives, she still promised to do what she could.

"Look, Faith. You don't have to do this. If I'd known you

were coming… It's just been a hard time. I'm sorry for what I said about Dad—Pops. I don't know everything. Not about the two of you, anyway. I do take issue with what you said about Rob, though. I know him better than I know myself."

Karol's mother slid into her SUV and put on her sunglasses. She told the kids to buckle up while she rolled down the window, speaking barely above a whisper.

"Honey, you know nothing about that man. If you did, you'd realize that it was he who sent your little friends next door away. I'm shocked that it took him so long to do it. Your Eric would have moved you away from here years ago."

Before Karol could reply, the window closed and the car took off, leaving her in a wake of dust and no small amount of doubt.

*She knows.*

It was all Rob had written in his late-night e-mail to his friend Singh. He couldn't say more because he didn't know more. In fact, he didn't know anything for sure but he'd been married long enough to know when "I'm okay" meant just the opposite.

For two days, Karol had been stiff and quiet, cleaning and cooking like some kind of Stepford Wife. Usually, Karol focused on the children during the day and except for the dishes, which Rob hated, they did the housework together when he got home from work. When his mother-in-law returned with the children on the day of her visit, Rob knew that something was wrong. It had started with the children greeting him at the door wearing coordinating outfits and fearful looks. Rob wasn't sure how, but Faith had incriminated him in some way. She'd seen through him despite all his efforts.

Karol turned over slowly, but he knew she wasn't sleeping. He rested an arm along hers, but she turned away, toward the wall.

This was war, and Rob knew it.

And war required time and strategy that Rob didn't have.

He could have held her shoulder and whispered the truth into her ear, but an all-night argument seemed less than appealing. If only Singh had done his part and told Hope, he wouldn't have been in this predicament, but Singh had it hard on his end, too. No man wants to fall beneath his woman's expectations, to remind her that underneath it all, he is just…a fallible human. A sinner. And yet, that was the truth of it for husbands and wives, too. But it's the man who takes it hard when his wife's eyes don't look at him the same. Rob knew the feeling firsthand, he'd gone through it just today.

*Lord. I don't want to fight.*

They didn't fight much. They'd only had a few really bad fights, early in their marriage, but he knew that once Karol got going on this one, there wouldn't be a quick resolution.

And then there was his friend to think of. Singh obviously hadn't told Hope the real reason they had moved away. At this point, Rob would be in even more trouble if Singh had told his wife and Karol talked to Hope and found out that her best friend already knew.

*Wake her up. Tell her.*

But then, maybe Karol knew nothing. Maybe she was really okay after all. Maybe he should just go to sleep.

*She is not okay.*

Karol turned back to him and opened her eyes. "Thanks for being so kind while Faith was here. I know these visits are a lot to take. Thank you."

With a deep sigh, Rob curled closer around his wife, smoothing his hand over the scarf tied over her hair. "I don't mind. I love your mother. She gave me you, didn't she? It's you that I worry about. The kids, too. You all seem…upset."

He'd expected Karol to be an emotional wreck after her mother left and they had time to be alone, but she wasn't. Her tears had dried into a steely resolve. She'd apologized for not having the kids in hand since Hope's departure. Rob countered, assuring Karol that the children were his responsibility, too, but by then she was far gone into superwoman territory, a land with only a narrow window of escape. He hoped that the minutes of pretend sleeping had calmed her down.

"I'm okay. Thoughtful, but okay. This week taught me a lot. It's going to keep teaching me if I let it." Karol didn't move away from him, but she didn't respond to him, either.

So much for her calming down. For Karol, yelling and screaming meant light at the end of the tunnel, but even icy words like this meant that plans were being made in her mind, questions were being asked… If Rob wasn't careful, he'd be accused and proven guilty without ever saying a word. This had gone on long enough.

Rob sat up in the bed and rested his back against the wall. Karol laid her head over in his lap, but she didn't say a word. She wasn't going to ask the questions this time. He was all on his own.

"I never meant to hurt you. You have to understand that."

Karol didn't indicate one way or another whether she understood it. She didn't move.

"It's not that I didn't love Hope and Singh. I did. I still do. It's just that I love you more. I missed you…"

She sat up slowly, arms crossed across her abdomen as if in defense. "So what are you saying? You asked them to leave?"

He reached for her arm, but she jerked away. The emptiness between them seemed to grow in the darkness. "It's not that simple. There was more to it—"

"Not really. Did you or did you not ask Hope and Singh to leave? Yes or no?"

Rob cracked his neck, one of Karol's pet peeves that he only did in private. He hadn't meant to do it now, but tension that rose up his shoulders and into his throat threatened to choke him. Rob wanted to tell the whole story, to spread the blame a little thinner, to leave a way for himself to get out of this, but he didn't. He couldn't. This was his wife asking about his actions, not anyone else's. The only way out was the truth. "I asked Singh to pray about it. It just wasn't healthy the way things were—"

Karol held a finger up to her mouth. "Stop. Talking."

"Wait. Look, I know you're mad, but that's not helping anything. We're going to have to talk this out—"

"Shh…"

When Rob quieted down, he heard what Karol had already, the beat of a drum. They almost bumped heads as they jumped up and headed downstairs. A drum set had arrived the morning before, a final gift for Mia from Faith, whose one request was that the gift not be returned or given away. Rob had shrugged it off and stored the congas in the garage. How much trouble could a four-year-old girl get into with a couple of drums anyway? he'd asked himself while hauling them to the garage.

A lot of trouble evidently.

As Rob and Karol raced down the stairs, he checked the clock on the DVD player—three o'clock. It seemed to take forever to get to the garage as they rounded the furniture in the new arrangements Faith had left behind. Just as they cleared the last chair, the drumming stopped. Karol and Rob stared at each other in the dim light, both looking afraid now instead of angry. Had one of Karol's tubs of unfinished projects fallen on their little girl's head?

A few more steps brought the answer and an unwelcome surprise: next to Mia and her new drum set was Neal, their now red-eyed neighbor.

Rob gave him a nod of thanks before grabbing Mia up and heading back upstairs, trying not to think of the bad things she could have gotten into in the garage alone. Behind him, Karol made ashamed apologies that Rob probably should have had a part in. He whispered a prayer for forgiveness, kissed his daughter, carried her upstairs and tucked her in, knowing that the best of his apologies this night were yet to come.

## *The Brat Project*

- Find out if there are city nuisance complaints for children—
  Neal says no, but go downtown anyway and get info.

- Read dog behavior modification articles—something has
  to work on these kids!

- Buy earplugs.

- Get new and additional locks for doors.

- Get an estimate on enclosing porch.

- Ask fence people to move up installation date.

- Take Karol to lunch and try to get her to understand where
  we're coming from. Neal's suggestion. I'm not up for it.

- Check on Fallon's presale numbers for her latest release.

- Update Heather on the final details of Fallon's black college
  tour.

—Dyanne's to-do list

## Chapter Five

Despite her husband's compassion for them, Dyanne was starting to think that maybe the kids next door were going to wreck her plans, after all. To keep that from happening, Dyanne put Project Pregnancy into overdrive. All she had to do now was get prepared for Fallon Gray's book tour and get her baby proposal tightened and printed up. Neal wouldn't be able to refuse her. He never had before. Not really, anyway. Still, she knew better than to push him too far at the wrong time. Like now.

Before Dyanne could reveal her plan, Neal beat her to it with a surprising proclamation of his own.

"I know we moved out here to relax, but it's turning out to be more work than our lives back in New York. I don't know if I can take it all. One minute it's maddeningly quiet and the next, there's some kid beating drums in the middle of the night. Maybe we should sell, once the summer is over."

Dyanne thought about saying that maybe that was God's way of getting him ready for the late nights with their baby, but that would probably only terrify him at this point. Neal's job, his business was steady. It's what he was used to. The biggest imbalance in his life was…Dyanne.

She, on the other hand, was intimate with the dizzying fear that everything could fall apart, including her marriage. She didn't wish that on anybody, the fear she felt all the time, as though something was chasing her to the next goal, the next step of the life she'd planned out for herself. Most of all, she was afraid of letting down her guard as her mother had: settling in and getting comfortable. She could still remember the look on her mother's face when her father had come home and asked for a divorce. Her mother had laughed, thinking it was a joke. All these years later, it still wasn't funny. It never would be.

"Don't give up so easy, Neal. Sure, it's going to take a while for things to calm down, but they'll be back in school in the fall. Just give it some time. You wanted this. We both did." She rubbed her husband's shoulders and tried to focus on him instead of wondering how far off schedule this was going to put her conception.

And of course, there was the biggest thing consuming her thoughts—Fallon's tour. She'd never get it all done if Neal wanted to do another move now. Dyanne needed to do some follow-up calls to a few bookstores on the collegiate part of Fallon's book tour. During the four days planned for Atlanta, Fallon would be speaking at a college, a megachurch and bookstore on almost every day. A noted psychologist and conference speaker, Fallon got some of her best sales after campus events. Other publicists never seemed to understand the dynamics of the process and rarely sent their authors on the university circuit.

Dyanne made it work because she analyzed the strengths and connections of each author separately and after seeing Fallon fill in at a graduation once, she'd created a university leg in every one of Fallon's tours. The key to it all was getting the kids to fall in love with you. Then, they called and e-mailed their parents, who told their friends and it all went on from there. Perhaps the same tactic would work with her neighbors' children….

Neal placed his hands over hers and turned to face her. "You're so sexy when you're distracted, you know that? If you weren't trying so hard to get a baby, I'd take you up those stairs and—"

"Don't let that stop you. A baby ain't gonna hurt nothing."

Both of them dropped hands and turned to the door. Dyanne had been thinking pretty much the same thing, but someone else, someone who was supposed to be far, far away had said it. It took them a few seconds to take in the large, lively woman standing in their open front door. Fallon Gray, Ph.D. Live and in color. The wrong color. Her blond dread-locks were now a black Afro cut close to her scalp.

Though Dyanne tried to recover quickly, knowing how easily Fallon was offended, she didn't move quickly enough. The woman swung through the door with a leather duffel bag, wearing an eggshell man's suit and low heels. The absence of her goldilocks, as Fallon had affectionately called them, gave her a totally different look. Dyanne's eyes were drawn to fist-size earrings dangling from Fallon's ears.

She took a deep breath and smiled, grateful that at least one thing hadn't changed. Her bestselling author still smelled of patchouli and oranges and hadn't lost her old woman's crush on Neal.

Fallon motioned to Dyanne's husband with a curving nail. "C'mere, baby. Go on out to the car and get my bags. Maybe that'll wear off some of that frustration from not taking Dee Dee upstairs and all."

Emerging from his shock, Neal started for Fallon with open arms, laughing as he went. "How in the world did you find us? And what are you doing here?"

Dyanne, who'd only managed to mumble a few half-formed words, wanted to know the same thing. Although she was a beast of a businesswoman when she had time to plan things out, impromptu and in-person encounters definitely weren't Dyanne's strong suit. And interacting with Fallon required some preparation. For all Dyanne disliked about her father's religious fervor, she had to admit being brought to her knees in prayer more than a few times by the colorful woman in front of her, who now looked nothing like the ten thousand promotional pieces that had been circulated the week before. Dyanne's anger brought her out of her shock.

"So what's with the hair? You know I sent out all those postcards with your locks, right? We talked about this. You have to stick with the image people know. Build the brand."

Fallon flopped down on their new leather couch. She kicked off her shoes as though she'd lived there longer than they had. "One thing at a time, baby. First, I have to answer Handsome here. Let's see now—" she fumbled in her bag "—how did I end up here? The company sent me some amended schedule talking about I was supposed to be going to Miami or somewhere by myself and that you had moved to Florida and they were considering matching me up with another publicist."

Dyanne hung her head. *They didn't,* she thought, knowing they had. She'd told everyone that they could still handle the department and contact her online if needed during her vacation, but the one thing they shouldn't try to deal with was Fallon Gray.

"Uh-huh. They did, girl. I can see what you're thinking all over your face. Anyway, this little white girl called me—Heather or something—and she was talking just as crazy as you please.

"Sweet thing, just confused. Real confused. Talking about how I wasn't doing the historically black college tour or signing at the Essence bookstores and they were cutting back and when would I be available to rethink my brand—"

The room started to spin. If Dyanne had been pregnant, she definitely would have had to lie down. This was beyond crazy. She tried to think, to remember where she'd put her phone, but

Neal was on top of it, shoving her new PDA into her hands. She tapped away, thumbs flying while Fallon continued.

"So you know me, baby. I called Steve."

The tapping stopped. Steve Chaise, publisher and CEO of Wallace Shelton Books, did not take phone calls. He took messages. Fallon Gray did not leave messages. The only way out of that call was a conflict, the thing Dyanne dreaded most of all. She was known throughout the company as being one who smoothed things out. Now she'd be swirling in this mess for months.

Still, she knew better than to try and correct Fallon on making the call or the woman would whip out her phone and call Mr. Chaise again. Nobody but Fallon's mama, now long dead, had ever succeeded in telling her what to do. The uncanny thing was that Fallon was usually right in the end. Still, this call thing couldn't have gone well. Dyanne cleared her throat.

"And what did Mr.—Steve say?"

Fallon rubbed her head, front to back, back to front, just like Neal did when he woke in the morning. Without those earrings, she looked a lot like Mr. Jennings, a math teacher Dyanne had in third grade. What a mess. Yet somehow when Fallon opened her mouth, nobody noticed what she looked like. Neal, however, kept staring at the author's head as if he was digging it or something. Men. They're intrigued by anything different, but it won't keep them. In the end, they wanted their women painfully the same.

Not that Fallon tried to keep a man. For all her flirting, Dr. Gray ran guys off after a month or two. She said after loving hard and true one good time, everything else was just something to do. Dyanne hated to admit it, but it was true.

"I don't remember everything Steve and I said. We laughed a lot and made some plans for me to fly in for lunch with him after the tour—"

"Laughed?" In all her years of working for him, Dyanne had never seen Mr. Chaise laugh. The one smile she'd thought she'd seen had turned out to be indigestion. If there was ever a driven person, it was him. Before now, she would have thought he only would have laughed if some bestselling business book suggested it—one he'd published, of course.

"Girl, yeah. Steve is something else, old dog. If he wasn't him and I wasn't me, I swear I'd have me a piece of that man. He's kind of fine in his way, don't you think?"

Yuck. "I don't think. Just cut to the chase. Am I fired?"

Fallon stretched and yawned. "Naw, Dee. Heather is. Poor thing. I tried to save her, but she got all snotty with Steve and well, you know the rest. As for us, we're good to go with an added ten grand for the tour budget. That spot we did on Gospel Broadcasting last week has broken us into the inspirational sector. Evidently, the first print run is almost gone. He thinks you're a genius and said to tell you so."

It was Dyanne's turn to sit down. The TV spot on Gospel Broadcasting Network had been a fluke more than anything. She was trying to build up her contacts in preparation for rolling out the Christian line and a friend of a friend of a friend from college had turned out to be the network director. Dyanne had been shocked to hear the woman's voice on the line, since she'd been one of the students adamantly against "the white man's religion" in college.

"Me, a Christian. Can you believe it? I tell everybody from back in the day that God has a sense of humor. He delights in turning big mouths like I was into believers," the woman had said before offering a slot on an upcoming show on woman's issues.

With no one else available at the time, she'd offered up Fallon Gray as a guest, thinking she'd be rejected, but her pseudo friend had been delighted. "Oooh, I love her! Though she doesn't say it, everything she writes comes straight from the Word. I'd love to have her on and let her discuss her faith more openly."

Dyanne had tried to explain that there might not be much faith to discuss, but Fallon had done the date and proved her wrong again. Not only had Fallon kept up with the host's Bible references down to the chapter and verse, she'd ended the segment with an a cappella rendition of "His Eye is on the Sparrow" that had brought the house down, leaving even the cameraman in tears.

Though everyone who watched seemed to have been amazed, Dyanne was a little annoyed about the whole thing. While it was great for Fallon to get such attention, the media exposure meant nothing since it was outside of the brand Dyanne had worked so hard to create.

How many of the educated, professional women in Fallon's reader base were up watching some Christian show out of the Midwest? Though she'd been glad for the favor from her old friend, she didn't want to confuse or even offend the readers who kept Fallon on the bestseller lists. This kind of thing could be done, but it had to be planned strategically. Or so Dyanne had thought.

"Did you say that the first print run is almost sold out? But the book just came out what, a week ago."

"Uh-huh. A hundred thousand copies so far, I think." Fallon was up now and heading for the kitchen. Despite her girth, she ate only raw foods and walked several miles a day. She said it was all the nuts she ate that kept her fat and that no man she'd known had ever minded.

"Sexy is all in your mind," Fallon always said in her books and speaking engagements. The women clapped, but like Dyanne, none of them really believed it. But looking at Fallon now, with no hair and only a little gold lipstick, Dyanne didn't know what to think except that this woman who so often drove her crazy had a beauty that didn't make sense.

Fallon pulled out a giant Vita-Mix blender from her bag and went straight for the spinach and mangoes she knew Neal kept on hand. That was how Fallon had first taken a liking to Neal. He had a mango in his cooler at a hot book signing in Dallas. Fallon had turned real slow to him and lifted her sunglasses at the sight of the fruit, saying, "Oh, I see, Dee Dee. You got you one of those sweet juicy brothers. Not every man can handle a mango, but I've never met a mango man I didn't like." And just like that, she'd made up her mind to like Neal as much she sometimes pretended to dislike Dyanne.

Fallon turned to the door to wave to Neal as he brought in her luggage before assessing the fruit. "I see you found a decent store out here in this wilderness. I was thinking there would be some good mango down here in Florida. It looks good, but this fruit ain't tasting like much. We're going to have to stock up in Miami."

Dyanne took a breath. Miami was not on Fallon's book tour schedule. In fact, the tour wasn't even supposed to start for another month. She still wasn't sure why Fallon was in her house, how she'd found it or how long she planned to stay— although the entire Louis Vuitton luggage collection Neal had just deposited in her living room gave her some idea. There was no point in trying to rush Fallon. If Dyanne were honest, she wasn't sure she wanted to. As much as they fought, somewhere along the way, the two of them had become friends. They just knew better than to admit it.

"Anyway," Fallon screamed over the whir of the blender creating the awful-looking green mango-spinach drink she loved above all else. "Steve and I got to talking about this Jesus thing and he was saying how sometimes he wondered about everything, too. You know, God and all?"

She stopped and lifted the lid of the Vita Mix, stirring things around. "He's getting old, you know. Even rich men start thinking about God when they realize they're not Him. It's always a shock, I think. Anyway, I told Steve about how Jesus brought me through when my husband took up with that girl and left me, how He helped me get through school and showed me how to write books to help folks…and he got real quiet. Sort of like you are right now."

Dyanne was quiet. She loved Fallon, but the way she could just disarm herself and strip bare, unloading her life in front of strangers, or worse yet, people she knew, like Steve Chaise, made Dyanne crazy.

And yet, backstage at that Gospel Broadcasting set, Dyanne had found herself swaying into the curtains with teary eyes, feeling weak and emotional. She'd wondered then if she wasn't already pregnant. It'd be an easier explanation than her show of feeling. She wondered if she'd ever be pregnant now. Fallon still had a bomb to drop, and Dyanne wasn't sure that she'd be able to catch it this time.

Fallon reached up and got two goblets and poured some of her Green Mama as she called it into both glasses until they were half-full. Dyanne took a sip without a fight, knowing that it always tasted better than it looked. Besides, the last pregnancy book she'd read had said that nutrition six months before conception was as important, if not more, than nutrition during pregnancy. Maybe there was hope of a baby after all since she was still thinking about such things.

"Steve and I talked about it and we agreed that I should write an inspirational book. You know, what I normally do, but with Bible verses and my testimony. He has some big people lined up for the launch of the Christian line evidently and he wants this book—"

Dyanne managed to swallow. "What book?"

"The one I came here to write. Pay attention, girl. It has to be done by the end of the month and then we're off on tour. Surprise! Now, where's my bed?"

After clutching the counter, Dyanne tossed back her whole glass of green mush, swallowed hard and pointed upstairs. It was all she had the strength to do.

* * *

"It's not so bad. It might even be fun having Fallon here," Neal said the next evening while caressing Dyanne's back. "Look at the upside, you'll probably get a juicy bonus out of this and you didn't even know what was going on."

Dyanne sighed and lowered her voice to a whisper. "That's just it. I still can't believe this. Maybe you're right. Maybe this vacation from work, this house, maybe it isn't realistic. I'm gone less than a week and Heather, who I trained and felt totally comfortable with, almost loses the author that keeps my department's lights on? Then the author calls the publisher and has a 'chat' with him? Do you know how that could have ended? Things are out of control."

"Out of your control, you mean." In the moonlight filtering through the window, the lines of Neal's body were even sharper, with deep cuts between the muscles on his back and down his legs. Fallon had made Dyanne forget about her ovulation timeline, but the silhouette illuminated by the moon was unforgettable. She reached out and traced his spine with her fingernail.

When he sighed with pleasure, Fallon happened to be walking by on her way to the room closest to them. She'd rejected the guest room at the end of the hall; too small she said. Besides theirs, it was the biggest bedroom in the house.

Dressed in a purple caftan and munching grapes, Fallon lingered in their closed doorway. "That's right, Dee Dee. Make him holler. You'll get you a baby yet. It's good for the skin, too," she said, laughing into the folds of her nightgown.

Dyanne slid under the sheets, covering her face in shame while Neal had another laughing fit. As usual, he found Fallon's brashness comforting. His wife did not.

"Mind your own business, woman. Aren't you supposed to be writing a book?"

"Feisty tonight, huh? I like it. Ain't you supposed to be

getting a baby? You tend to your business and I'll tend to mine. The moon is on the wane, but I think you can still squeeze something out of it. I love my room. Did you know I can see straight in your neighbor's upstairs? Those kids are something funny. Been waving at me all night. Their parents probably don't even know they up. I've got to go and meet them tomorrow."

Brilliant! Maybe they'd all keep each other out of trouble. "Go for it," Dyanne said, wondering if this was going to happen every night. At least the children next door were warming up to Fallon. Progress at last. "Those kids are something wild, especially that little girl."

"Good! I can't stand all these little fake kids people have now, small adults running around. If I'm going to spend time with children, I want them to be just that. Remember that when you ask me to babysit. Now go on, act like married folk. Good night. I'm turning on my music…."

True to her word, instrumental jazz replaced Fallon's voice a few minutes later, the latest intruder into their tranquil bedroom.

*At least she warned us.*

The sultry crooning of a bass guitar was just loud enough to be heard, but not too distracting. Neal must have liked it because he went after Dyanne with both hands—and a full heart.

"I love that woman," he said, going in for a kiss.

Me, too, Dyanne thought. "You'd better be concerned about loving this woman," she said, returning his playful yet passionate kisses. Still, she was relieved that Neal seemed happy about having Fallon around.

Once before, Dyanne had spent a week alone with Fallon on a huge rewrite and it wasn't pretty. There were still shards of Swarovski crystals in the carpet of their old apartment from the vase Dyanne had broken after throwing up her hands one time too many.

Things had been tight enough with just a month to get this house in order and finalize the book tour. Being successful in the African-American market meant making—and keeping—relationships. And that wasn't always easy with tight dead-lines and high personnel turnover. For every bookstore owner, university official or organizational chairperson, there were keep-in-touch gifts, e-mails and calls and down-to-the-minute checking and just-in-case plans.

Even then, many of Dyanne's contacts worked on what her grandfather had called "colored people time," an entirely different construct than the European concept of planning down to the last second. Dyanne's grandfather had explained that the African sense of timelessness was the one thing that couldn't be beaten out of them. What some thought was laziness was a virtue of watching people over clocks. "The sun, moon and stars told us what we needed to know. And our bellies of course. When you're hungry, it's time to eat."

Right.

Unfortunately, publishing—or the rest of the world for that matter—didn't run by sundial. To compensate, Fallon traveled with pop-up tables ("Someone is using the table now, but if you come back at four…"), extra books ("We ordered them, but they didn't come in"), media contacts ("They did a press release, but nobody called…") and all that was just for the regular stores. Once they hit the "chitlin circuit" as Fallon called the drive to the black bookstores, lodges, gymnasiums, historically black colleges and now more than before, churches, it would be Dealing with Divas 101 time. The thought of it all made her tired, but excited, too.

Neal was kissing her elbows now, totally erasing her train of thought. She let out a contented sigh of her own. Maybe this was enough, the two of them. Maybe this wasn't the time to have a baby. What would she do with a kid the next time Fallon showed up needing a month—or two—of attention?

*Trust Me.*

It wasn't a voice or anything flaky like the experiences her father talked about, but the words were impressed on her mind, overflowing Dyanne's heart. All she could think of was how hard she'd prayed for her parents to stay together, for her mother to keep the baby boys she'd miscarried again and again, each time taking her mother farther from them into her own little world.

Though Dyanne couldn't deny that God had been good to her, the one time she'd needed Him, truly trusted Him, He hadn't come through. She couldn't make that mistake again. Her father had spent the past few years trying to teach her about God, but the first lesson he'd taught her about Him still held true—the only person a woman can trust completely is herself.

As if he'd read her thoughts, Neal's hands and lips stopped moving. "You really want this, don't you? This baby?"

Dyanne nodded slowly, surprised at the vulnerability in his voice. For months, she'd tried to get her husband here. Who'd have thought that Fallon Gray would be what brought him around? Never one to miss an opportunity, Dyanne reached over and clicked on the light.

Neal shielded his eyes. "What are you doing?"

Dyanne tiptoed to her briefcase and produced her master-piece—the baby proposal.

Speechless, her husband flipped through the pages of flow charts, family cost predictions and couldn't believe what he saw.

"You got an endorsement from the doctor who wrote all those baby care books? You've got to be kidding me."

She wasn't kidding. Mr. Chaise—Steve—had snapped up the doctor in a five-book deal last summer and Dyanne had spent over an hour talking to him about children. He'd made a few quotes in the conversation and when she'd asked later, he'd given her permission to share them with her husband, although he said he didn't recommend it. Now, watching the look on her husband's face, she wondered if he hadn't been right. "Just read it. I did a lot of research. It's all there."

He slammed the folder shut just as he reached the best visual in the whole thing. "It's not all here, Dyanne. This is a business proposal. Babies come from love. I wanted to believe that this was about love, but as usual it's about something else. I'm not sure what quite yet, but I don't think I want to find out. No baby for the immediate future, and that's my final answer." He stormed off down the hall, not stopping until he reached the guest room that Fallon had turned down earlier.

Fallon. She'd probably heard all the yelling. In a strange way, Dyanne almost hoped so. She wanted to throw herself in Fallon's arms and have a good cry, but she couldn't. She wouldn't. Work was work and home was home. No matter how close they seemed right now, they had to remain separate. Dyanne hoped that she and Neal wouldn't remain separate, too. His negative response to her proposal had sent her reeling, both with its quickness and its finality. What guy didn't want a baby?

Maybe he just didn't want one with her.

*Trust Me.*

Dyanne turned out the light and wrapped herself in a sheet before following her husband. She didn't know who to trust, but she was running out of options.

## The Never Enough

It waits for me at the edge
Of laundry baskets,
Holding my best hopes.
Hungry, it swallows possibilities
Spitting reality at my feet.
"Never," it whispers, blowing
through the pages beneath my bed.
"Enough," He says, this
Brightness with no darkness
At all.
I awake, dancing
On the curve between night
And morning, hearing
Only, "Never enough."

—Karol
Upon waking after dreaming about mangoes and
Ferris wheels

## Chapter Six

"They got company over there," Karol's son Judah proclaimed at the dinner table. "She looks old, but not boring old. Fun old, like Grandpa."

"Don't call people old. That's rude," Karol said.

Ryan shrugged. "Not really. We're all going to get old. Why are people so touchy about it?"

Karol didn't know quite what to say to that. Or maybe she did, but she didn't want to hear it. She'd seen the hybrid SUV pull up and the tall woman with a teeny-weeny Afro get out of it. The lady had looked familiar in a way that made Karol catch her breath, but she didn't think much of it. She'd exhaled like that the first time she saw Hope, too.

She took a breath at the thought of Hope and Singh. She'd picked up the phone a million times to call Hope and apologize about what Rob had done. Why her husband would have asked her best friends to consider moving away still eluded her. Granted, she and Hope may have been closer than was healthy. Karol could see that now. Why wouldn't Rob have just said that? She'd have listened.

*No, I wouldn't have. I'm not listening now.*

The thought hit hard. She'd dreamed of fruit and carnivals

and the guest next door. Probably too much pizza, but sometimes it turned out to be important. The new woman seemed important somehow, more than the new neighbors even. Some people just had that way about them, as if you'd known them before. At first, she thought it might have been Dyanne's mother, but somehow she didn't think so. Instead it was probably a friend—the one thing Karol didn't have right now.

*That's silly. You have loads of friends. You could call any woman in the church directory right now and she'd love to hear from you. Other mothers from the children's school, people you used to work with...*

Maybe. Maybe not. After her little trust God speech the other Sunday, the same mothers who had thronged around Hope had barely waved at her during the last service. And Karol really didn't care. The thought of finding another best friend, telling all the stories, breaking down all the walls... Just the thought of it made her stomach hurt. She couldn't imagine anyone else getting her corny jokes or having a husband who got along with Rob as well as Singh had. Outside of the new guy next door—and that was just being neighborly—Rob hadn't been spending time with anyone new, either.

*Rob was right. We were too close. All of us.*

She piled another pancake on Judah's plate, grateful that the younger ones were quiet this morning. They seemed too tired to talk.

Be afraid. Be very afraid, she thought. Silence always had a deeper meaning, with these kids at least.

Karol put down the syrup and headed for the bar where the children were sitting. She checked their heads for fever one by one.

"They're not sick," Ryan said. "Just sleepy. They were up half the night playing Flashlight and 'I See You' with the new lady next door. I told them to cut it out, but you know how they get."

Boy, did she.

With a smile, Karol served the last pancake and offered warm syrup to the boys after pouring Mia's. Prevention was ninety percent of the equation with that girl.

Ryan took the bottle himself and looked a little offended that his mother was still trying to fix his pancakes. He grabbed his knife and moved it to the other side of the plate.

"Just in case you get any other ideas," her oldest son said, looking weary as usual of the error that his mother usually realized too late.

Karol tried not to laugh and turned her attention back to the younger children. They were harder to keep up with but easier to figure out. "When that happens, come and let Mommy know, okay? Even if it's the middle of the night. Things were fine when Rob—Dad—and I came to tuck you all in. I didn't hear a thing."

Mia rested her head on her fist, fighting to keep her eyes open. "The lady started it."

Judah nodded. "I didn't know that any grown-ups knew how to play Flashlight."

Ryan rolled his eyes. He was growing up and the antics of his younger siblings embarrassed him more than amused him these days. "These pancakes are awesome, Mom. Did Dad make them?"

He had made them. Rob had slipped out of bed and made the pancakes before work, leaving breakfast and a love note behind. Things were still a little shaky between them after his admission of being behind Hope and Singh leaving. Even now, Karol wanted to call Hope to discuss it, but something held her back. During her Bible reading time, God had given her the scripture to confirm it. One she'd read on many other occasions but never with such a personal meaning:

"…as His divine power has given to us all things that pertain to life and godliness…"


"Yes, Dad made them. I just heated them up."

Judah shrugged his shoulders. "Figures. Your eggs are good, though. The best."

*Except for Dad's omelets.*

Ryan held up a finger. "Except for Dad's omelets, but still…"

Karol had to laugh. She'd prayed to have a husband like Rob, a sensitive, caring man. She wondered now if she hadn't forgotten along the way that no matter how sensitive Rob was, he was still a man. Her mother, Faith the Second, had her shortcomings, but she always saw Rob as the man he was, even if she didn't always treat him kindly.

She decided right then to make Rob a cake for dinner— 7-Up cake, his favorite. And after dinner, once the kids were asleep, she'd offer him something much better than her cooking. Until then, she had a day of parenting—no, discipleship—ahead of her. It was time for Karol to let go of Hope and come into her own as a mother, even if it meant starting all over again to find her way.

After breakfast, Karol and the kids did something they hadn't done since their neighbors moved away. They had Bible time together.

"It's not the same without Eden doing the voices."

"Or Bone barking."

They were right. It wasn't the same. Though Hope and Singh taught their children at home and Karol's children went to public school, they'd all gathered each morning for prayer and Bible study in the tree house that Dyanne had torn down. Hope had chosen the stories, usually ones she and her children were studying during their other subjects.

Karol's job had been bringing whatever supplies were needed for the day's illustration. She generally brought whatever Hope recommended on the list she gave Karol on the weekends. If there was a project with the story, all the children worked on it together once the boys were home from school. During the day, Karol and Mia went back and forth between houses. Her daughter often came home with a "school" paper of her own, custom made by Hope on her computer. No, Bible time wasn't the same. It never would be. But it was theirs.

"How about we do the voices? All of us. Just follow me. I'm not Miss Hope, but I'm your mom, and I love you. And God loves you, too. I'm sure that Miss Hope would want us to find our own way to have time with God's Word."

"Do we have to go outside?" Mia asked.

Karol shook her head. "No. We can do it right here. We can even sing if you want."

Karol's younger son, Judah, raised his hand. "Can I do that part today? I learned a new song at church on Sunday."

And on it went. Ryan headed up the prayer time, even stopping to take requests. Judah led them all in a beautiful, off-key worship song and Mia acted out the story—voices and all—as Karol read it. At the end, instead of the usual short sermon that Hope used to give, Karol went another route. She let the kids ask questions.

They stared at her, stunned. "We can ask things?"

"Sure," Karol said, wondering if Faith the Second wasn't right about their creativity being stifled. Had Karol been so caught up in preserving the status quo that her children didn't think that they could ask her questions about life? About God? Karol hoped she was wrong, but she filled in the silence with her own questions for them until they worked up their nerve.

When their curiosity kicked in, the children's queries were more numerous and complex than she anticipated. More than once she had to admit something they rarely got to hear from their mother's mouth: "I don't know."

They seemed glad to hear it. So did the tall, beautiful woman visiting the people next door. Unlike the new neighbors, who always approached cautiously, tiptoeing around the edge of the yard, this big, beautiful woman cut right across the lawn and up to the front door. And she didn't ring the bell, either. She knocked a rhythm that sounded like music. Like a secret.

Karol's little disciples scrambled away from the table to meet her as though they'd been expecting her all along. Mia made it to the door first, swinging it open without asking who it was. Karol frowned, pushing herself up and following behind. Even if they'd watched the woman approach through the window, the lady was still a stranger. Karol would have to get on her daughter about it later. At the moment, though, she was as excited about the visitor as the kids were, only she couldn't figure out why.

"Hi! We were hoping you'd come over," Mia said, taking the lady's hand as though she'd always known her.

"Well, of course I was coming over. We had such a good time last night. I had to come and meet you all. Your mom and dad, too." She reached out to shake Karol's hand. "I have the funny feeling that I've met your mom already. I just can't put my finger on where."

Karol's breathing quickened as she took the woman's hand. So it wasn't just her imagination. She stared at the lady, squinted even. "Did you have long hair before? Locks maybe? I'm Karol, by the way. Karol Simon."

The woman's eyes narrowed. "Yes. I cut my locks a few weeks ago. You may have seen me speak somewhere. I'm Fallon. Fallon Gray. It's not my real name, but it's sort of stuck on now. Just like your face.

"I'm not placing Simon, but your eyes are familiar. Very familiar. You look like Eric Ware, a professor I once knew from Morris Brown College. Do you know him? I'm reaching. You've probably never heard of him. He teaches—"

"Anthropology. He's my father."

Ms. Gray, the embodiment of self-assurance and poise, crumpled a little. She patted Mia's hand and then her own. When she spoke again, her words came at half the speed and volume. "You're Eric's daughter? He talked about you so much…" Like an intake of breath, she came back to herself. "Come here, girl. You 'bout like family. Where's your mama? Or is she still calling herself Faith number two?"

Karol was too stunned at first to respond. She was still hung up on hearing her father's name so many times on this stranger's lips. Eric. She'd said it all in one breath each time, as if it really meant something.

"Faith the Second," Mia corrected, holding up two fingers. "She brought clothes. Drove a big car. You just missed her."

The visitor sat down on the couch and slipped off her Etienne loafers. Mia jumped right into her lap.

"Imagine. Dee Dee moves in next door to Eric Ware's daughter. God certainly has a sense of humor. And irony, too. Always with the irony. People miss that about Him."

Karol didn't miss it. She didn't miss a thing. "Dee Dee? Do you mean Dyanne?"

"Uh-huh. She goes by that, too. I call her Dee Dee Thornton. She's my publicist. Oh, I'm getting ahead of myself. I'm supposed to be telling you why I came over. Your kids were so cute in that window last night and I had a dream, you see…"

Karol stiffened. Her own dreams were one thing, but she didn't go around telling people about them.

Fallon continued. "I dreamed about mangoes and Ferris wheels. It's not the first time, either. I had that dream when I first started writing and sometimes I get it when I'm about to meet somebody important. Folks that stick. Always people. Do you all know what I mean?"

The children nodded furiously. Karol nodded slowly, trying not to cry.

"Well, anyway, see. The devil messes with us all, tells us we're not good enough, that we'll never be good enough and God sends us always people, folks who always know what to say and do to make us feel better. Mangoes make me feel better. And I'm terrified of Ferris wheels. Sometimes I dream of big, juicy beautiful things that I can't afford to be scared of. I think one of those things is you, Karol. Or maybe all of you."

After a moving, emotional silence, Judah farted.

All of the kids squealed. Mia threw a pillow at him.

"Sorry. I ate my pancakes too fast. Now I'm hungry all over again."

Their visitor laughed a long throaty laugh. "Don't be sorry, baby. I thought that was me. We can do lunch together. Your place or mine?"

Before Karol could answer, Mia threw up a fist. "Our place!"

Fallon Gray threw back her glorious, glossy head and laughed again. "Lead the way to the kitchen."

When she'd left this morning, Dyanne had asked only one thing of Neal—to keep an eye on Fallon Gray. And that was the very thing he'd failed to do.

"So where is she?" Dyanne asked, skimming a hand through her freshly relaxed hair and putting down a bag of fruit from the farmer's market. She had something to tell Neal, something she should have told him before anything else, but Fallon's absence took priority.

Neal, who'd spent the day catching up on his own Internet security business, shrugged his shoulders. "She's a grown woman, honey. She'll be fine."

His employees telecommuted from across the country and had things pretty well in hand for the next few weeks, but Neal never let too much time pass without checking on the servers and all the monitored accounts. People would be amazed to know how many hack attempts there were to sites with even the highest levels of security. Neal knew better than anyone that there was a slim line between a breached system and a secure one. He was starting to think the same about his marriage.

"I didn't ask you her age or whether she'd be fine. I asked you where she was."

"Who, Fallon? I don't know. She went out. Taking a walk, maybe? Her car's still here."

"No. It's not."

"Well, it was."

Dyanne gave up. Neal hadn't even raised his head to look at her. Usually, she would have been right beside him—or in the next room—head down and nose to the grindstone, too. Today she was irritated by his lack of eye contact in the same way Neal had often been with her. She'd have to process that later. For now, she had a bestselling author with a deadline, missing in action. That was not acceptable. "I'll find her. Wait up for me. I bought something today. I need to talk to you about it."

"Right," Neal said, typing faster than most secretaries and still not looking up.

Gathering her courage, Dyanne tugged down the beautiful linen dress she'd picked up from a quaint little shop in town when she'd stopped to feed the ducks at the man-made lake and park where the farmer's market was held. Dyanne had liked the dress so much that she'd put it on right there in the store and carried her own clothes out in a bag. She'd raced home to show Fallon, thinking she'd get a kick out of it. Aside from fitting Dyanne perfectly and giving her the appearance of curves she didn't possess, it was the color of mangoes. She'd bought something else, too, something that had seemed like a perfect fit at the time, but now didn't seem like such a good idea. Oh, well. It could go back.

For now, she had to find Fallon, who was still nowhere to be seen. Dyanne had a sinking feeling about what might have happened to her. The neighbors. Or knowing Fallon, it might have been her that "happened" to them. Either way, it was not okay. Fallon Gray had come to Dyanne's to write a book and that's just what she was going to do. No matter how much Steve Chaise laughed with Fallon, he wouldn't be smiling if there wasn't a publishable manuscript on his desk a month from now. Dyanne wouldn't be smiling, either. She wasn't smiling now, not even when Fallon's car pulled up—without her in it.

Her neighbor Karol put the car in Park and got out slowly. "Your guest came over. We made lunch. She wanted some fruit to make the kids a smoothie. Our van takes a lot of gas. She insisted that I take her car—"

"She shouldn't have."

Her neighbor smiled, as if she wanted to laugh. "She said you'd say that. That she shouldn't have come over, that I shouldn't drive her car—which I don't think I should have, but she's quite persuasive and has full coverage. Look, why don't you come in for a minute. I know things have been a little bumpy between us, but we really are good people. The kids, too. They're just…kids."

Like a fool, Dyanne fell for Karol's speech and followed her inside after her neighbor complimented her new mango-colored dress. Karol's house seemed cleaner than Dyanne remembered. Quieter, too. Maybe she'd gotten her kids under control after all.

"Surprise!" Fallon jumped out of the hall bathroom with Mia on her shoulders. They tossed a water balloon at Karol, but hit Dyanne instead.

Karol looked as shocked as her neighbor, but she recovered quickly and led Dyanne through the dining room to the kitchen for a paper towel.

"I'm so sorry. They were trying to surprise us I guess…."

"Yeah. I got that."

In the kitchen was another surprise, the boys had dragged in a china cabinet Karol said she had picked up at a flea market from the garage and turned it on its side. They were bowling in it. With a real bowling ball.

"You know what? I think I'm just going to go," Dyanne said, turning back toward the door.

"But wait—"

"Fallon! Let's go. We've got work to do."

"Dee Dee, wait. This was all my doing. Karol had no idea."

"I'm leaving, Fallon. I'd appreciate it if you'd come with me. Now."

Fallon followed Dyanne reluctantly and the children ran after her.

"Come back soon!" the middle boy cried. "We're always people, remember? Mangoes and Ferris wheels. Don't forget us."

Dyanne almost stumbled at the little boy's words, but she didn't. She made it over the threshold of Karol's house with a sure foot. Once outside, she was met with something, someone that made her want to run back inside. Neal leaned on the porch with his hands folded across his chest. He was staring at the ground. Not a good sign.

"I found Fallon. Let's go home," Dyanne said, trying to escape before her husband made a scene.

Neal didn't move except to point at finger at the vehicle next to Fallon's: a brand-new minivan. "What is that?"

"Let's talk about this at home," Dyanne said waving to Fallon, who had stopped all progress to follow her back to their house.

"We are home. The house is right there. Now, I need to know. What is that vehicle and who does it belong to?"

Though Neal didn't raise his voice, his tone had an edge that sent Karol's children running back into the house. He had the intimidation part of parenting covered. Now it was the marriage part that was at issue—and this time Dyanne knew she'd overplayed her hand.

"I need an answer, Dee. Whose is it?"

She winced a little before giving her answer. "Ours? Look, don't be mad. I have twenty-four hours to take it back—"

"No, you have twenty-four minutes to take it back. Where is the other car?"

Gulp. "I traded it—"

"Oh, no. Ohhhhhh no. Give me the keys. Fallon, can you follow me with Dyanne?"

Fallon was already down Karol's front stairs and headed toward her own car. "I'm one step ahead of you, chief."

Dyanne followed Neal with her wet, not-so-cute dress clinging in all the wrong places. "What? Why should we follow? I want to ride with you." She wrapped herself around his arm.

He shrugged her off. "No, you don't. Not right now. Trust me."

Her heart sank. She'd heard those words before.

# *To-Do*

- Buy percale linens for guest room—Egyptian cotton

- Drop off prescription for next month's birth control

- Have flowers delivered to Neal at the gym

- Get 1000 good words out of Fallon

- Confirm all new stops on Fallon's tour

- Send a note to neighbors apologizing for arguing in their yard

—Dyanne
The morning after returning the van

## Chapter Seven

Sound carried between the two houses. The guest room, where Dyanne was sleeping alone—wasn't it the husband who usually got kicked out of the bed?—was directly across from Rob and Karol's bedroom. And tonight, despite their neighbor's argument on their porch, down their stairs and in their yard, the Simons were not quiet. The Simons, John Boy and Chaka Khan, were making love. And not just any kind of love, either. Mango love.

After five minutes of it—yes, that long—Dyanne closed the window and put the new pillow by her face to drown out her crying. She shouldn't have bought the new car—or traded the old one—without talking to Neal.

And sure, he'd said no babies and yes, she'd heard him, but the salesman made it sound so good, so safe when she'd gone back to the dealership to explain that she wouldn't be needing a van after all. The salesman told her some lame story about how getting a van had made him realize there was room in their lives for children and Dyanne had fallen for it. She'd wanted to fall for it, to believe that her dream of a family was going to endure instead of shattering into a million pieces because one person fell out of love or got seduced by the secretary or some random thing.

Dyanne knew business. She knew how to invest in things, in people. She knew that investments made people stay around when they felt like leaving. Children were the next investment for her and Neal to make. Though he thought her love didn't equal his, Neal had no idea how many times Dyanne had gotten off a plane without seeing him right away…. She couldn't imagine the thought even for those few seconds of him not being there. And then she'd see him, with a bag of Jelly Bellies and a dashing smile. Waiting.

She wanted him to know that he wouldn't always have to wait, that there was more for them, the next level. They'd done the groundwork: retirement plan, good medical and dental, a house with fresh air and slow times. Somehow, in trying to bring them closer together, Dyanne had driven her husband away. And so she lay in the guest bed, crying into her new pillow, haunted by the sounds of love from a couple she'd thought nothing of when she met them. And yet, like Fallon, the Simons kept turning up over and over again….

Dyanne heard the door open and tried to stop crying, but she couldn't. She knew by the smell of licorice, that Fallon had applied her cream and padded down the hall to give Dyanne yet another piece of her troubled mind. As the bed squeaked in response to Fallon sitting down, Dyanne prepared herself for the discourse on what a good man needed and all that nonsense Fallon spouted to packed auditoriums week after week. What she got was something else entirely.

It began with Fallon lowering the pillow slowly and pulling Dyanne into her arms. She kissed the head of her up-and-coming publicist and sang her a lullaby. When the song was done, the gentleness went with it and good old Fallon returned.

"All right, little sister. That's enough of that. Fix your face and your nightgown. Your man will be coming down the hall in a minute."

Dyanne laughed, or at least she tried. "You don't know Neal. When he's mad, he's mad. He'll sleep like a baby."

"Mark my word, baby. He's coming and when he does, don't start running your mouth. Take him to that downstairs bedroom and—"

"Downstairs?"

Fallon got up. "Yes, baby, downstairs. Alone. I'll see you in the morning. I'm already a day behind on this book."

Before Dyanne could say anything else, there was a knock at the door. Dyanne sat still, unbelieving. Fallon opened the door and disappeared down the hall without saying a word. Another first. At the sight of Neal, the tears that the author-friend had wiped away came flooding back again.

Though she'd planned a silent stone wall. Dyanne caved at the sight of him. "I'm s-s-sorry. I just want-ed to—"

"I'm sorry, baby. I handled it wrong. All of it. Shh. Don't cry."

When she couldn't stop crying, Neal picked her up and lifted her into his arms. Holding her close, he carried her… downstairs. The crooning of Luther Vandross followed them from Fallon's room. Like their love, the music seemed to fill the house.

For a moment, Dyanne worried if all this going on wasn't making too much noise for the neighbors.

Just for a moment.

The next morning Fallon was downstairs in the kitchen singing and cooking when Dyanne and Neal woke up.

She pulled on her nightgown and went out of the room. She could barely look at Fallon when she said good morning. Whatever professional-personal barriers may have been between them had been demolished last night and Dyanne wasn't so sure she liked this new open territory. When the pan crackled she realized what other barrier had been crossed. Fallon was *cooking.*

"Um, I thought you were a raw foodist."

"I am, except when I'm not." Fallon flipped a spinach and red onion frittata for Neal. His favorite. He'd ordered if for breakfast once when they were at a convention together and mentioned how he loved it. How did Fallon remember things like that?

"So all those times you had Neal going for organic fruit and me searching for raw chefs, we could have pulled over at Burger King?"

Fallon ground a bit of white pepper and dashed it on top. "No, I was a raw foodist then. I'm just not one right now. Don't think so hard. Just go with it, okay?"

"Okay." Why was that so hard, for Dyanne, to just go with it? She wanted, no needed, for people to be what they were supposed to be, what they said they were and to stay that way. Unfortunately, something in human DNA made such people rare. She'd thought that Fallon was that—rare—even though she tried her best to act common. Maybe Dyanne had been wrong about her, too. She'd certainly been wrong about herself. About Neal. Before this baby thing, she'd thought they had a rock-solid marriage, so strong that nothing could come between them. She now knew that a minivan and a baby proposal could put them in two different beds.

"Don't look so disappointed, honey. The only thing I am all the time is a Christian, and sometimes you'd think I'd given up on that, too. But I haven't. That's the one thing I can't give up on, because God won't give up on me. He keeps at me, saying, 'Fay—' He doesn't call me Fallon '—don't do that, baby. It ain't right.' Sometimes I have my eyes closed expecting a whippin' and He's like, 'What are you doing over there?' You have to learn the difference. All these years and I'm still learning."

Dyanne rinsed off an apple and took a bite before remembering that she'd been on her way to get Neal some clothes from upstairs. "I'll be right back."

"He's got some jeans and T-shirts in the bureau down here. Top right."

This was getting freaky, Fallon's little knowings. "Thanks."

"Sorry for going through your things, but I caught up the laundry yesterday and there was no more room on Neal's side for some of his clothes." She cleared her throat for emphasis.

The message came through loud and clear—Dyanne had too many clothes and shoes and accessories and well, just too much stuff.

*And here I am worried about getting a baby which would mean even more stuff.*

"Maybe we can go through some of my things one weekend before you leave."

Fallon smiled. "Maybe."

Neal didn't seem surprised when Dyanne told him where to look for clothes. He shrugged and grabbed them. "Is that spinach I smell? And feta cheese?"

"Your favorite frittata."

He laughed, and then froze. "Wait a minute. Isn't Fallon a—"

"Raw foodist? Only when she isn't."

Neal shook his head and pulled her close. They were just about to kiss when the shrill scream of the little girl next door cut through any remaining romance between them.

Dyanne rolled her eyes. With these kids around, Neal would have a vasectomy before the summer was out. She was just about to apologize to her husband for not having gotten Karol straight yet about her kids when Neal ran past her in his bare feet and half-buttoned shirt and out the door.

"She had a bad dream," Neal explained when he came back to the kitchen with Mia on his hip. Both her little arms were latched around his neck as Dyanne's hands had been not long before.

Fallon rubbed Mia's back and tried to take her, but the little girl shook her head.

Dyanne shook her head, too. This was ridiculous. "Well, let's take her back home so we can get on with our day—"

"They're all sleeping, honey. The sun isn't even up and it's the weekend. I'll take her back soon. Evidently she used to get up and come out to that tree house you knocked down. She got up and toddled out here and remembered the whole thing was gone." He stroked the little girl's hair. "Poor baby. She must have forgotten."

Fallon smiled and shaped a biscuit with the bottom of a glass while Dyanne tried to find her voice. Poor baby? Neal must have forgotten something, too—his mind! First, Dyanne couldn't have a baby, and next he's treating the ruffian from next door like she's a princess? Well, she was sort of cute, but still…

"Neal, we can't do this. Her parents will be worried and it's starting a bad precedent. You know, like with puppies? If you let them on the furniture—"

"Puppies?" Neal asked, giving Dyanne the same sour look that Fallon and the little girl were making.

A violent ringing of their doorbell, followed by banging, kept Dyanne or Neal from saying more. Dyanne made it to the door first, eager to give Karol a piece of her mind. What she wasn't prepared for was receiving a chunk of Karol's husband's angry thoughts.

"Are you crazy?" Rob said, stepping inside the Thornton's house and plucking his daughter from Neal. "We've been looking everywhere. Why didn't you say something?"

This was not John Boy. Not by a long shot.

Neal looked surprised, too. "Look, man. I'm sorry. You all were sleeping and she said she was hungry so…"

Rob closed his eyes. "No, I'm sorry. I didn't mean to raise my voice. Since the Waltons moved away, things with the children have been, well, difficult. Especially Mia. She spent a lot of time over here with her friends and she hasn't been sleeping well. I woke up and she was gone and there was no stick—"

Fallon piped up from behind. "Stick?"

"Yes. I'm sorry. I have to remember that you all are new. So new. And not even any children of your own. How could I expect you to understand? We're probably driving you all nuts—"

Finally somebody was getting down to reality, Dyanne thought. "About that—"

Neal gave his wife a stern look. "The stick. You were telling us about the stick."

Rob hugged Mia closer. "Well, when Mia woke up and came over here, Hope would have one of her kids leave the stick, it was more like a cane really, a big rain stick Singh had brought back from somewhere. We'd usually hear the kids shaking it on the way over and know that Mia was okay. Now everything is different. She can't just go running off. She doesn't understand that."

"Neither do I," Fallon said. "Life's too short to have to stay in your own yard. I don't have a rain stick, but I've got a maraca in my trunk. Will that work?"

"Fallon, I don't think it's appropriate—"

Rob smiled. "That'd be perfect, ma'am. I appreciate it. We'll be getting home now. I'll call you soon, Neal, about that deck if you're still thinking about it."

Deck? What deck? It was Dyanne's turn to fold her arms across her chest and stare at the floor.

Neal cleared his throat. "Nothing for certain yet. Still need to talk it over with the wife."

"Ah. I see. Well, we'll look to see you all in church then. Don't be late. It's Mother's Day. It's no Easter, but the pews fill up pretty fast. Thanks again."

Dyanne stared at her husband, who mustered a half smile. What else had he signed them up for, a reality show? He hadn't said anything about going to church. And on Mother's

Day, too? She could still remember the humiliation of the childless women on those days, coming out of service with no flower in their lapels. She wouldn't be one of them.

Fallon clapped her hands. "Church! This should be fun. And I know just what I'm going to wear." She lifted the first batch of perfect biscuits out of the oven and offered the first to Dyanne. "Have one?"

Dyanne shook her head and spooned raspberries into the oatmeal she'd planned to eat for breakfast. "No biscuits for me. I've got enough on my plate. In more ways than one." With that, she headed into her downstairs office.

Alone.

Ksimon: Happy Mother's Day!!!

Hope4Today: Same to you!

KSimon: Going out for lunch after church?

Hope4Today: No. The church here is having a big brunch. All the dads and sons are cooking. The boys are leaving now if I can find another pair of shoes. The boys are like weeds now, all arms and legs. Shoes fit one Sunday, the next week, they can't get anything on.

KSimon: The brunch sounds like fun. Send more pictures or I won't know the kids when I see them.

Hope4Today: Of course you will. Once they open their mouths, you'll know! Speaking of pictures, have you lost weight? You look slimmer in that picture you sent. Maybe not having me and my goodie bags around is a good thing.

KSimon: Maybe not. ☹

Hope4Today: LOL At least somebody loves me.

KSimon: A whole lot of somebodies love you, one in particular.

Hope4Today: I guess. Sometimes I wonder.

KSimon: It was great to finally talk. Should I call you again?

Hope4Today: No. The little girls need their hair braided. I've got to grow up some time.

KSimons: Me, too, I guess.

Hope4Today: We're supposed to discuss, but he's putting it off. I'm not to happy with him or Rob.

KSimons: I'm sorry.

Hope4Today: Not your fault. Enjoy your day. You deserve it, Mama!

KSimons: Sometimes I wonder…

Hope4Today: Don't start, okay? ☺

## Chapter Eight

"Mom! I got you a flower and Ryan stepped on it and now I don't have nothing to give you and Dad said it's a surprise but it's not a surprise 'cause Ryan got the flower and—"

"It's okay, sweetie. I appreciate the thought—"

"He's lying! Do you hear me, Mom? Lying through his teeth. And on the Lord's day, too."

"Am not!"

The boys tussled until they fell onto the porch where they all waited for Rob to emerge and drive them to church. Instead of taking the boys on ahead, he'd insisted that they all ride together. From the not-so-quiet whispers buzzing through the house, Karol gathered that some kind of surprise was in the works. If Karol survived until Rob came out of the house, that is. The kids were in fighting form, and Mom was the word on all their lips.

Just as she was about to go inside to tell Rob to just come on and forget whatever surprise he was rigging up, Judah jumped on his older brother and punched him in the face. In their new blue suits, both boys went down and rolled down the front stairs and right into the yard.

"That's it," Ryan said quietly amidst the tumble. "Younger or not, that's unacceptable."

Karol rolled her eyes as she pulled them apart. Her Ryan, always the gentleman, even in a fistfight. He'd been born far too late.

"Boys! Why? Now look at your clothes. Wait, Mia. Don't!"

Like a fairy without a flying license, Karol's beautiful little daughter tried to follow after her brothers, still wrestling around in the dirt. Her new patent leather shoes caught on the hem of her dress, a hand-me-down from one of Hope's daughters. With a yell fit for Tarzan, the little girl tripped over the last two steps and fell with a thud on a patch of moist dirt next to her siblings.

"Mom!" they all three cried at once.

Karol forced herself up to see if Mia was all right, not wanting to admit that for one second she'd been frozen still, reluctant to deal with any of it. Meeting her children's every need, even anticipating their needs before they occurred, had once been the mainstay of Karol's life. These days, she wished that they'd just grow up a little bit and stop doing silly things like this. Maybe she still had a bit of growing up to do, too, she thought as guilt washed away her earlier feelings.

Before, she and the children would have gone next door and helped braid hair and put on lip gloss while the boys talked among themselves. Now they were alone and suddenly everything seemed so hard, especially being a mother.

*It's this thing with Hope. The way the guys just decided we should be apart. Lord, it's eating at me still. Can't I have something? Someone?*

"Mia, are you okay? Wiggle your fingers. Wiggle your toes. Wiggle your nose!"

The little girl happily complied and held out her arms, but the front of her dress was so dirty that Karol didn't bother to brush it off. She unzipped it and began to pull it over Mia's head. "Go on in the house, all of you. Mia, Mom is going to have to give you a bath."

Ryan, who'd been concentrating on dispensing justice before, looked stricken now. "What about…Mother's Day?"

What about it? Karol thought.

The day didn't get better. With everyone scrubbed, played with, read to and set up with age-appropriate games and snacks, Karol curled up on the couch with a novel she'd been trying to read for a month. She gave up after starting over for the third time.

Rob—bless his heart—had tried to get her to go out to lunch and salvage what was left of Mother's Day, but Karol just didn't feel like it.

Until the washing machine overflowed.

The bubbly flood, along with the mysterious electronic charge emitted by her oven when she tried to retrieve dinner, also known as Tazer Chicken, reduced Karol to a puddle of tears.

When her husband rushed to the kitchen from the laundry room to see what was the matter, he got more than he bargained for.

"Mom! What's wrong? Are you okay?"

She wasn't okay, and for once, Karol didn't try to hide it. "No, Rob. I'm not okay. The stove just zapped me like a stun gun. And I'm not your mother, either. You can't call me that anymore. In fact, no one can!"

Instead of the look of disappointment she expected, Rob offered his strong warm shoulders. He kissed her hair. "Go and get it, Ryan."

Karol struggled to turn and follow her son with her eyes, but Rob held her close. Her son returned, dragging a huge notepad of some kind behind him. Mia, who had disappeared, too, came dancing by with a banner that read We love you, Mom! She could see the front of the huge pad Ryan held now, too. It read: The Just for Mom coupon book, Gifts of Time and Talents.

Judah approached with a bouquet of flowers, black-eyed

Susans, her favorite. She'd had the children do this before, creating a coupon book for Rob on Father's Day but never on such a grand scale. The cover was glossy and the booklet, a bit larger than poster size was bound together perfectly, like a real book.

She buried her face in Rob's shirt. "You shouldn't have. I'm so sorry."

Her husband pulled her closer and led her over to the coupon book, which took both Ryan's hands to hold up.

"Open it," Rob said.

After taking a deep breath, she did. What she saw there took her breath away. There weren't many coupons but just one, with blank pages behind it. It said:

This entitles Karol Simon, the greatest mom ever, to twenty-one child-free afternoons to herself. These pages are to be used as a scrapbook for her adventures. Fill them with your beauty and grace as you have filled our home. With love,
Dad and the kids

Rob squeezed her hand. "Now you can work on your book. Get a good start. I can't wait to read what comes out of this."

"Um…" Where Karol had felt overwhelmed with emotion at first, she now felt terrified. Her first attempt to be published had broken her heart. The children had mended it and created a safe hedge from having to deal with the words always swirling in her head, the stories that tugged the corners of her eyes in the twilight of morning. Rob had always known about her "promise boxes," the crates of notebooks under Karol's bed. He'd been encouraging, but content to let her write or not write. Since Hope's departure, though, she'd been writing again. Poems quite different from the inspirational book she'd sought to publish years before. Different but somehow the same. She'd given a few of them to Rob to read. Karol saw now that may have been a mistake.

"It isn't possible. Hope isn't here anymore. Faith just left. You have to work. Forget about it. Just the thought is enough."

Too much, in fact. Karol had earned her Master of Fine Arts in literature at Florida State University. She'd taught and learned writing techniques all over the world. But that was before Rob. Before kids. Before God. Though she still taught adjunct classes some summers, that part of her life had been tucked away safely into the plastic tubs under her bed. Her pulse raced at how easily it all could have overturned and spilled out, for everyone to see. But it wouldn't. It couldn't. Rob didn't have the time.

"It's a done deal. I did some work for some of the network specialists. You remember, the fence Singh and I put in before he left? I've been planning this for a long time. Even before they left. I figured that this might be the someday we always talk about. When you started writing again, I knew this would be the best gift. Now is the time."

Ryan kissed his mother's cheek. "I agree, Mom. All the inspirations you've written over the years for the church. Your poems. The stories you make up for us. You taught me to love books. One day, I want to hold one of yours in my hand. Of course, you can do whatever you want with the time. Read if you want to. It'd be great for you to write seriously again. You've done so much for us. Let us do this for you. I know we've been acting up lately, but I'll help Dad with the kids. I promise."

She swallowed hard at her son's apology. He had grown so much this year and it wasn't quite summer. She could remember when he had to lean on tiptoe to kiss her cheek. Would she be looking up into his eyes one day? Probably. She hoped there wouldn't be anger there waiting for her. Karol bowed her head with the weight of the moment, the love surrounding her as Mia hugged her leg and Judah tucked a flower in her hair. She had some apologies of her own to make.

Fighting back tears—and losing—Karol raised her head and pulled her family to her.

"I've been a wretch. To all of you. I am so, so sorry. When Miss Hope moved away, I just sort of—"

"Went crazy?" Ryan offered with a smile until his eyes met with his father's. "Sorry."

"I'm sorry, too," Mia said. "For the drums and going next door."

Judah's lips rolled inward. He closed his eyes. "I'm sorry, too. About the burgers and stuff. And messing up Mother's Day."

Karol kissed his forehead and assured him that he hadn't messed up anything. She was moving on to Mia, when Rob surprised her. Again.

"And I'm sorry," her husband said. "You're right. You're not my mother. And I'm not your dad. It's been a rough few months. I'd wanted to just give you the afternoons to write but after this morning, I think you need twenty-one days without having to be a mom at all. If you can umpire in the mornings, Ryan and I will do all the chores. Even the dishes, the cooking and the shopping." He kissed Karol's cheek. "And…we won't call you Mom. Not for the whole time. You can be Karol the First if you want to. You're definitely number one with me."

Embarrassed, Karol shook her head. "No. You don't have to do that. I don't know what's wrong with me. I love my kids. I love you. I love being a mother. I'm just—"

Rob shook his head, too. "No. It's time. You and Hope were so good about giving one another a break. I went to the men's retreat with the church and all those conferences for work and started to understand why you need time for yourself. I want to do this, but on one condition."

Karol wiped her eyes. This was crazy, but she didn't want to interrupt him. He'd forget about it in the morning. There was no way he could take care of the kids himself for three weeks. Besides, what would she do all that time? Eat bon-bons? "What's the condition?"

This time, he kissed her lips. "That you find what you love to do, something that doesn't have anything to do with the kids or with me. Something that makes you want to jump out of bed in the morning—besides me… Just kidding. I want you to get all that stuff out of the garage that you've tried and quit, take a class, go back to the gym—"

"Rob!"

"Dad! Mom's not fat. Not really. Just like mom fat. She's supposed to be." Ryan was really enjoying himself today.

"Son."

"Sorry, Mom."

"Look, Karol, I didn't mean it like that. Goodness, this is hard. I thought it'd be more fun. I want you to find your passion, like you're always telling the kids. When you've done that, then we want you to be our 'Mom' again. For good. No more freak-outs, no matter who's living next door. Deal?"

Ouch. "Deal."

Rob smiled. "And I'll work on trying to call you something else in the meantime. Again, I apologize. Just habit, I guess."

"Honey, I'm sorry. Forget it. Please…" Karol turned away from them and rested her forehead against the cool of the refrigerator, ashamed to see her children standing hesitantly in the kitchen door.

"I won't forget it. Now get dressed, *Karol*. We're going to dinner."

As she turned to leave the kitchen, Judah tugged at her sleeve. "So what do we call you now? Mommy woman?"

Rob whisked him away before he could hear Karol, whispering into the empty hall. "Call me anything you want, honey. Call me anything you want."

## *To-Do*

- Get Fallon set up on voice recognition software

- Go out to dinner with Neal

- Go to church this Sunday? Maybe…

- Call Dad. Probably not…

—Dyanne

## Chapter Nine

In the weeks since the blowup over the minivan, Dyanne and Neal had made a shaky peace with their neighbors. They seldom saw them, although Neal often reported Rob's departure for work when he came in from his run. Dyanne had been using the treadmill lately. The Florida heat was still a bit much for her most days.

Her marriage, however, was running cold. Tonight she and Neal were going out to dinner alone for the first time since Fallon had arrived. A much-needed outing put in peril by her husband, shielding his eyes from the sun and heading next door where Rob Simon and his brood struggled with bags and boxes of what looked like a month's worth of food, even for a family their size.

Neal strode away from her with ease. "Looks like you've got your hands full there, Rob. Need some help?"

Dyanne watched in horror as her husband crossed into the next yard to help their neighbor with the endless bags of groceries he and his children were carrying. The neighbors weren't going to spoil things. Not this time.

"Um, honey? We're going to be late."

Neal shrugged and headed into Karol and Rob's house

with two bags in each hand. The children clung to him like vines, with the youngest, the girl, chattering on as though Dyanne's husband was her long-lost big brother. Just as Dyanne was about to huff her way inside and drag her husband to the car, the oldest boy, whose name didn't come to mind, walked over and took her hand.

"You can still make it. The Interstate is fast here. Come on in. He'll be right out, I'm sure. You look lovely. Green really looks great on you. Brings out your eyes some. Don't you think?"

Her legs faltered forward. "Why, yes. I...uh...do think that. Not that my eyes are green or anything, but—"

"In the right light..." She and the boy said together as they approached the front door and Neal bounded out of it.

"Just a few more," Neal said squeezing past them. "I'll be right to the car, babe."

"Sure," Dyanne mumbled. She was too taken with the boy beside her. The boy was tallish with the type of shoulders Neal had once had—narrow and spare. She'd thought the boy younger before, but without his younger siblings running around him, he seemed much more mature. They paused again as the children ran out after Neal.

"How old are you again?" Dyanne asked.

"Ten. I'll be eleven next month, but it's no big deal. Not now anyway."

That stopped Dyanne in her tracks. Birthdays were always a big deal. For her anyway. "It'll be great, I'm sure of it. Have you invited your friends, planned your party?"

He shook his head and helped her up on the porch. "Usually it's just us and the kids next door. Don't look like that. We liked it that way. With so many of them, we all ended up having a birthday to share with someone in their house. It was fun. We all made cards for one other, a huge cake, the park, books..."

That got Dyanne's attention. "You like books?"

His eyes lit up. "Of course. Don't you? Books are like…everything. Anything you need to know, anywhere you want to go. I like games, too, of course, but there's nothing like a book."

She couldn't have said it better herself. They'd barely made it to number five of their all-time favorite novels when Neal ran up behind her.

"There you are! Ready to go?"

A few minutes before, she'd been more than ready to go, but now she wasn't so sure. This boy had read things at ten that she hadn't read until college, all while managing to fit in the usual fantasy, sci-fi and reading the entire Bible through every year. At his age, she'd still been reading *Sweet Valley High* and *Seventeen* magazine. And such a gentleman, too? The kid was amazing.

"Just a second, sweetheart, Ryan and I—it is Ryan, isn't it? Yes, well, he's just been telling me the most amazing things. Just amazing…"

Rob wove through them with a stack of frozen pizzas. He tossed one in the oven, then another. Dyanne leaned down to tell the boy she'd talk to him later when she saw Rob jerking back and forth in front of the oven.

The younger boy, Judah, jumped up and down in front of Neal. "The oven got him! Tazer Pizza! Mayday Mayday. You gotta call Mom!"

Rob swallowed hard and sat down in the nearest chair. "Don't call Karol. And don't call her Mom, either. We've made it this far, haven't we? Three days. We can do this. Totally."

Ryan, still standing near Dyanne, shook his head and whispered in her direction, "We totally cannot do this."

Neal and Dyanne looked at each other, confused and trying to figure out what "this" was. In one long breath, Ryan explained.

"Mom is having a midlife crisis or something. Well, not

really. We've been out of control and screaming 'Mom!' all the time and then Dad calls her that, too, which I always thought was weird, even though Miss Hope did it—"

"Ryan..." Rob had his face in his hands.

"Right. Anyway, Mother's Day was horrible. We got in a fight in the yard and messed up our clothes, the washer broke down, which Dad was too busy fixing to get to the oven—by the way, can we still call you Dad?"

When Rob didn't answer but narrowed his eyes, the boy continued. "So, Dad promised Mom that she doesn't have to be a mom for twenty-one days. We gave her a big coupon book and everything. We can't call her Mom, either. It's like some crazy project, you know? Mom's the word!" He held a finger up to his mouth.

Dyanne held a hand up to her own mouth. What a loving, wonderful thing to do. She hoped Rob didn't kill himself in the process, but it was a beautiful gesture. Maybe if her father had done the same after her mother lost those babies...maybe things would have been different. For all of them. She forced the thought from her mind.

"We'll help."

Shocked at the sound of her own voice, Dyanne pressed her lips together. She turned to Neal, expecting a glowering look, but instead there was pride in his eyes.

"Yes," Neal said. "We'll help. I just changed my schedule so that I'm free every afternoon. Rob, you can do errands—"

"Take a nap..." Dyanne said playfully, though wondering if Neal had lost it. Every afternoon wasn't the kind of help she had in mind. Neal had altered his schedule so that the two of them could spend more time together and so he could help Dyanne with Fallon's book. With just a few weeks before the deadline and the book tour, now was the worst time to sign up for daily babysitting duty. She'd been thinking more along the lines of Sunday afternoon playtime.

The relief on Rob's face made Dyanne feel guilty for not wanting to do more.

"Are you serious?" he said. "I've been praying and praying. I had it all planned, home office set up and everything, but we've got a new contract to install software in all the schools. They're going to need me on-site every afternoon. I just found out and I had no idea what I was going to do. I didn't want to back out on Karol. I don't think she thinks I can do this, but I can. I want to."

Ryan rolled his eyes in the way that only an oldest child can. Dyanne wanted to laugh but she didn't dare with Rob and Neal looking so serious. No wonder the boy thought his birthday would be forgotten this year. In the midst of all of this, Rob would be doing well to brush his teeth and get dressed every day.

As Rob and Neal shook hands, Karol walked into the kitchen in a workout outfit that had seen better days. Her expression matched her clothes. Surprised. "Dyanne? Neal? Good to see you. If I'd known you were coming—"

"They helped with the groceries, honey."

Karol's eyes widened at the heap of paper and plastic bags. She kissed each of her children and then Rob. "Sweetheart, did you buy all this? Today?"

Rob beamed. "I did. I took it right from the master list."

With a sigh, Ryan headed for the door. "I tried to tell him that was the wrong list, Mom—I mean, woman who gave birth to me."

Karol made a face at Ryan, but hugged Rob. "That's what I buy for the month, but you don't have to get it all at once. It's broken down into weekly shopping on another page. But you know what? It might be easier this way. Thank you, honey. Thank you so much."

Rob waved thanks to Dyanne and Neal, who headed to their car, where they sat alone and silent before heading to dinner. Without saying it, they both knew what the other was thinking—though their lives had been full of travel and success, there was emptiness, too. The Simons had something that they lacked and it wasn't just children.

On Monday, Rob made good on their offer. School was out and all three Simon children arrived bright-eyed and bushy-tailed—or bushy-haired in Mia's case—despite Rob's suggestion of a nap. Dyanne would have joined Fallon, Neal and the children in the yard, but as she'd explained to her husband and her friend—yes, Fallon was officially Dyanne's friend—earlier, she simply couldn't be disturbed.

Evidently no one had given Ryan the memo.

"Hi. What are you working on?" He entered the office slowly, staring up at the wall-size poster with book covers for the new line. Covers Dyanne needed to analyze and prepare input for her phone meeting the next morning. That would have to wait until she'd transcribed Fallon's audio files from the new voice recognition software Neal had bought her. They'd expected a longer learning curve, but when Dyanne told Fallon that the children would be coming over, she'd locked herself in the room and made it happen. So far that had been Dyanne's best use for the kids next door. Except for Ryan, of course. He was different. Still, she had no time to talk even to a fabulous kid like him.

"I'm working on Fallon's book. It's due around the time your mom's whole experiment is up. Right before your birthday."

Ryan smiled. "Maybe we can celebrate everything all at once."

Dyanne still had secret hopes to do something special for Ryan, all by himself, but she went along. "Maybe. I've got to get to work, though, or there won't be anything to celebrate. Sorry I'm not a good playmate. How'd you end up in here anyway? Aren't they playing outside?" From the sound of Mia's muted squeals, they were definitely up to something.

Ryan leaned on the edge of the desk and stared out the window. "I'm ten. Been there. Done that. Besides, you're the only one left. Mia's got Neal wrapped around her finger…."

*Tell me about it.*

"Judah and Fallon are like brother and sister—well, maybe boy and great-aunt."

Dyanne couldn't argue there. "So you're left with me?"

"Pretty much. You like books and you smell good. That's a plus. And I've always wondered what it'd be like to have an older sister."

In the years when her mother had lost so many little boy babies, Dyanne had wondered what it would have been like to *be* a big sister. She just wasn't so sure that now was the time to find out. "Look, Ryan, you seem like a mature kid so I'm just going to shoot straight with you. I didn't want to do this, look after you and your brothers and sisters."

"But you said it first—"

She tried to overlook the frustration on the boy's face. "I know. I wanted to help out on Sunday afternoon or something, but every day? No way. I'm drowning here. I've got this book to transcribe, covers to critique, book tour stops to confirm…. My back is against the wall and I just…can't…get it all done!"

The emotion in her voice surprised her. This should have been easy work. She'd tackled projects five times the size in less time before. But this wasn't before, it was now. And she wasn't holed up in some hotel with room service, she was home with Neal and dirty dishes and ringing phones and Fallon cooking and neighbors arriving…. Tears sprang up from some unknown well and poured down Dyanne's face.

"Now you're probably wishing you were outside, huh? I don't think I'd make a very good big sister. I don't think I'd make a very good mother, either."

Ryan laughed. "Oh, you'd make a very good mother. You've already got the drama down pat." He straddled the stool next to Dyanne and handed her a laminated note card before attacking Fallon's already transcribed pages with a red pen.

"Don't! I have to mark those with proofreading symbols. Ugh…"

Ryan went on, slashing phrases without mercy. "Got it. Mom used to be an English professor. She still teaches some summers. She wrote a book once. I helped Miss Hope edit it."

That stopped Dyanne cold. "*Your* mother wrote a book?"

"Yes, *my* mother. She's not the slug you think she is. Not hardly. You just caught her at a bad time. All of us really. Now read the card. Three times aloud. I should be done with these by then. We'll start the covers next. The one in the middle is awesome but the others suck. Big time. Too busy."

Dyanne's eyes widened. She'd thought the same thing herself. How a ten-year-old could know just what to say she wasn't sure, but it seemed best to follow his advice. She held the card up in front of her and began to read:

"I am strong, beautiful and created for the glory of God. Though I bend, I will not break. Though life often asks more than I can give, I will not give in. Blessing and wisdom flow from my mouth. Power and grace come through my body. My hands heal and comfort. I am quick to listen, slow to speak and slow to get angry. I do not need the counsel of man to obey the word of God. I have a secret place in the Most High. It is available to me always. God has given me a flow. He has made me a river. God is within me. I Will Not Fail. He will help me at the break of day.

"I agree with what the word of God says about me and ask God to give me supernatural wisdom. May my family and I fulfill our eternal purposes in every word we say, every move we make. In Jesus' name, Amen."

By the time Dyanne had read it aloud the third time, the tears were flowing again. Ryan kept editing, but snatched a tissue from the box on her desk and handed it to her.

"Thank you. Thank you so much. You wrote that, Ryan?"

"No. My mom did. It's based on Psalm 46. She's done tons of those. That one's for emergencies. I figured you might need it so I brought it along."

This kid was going to make somebody a killer husband. "You knew?"

He nodded. "I always know. Nobody listens to me, though. I get that. It's part of being a kid. It'd save a lot of time if they listened. I tried to warn Dad about this Mom thing for months. It's because of Faith the Second—my grandmother—you met her. Mom is always like this after she leaves. Miss Hope was usually over to our house double the usual time for the week after." He passed a stack of pages to Dyanne. "Here. These are done. I'm going downstairs for a snack before we start on the book covers. Hungry?"

Dyanne found her voice. "Starving."

# *Nowhere To Hide*

Folded into myself, looking for
What You alone possess, I
Can only find the corpses of my
Long, lost dreams. Their
Beauty faded, allure lost,
They wait in the abandoned corners
Of my soul, waiting for another
Chance to ensnare me.
You are waiting, too, pierced
And poised, arms wide-open.
No case to make, no questions
To match my answers.
Only true or false instead
Of good, better, best. Only
Here and there and everywhere.
Nowhere to hide from Your love.

—Karol, day 5

## Chapter Ten

Having time alone wasn't as easy as it seemed. The last time Karol and Rob had gotten a sitter, they'd gone to buy a microwave before dinner. They'd promised not to talk about the kids, but somehow Ryan came up during their hurried meal. She'd fallen asleep during the movie after seeing the ending from afar off. These afternoon times seemed much the same, so much bigger than Karol knew how to fill. She'd started with the gym, surprised to discover that their membership had not expired. Her courage, however, was in serious decline.

"Good afternoon," the receptionist said, looking at Karol over a fringe of spidery lashes that looked meticulously applied. Her body had the same wispy falseness, but the men in the room didn't seem to mind.

*What am I doing here?*

Karol had asked herself the same question on the first day, when she had become painfully aware that her penchant for spandex and step classes had gone the way of the dinosaur. There was spinning, Latin dance, Pilates and all sorts of other stretchy limber things that Karol could never quite manage.

She wasn't giving up, though. Three times a week, she came here for an hour. Afterward, Karol had walked at the lake, gone to the library, taken a short-lived painting class, knit a baby blanket and gone to the pool, all by herself, and dived into the deep end. She'd had lunch with some of her old colleagues from Florida State, many of them now mothers themselves. She'd attended afternoon prayer at the church and visited new moms from the congregation who'd just given birth. Karol prayed more, praised more and pulled herself from place to place frantically trying to outrun the words swelling inside her, screaming to be written down. Trying to outrun her destiny.

"Hey! There you are. I wondered if you'd make it," a woman from the Latin dance class said, waving at Karol.

Karol smiled and caught up with the lady, who she recognized from church. Had she been in that class the last time, when Karol made a fool of herself trying to swivel her hips like the exercise instructor?

"I'm so glad you came back. It's a blast. You looked like you were having a ball the other day, but you left before I could say hello."

Yep. She'd seen it all.

Salsa music boomed from the stereo system as they entered the workout room. In the last class, Karol had been in the front row and come in early. She'd never looked back to see who was in the room. Now as she took in all the smiling faces and waving hands, she wanted to run back to her car. Almost the whole women's ministry was here! And not the mom-kind, either. The pretty, poised church ladies who had sitters for everything, even their weekly hair appointments.

"Got out from under those kids, I see," a slim blonde said, clapping Karol on the back. "It's about time. You'll love it here. And we'd love to get to know you better. You and Hope were always so close. There was no getting between the two of you! Oh, class is starting."

As the music rose and their bodies dipped, Karol stared at

the mirror. The woman in the back row, tall and brown, had her own face, but Karol wondered if she really knew that woman at all.

After dance class, Karol joined the ladies for lunch, but she left long before they set out for the mall and the grocery store. She missed her children, her home. The very things she'd wanted to escape called to her now, blurring the words of these women who seemed so different from herself. But she tried to listen. She smiled as much as possible, knowing that something had changed and that no matter how hard she tried to swim back to the shore where she'd felt safe, she could never reach it because it no longer existed. With her own words, she'd washed it away.

More than anything, Karol wished that she could take it all back. Every thought of running away, every feeling that being a mother was somehow not enough. Her heart broke thinking about how her children tiptoed around her now as though she were one of the china dishes so often broken in her own childhood home.

The fear in their eyes scared her, too. She'd been so afraid that losing Hope had somehow meant losing herself, her ability to be a mother. Now Karol realized that her concerns had been misplaced. It was her own family that she needed to worry about. Rob was frazzled around the edges and quickly coming undone. And the only person she could discuss it with was ten years old and he was more than a little bit overwrought himself.

Ryan was changing, his slim frame filling with muscle and wind, his angular, thoughtful face rounding with manhood. He'd even started growing his hair out into an Afro. Rob hated it at first, but they both had to admit it suited Ryan, who, like his mother, always seemed to thrive when going against the grain.

That night, long after dinner and the reading of too many stories, Karol tiptoed to the kitchen to save the unwashed dishes left behind in Rob's brilliant reenactment of the battle of Jericho during Bible time. When she entered, her son was already there, smiling shyly and running water.

Karol grabbed a dish towel. The boy didn't give his usual protest. It'd been a while since they'd been able to talk, just the two of them.

She spoke first. "It's too much for him, isn't it? All this running around your dad is doing trying to take care of you kids, the house, his job…" Karol asked Ryan in the dim kitchen. Ryan had probably agreed to do the dishes tonight, but Karol figured he could use a little help. It didn't hurt that it was keeping her sane, as well.

Ryan yawned. "It's too much but he'd never admit it. You started this. It's going to have to play out to the end."

Karol tightened the belt of her robe and dried another dish. Her son was right and she knew it. Talking to him like this wasn't something she'd done much before. She wasn't sure it was the right idea now. Hope had warned about trying to be too chummy with your children. She was usually right about those kinds of things, but Karol didn't know what else to do.

"I wish that Hope was here," she said into the darkness.

"I'm glad she isn't," Ryan answered back.

Karol almost dropped the dish in her hands. "What did you say?"

She could see him shrug in the evening light coming through the window. "Look, Mom. I love Miss Hope. Mr. Singh, too. It's just that, well, they've learned what works for their family. We need to do the same thing." He turned off the water and kissed his mother on the cheek. "I'm kind of glad to be able to just be myself. It'd be great if you and Dad would catch on."

Her heart pounded as she put down the dish and towel and

gave her son a crushing hug. "Who are you and where have you been all my life?" she asked with a laugh in her throat.

"I've been right here, Mom. All the time. You just didn't see me," Ryan whispered, returning his mother's hug just as his father walked into the kitchen.

"Well, look at this. Kitchen elves and a group hug. I think I'll join in."

As Rob wrapped his arms around them, the truth in her son's words pierced Karol's heart. She'd been so busy trying to be the perfect mother and wife that she'd forgotten that sometimes people—especially children—just need to know that someone sees them.

*I see you Ryan Andrew Simon. And God sees you, too.*

Things had been tense between Karol and Hope since Karol admitted that Rob had something to do with her friend moving away. Singh had had a part in it, too, but Hope didn't seem to see it that way. Though her friend never said it directly, Hope seemed to be bearing a bit of a grudge against Rob, maybe Karol, too. In time, Karol thought that it would blow over, die down.

She couldn't have been more wrong.

"So how long are you going to let this go on?" Hope sounded a little irritated on the other end of the phone.

Karol tried to hide her surprise at her friend's tone. "Until the twenty-one days are up, I guess. I've tried to get Rob to forget about it, but he won't. He says that I have to fulfill my end of the bargain and find something I love to do."

Hope groaned. "Oh, please. You have lots to do—laundry, dishes, shopping, cleaning… Are you all doing that unit study I suggested? The one on insects?"

Not this again. The two families had always studied things together in summer. But this time, it just wasn't meant to be. They were doing a unit study on love, written by God Himself.

"No. We're not doing that, Hope. God has us doing His uni
study right now. Mia's having a ball with Neal. Judah is
learning to be a gourmet vegan chef from a bestselling author
and Ryan is basically doing a publishing internship with one
of the top publicists in the country. I couldn't have planned it
any better if I'd tried."

The tension Karol thought she'd imagined became real
and stretched thin. "I just don't think it's wise, Karol. The
Thorntons are nice enough. I mean, we sold our house to
them. You don't know those people, though. Not really. And
that Fallon Gray? She's questionable theologically. Have you
read any of her books? They're self-help, I've heard—"

"She's a believer, Hope. Better than that, she's a friend.
She's even asked to take a look at some of my writing. I doubt
that I'll show it to her, but it's nice that she's interested."

The conversation went on like that, back and forth with
Hope expressing concern that Karol was losing her founda-
tions, both as a Christian and a mother and Karol countering
that the opposite was happening—she was being rooted and
grounded all over again.

"None of this sounds like you, that's all I'm saying. It's not
just me saying it, either. Everyone says so."

Tires squealed in Karol's mind. "Everyone? Who is
everyone? Are you talking to people about me behind my back?"

Hope cleared her throat. "I'm just concerned for you, okay?
I made a few calls after people contacted me asking if things
were all right. They said you all have missed a few services
and that you're hanging out with a different crowd, wearing a
lot of makeup…? They say that Ryan is changing his behavior,
his hair. Dressing differently. Reading different books—"

"And that's a crime?" This was rich, really rich. This
wasn't their first disagreement, but Hope had never seemed
so…controlling.

"No, it's not a crime, but it can lead to so many dangerous

things. Look at all the other couples in the church who divorced, the children who have gone astray. You don't want that, Karol, I know you don't."

She didn't want that, but she certainly didn't want a house full of robots. Karol wanted her children to have a living, active faith that could endure the real world, a faith that belonged to them instead of being borrowed from her. "I don't want any of those things, Hope. You're right about that. I'm scared to death that my marriage might fail or my kids might grow up and make bad choices, but you know what? More and more I'm coming to see that life isn't safe. Even life in Christ.

"And for the record, I'd appreciate if you or any other anonymous people who care so much about me, would let me know your concerns directly instead of holding a powwow about the spiritual condition of my family."

"That's what I'm trying to do now, Karol, come to you. That's why I called. I thought that this might have been tied to, you know, that problem you and Rob were having a while back. Since I'm not there for us to talk about it, I thought maybe you'd let it get the best of you again. Brent Waverly is counseling anyone at the church for free now. I talked to him a little about the situation and he said—"

"What?" Karol felt faint. Rob played golf with Brent Waverly. He and his wife had been to their house for dinner.

"Oh, it's fine. He said that Internet pornography is a huge problem. He's seeing half the families in the church about it."

Karol swallowed. Hard. "Hope, I love you, but you were totally out of line. I still don't know that Rob ever looked at anything. The site I saw was an Internet pornography addiction support site for Christian men. Rob said that he was there on an accountability thread for a friend—"

"Come on, Karol. Don't be obtuse."

Since when was this a geometry lesson? "I'm not being obtuse. Or concave or whatever else you think. I asked my husband about it and that's what he said. Yes, I let my fears run away with me, for a long time. I can see now that it's affected every part of my relationships with my family. That was my fault. In the end, there's nothing I can do but trust God. Rob is a grown man. If something was going on, at least he was getting some help," Karol said, her heart racing. Though her words came out articulate and confident, she was anything but. This conversation brought all her old insecurities crashing down on her again.

"I'm praying for you, Karol. I'm sorry that you're angry at me. Maybe I did go too far—"

"You did."

"Right, well I'm sorry."

"I'm sorry, too. I'm sorry that this changes things between us much more than your moving did. I guess Ryan was right."

"About what?"

*It's time for us to figure out what works for our family.*

"Nothing. I'll talk to you soon, Hope."

"We're still on for Ryan's birthday, right? And you're coming here? For Eden and Mia's birthdays? I was going to tell the children next week for sure."

Karol closed her eyes. "Don't. I'm not sure what we're doing."

"No? I thought we decided on the beach." Hope's voice was trembling.

"You decided on the beach. I haven't decided anything. Gotta run. Kiss the kids for me."

For a long time after the phone line went dead, Karol stood in her kitchen holding the receiver. She wrapped a hand around to her back, grasping at her T-shirt for the invisible knife she felt cutting into her soul. She'd seen a side of herself today that surprised her. She'd seen a side of Hope today that scared her. That hurt her.

What hurt worse was knowing that she'd put the knife into

Hope's hands with her endless droning about every problem in her life. Some things, she realized, weren't safe to tell. Another thought stabbed at her mind. If Hope had thought nothing of calling up people from the church and telling them about Karol's problems, surely she'd told Singh, her husband's best friend. Though Rob might have told Singh anyway, she hated to think what Singh would think of her now, spreading their family's problems all over the church….

Her hand moved back to her belly, moving up until it rested just over her heart. The phone made a loud beeping sound, forcing her to turn it off. When she did, Karol heard the sound that wounded her most of all—Rob's boots against the hall floor.

He'd probably heard it all.

# *To-Do*

- Reconsider baby plan!

- Order Ryan a Montblanc pen

- Finalize Fallon's church engagements

- Talk to Fallon about the mess in the kitchen. Be diplomatic.

- Go to church.

- Call my father—maybe

—Dyanne
After a week of watching Karol's children

## Chapter Eleven

"You're playing right into his hands, you know."

Dyanne looked at Fallon with the usual confusion, trying to figure out whose hands she was playing into. She'd come down to the kitchen to talk to Fallon about all the mess she and Judah had been making in the kitchen and somehow gotten sucked into helping make apple bacon omelets, which, despite their disgusting beginnings, tasted exquisite. "I'm playing right into whose hands? Neal's? Or yours?"

Fallon scraped the edges of the pan while Dyanne started on the dishes. She folded another omelet over neatly before waving the spatula in the air. "Don't try those evasion techniques with me, Dee. You know just what I mean. You were crazy for a baby when I got here and Neal messed with your mind a little bit and you folded like a card table."

Dyanne rolled her eyes. Fallon was fun but she oversimplified things. Very complicated things. "He's just not ready for children. I'm figuring out that I'm not, either. When those children leave every afternoon, we're all exhausted. The kitchen is a mess, the yard is full of stuff and I'm more concerned about what I can teach Ryan next—or learn from him—than I am about doing my job. No, the Baby Project is definitely on hold. It's for the best."

The fluffy eggs lifted right off the pan. Fallon managed to bring them to the plate safely before she broke out in a fit of laughter, one of many things about Fallon that rubbed Dyanne the wrong way.

"Please don't laugh at me. I'm serious."

Fallon lifted a goblet of spinach-mango juice to her lips as though she were swallowing the humor down her throat. "I'm not laughing at you, baby. I'm laughing with you. You finally gave up on your proposal, huh? He showed it to me, you know. If I didn't know you, I wouldn't have believed it, but I know you meant every word just as much as you meant what you just said. I see where you're going with it now. Surrender is a powerful thing. That's something God can work with. I hope that baby likes mangoes. Drink up, now. You left half of your juice yesterday."

Did this woman ever listen to anything but her own crazy self? "Do you hear anything I'm saying, Fallon? No babies now. None. Let's get this food done and get upstairs and get you back to work. Yesterday's pages were decent. We can make some progress today if you actually listen to me."

She laughed. "Oh, I'm listening, baby. All I'm saying is, when love calls, you better answer…." With that and a few swirls of her hips, the table was set and the day started.

Dyanne wasted no time in taking her seat and starting to eat. Neal had risen hours ago and was now probably miles into his long run. With their afternoons now full of children, mornings were tight, especially with the new Bible study Neal had added to their schedules. *A Brave Surrender: Letting God Reign through the Book of Romans* was one of the titles in her new life, but Dyanne hadn't planned to actually read that one word for word. A good skim would give her a feel for the market. It was just a product, after all. Or at least that's what she had thought until with apple and provolone mingling her mouth, Dyanne realized that she'd just done the first assignment in the book—surrender the biggest area of disappointment in your life to God and tell someone.

Hmm…maybe there was something to all of this after all.

After a long day and an even longer night, Neal's arms were the only place Dyanne wanted to be. The crickets in Tallahassee had driven her crazy when they'd first moved in, but tonight they sounded like music.

"I missed you today," Neal said, twining his fingers in her hair.

Dyanne could see his smile in the moonlight. She added one of her own. "I missed you, too. It's funny, I never thought I'd miss you when we were in the same place."

Neal nodded. "I guess it's like that when you have children. You're together, but not, you know? It's kind of sexy, though." He kissed the nape of her neck.

"Oh, no, you don't. Don't you start that up again. I'm over the baby thing. Fallon told me this morning that you were playing mind games on me and I was falling for it, but I didn't even take that bait. So don't go talking about how it's sexy and—"

"Fallon was right."

That killed the mood. Dyanne pulled the sheet tight around her and sat up in the bed. "What?"

"I didn't mean to do it, but maybe I subconsciously thought that if we spent enough time with these kids you'd see how wrong you were about having kids."

Dyanne loosened her grip on the sheet a little. "Well, I don't like how you went about it, but it worked. I mean that little Mia is cute but she's nothing like what I had in mind. I wanted a tea party not a locker room. The two of you tracked mud all over the porch yesterday. And Judah? Sweet but the poor child can't aim a lick in the bathroom. Did you know I had to throw out my shampoo? Ryan's a dream, but he was born first, so I think one's enough. Not now, though. Definitely not now."

Her husband put the pillow over his head. He sighed as if someone had deflated him. "I figured you'd say that. I mean I said it first. Even got mad at you about that stupid van."

"Wait a minute. What are you saying?" Dyanne pulled the pillow away from his face. "Did you somehow change your mind? You didn't, did you? This is my surrender, you big dope! You know, from the book? I'm really trying here."

Neal blew out a breath. "I know that. Don't you think I know that? I thought I had this all figured out." From the look on his face, Dyanne could see that this was probably her husband's surrender, as well.

*Okay, God. This is just too much. Make up Your mind. And his, too.*

"And then what? You had it figured out and then what? What happened?"

He laced his fingers with hers. "God happened. I thought that being with those kids every day would make you not want to be a mother anymore. I didn't count on those kids making me want to be a dad. I know it's just because the kids are around. When this whole thing is over with Karol, I'll be fine."

"You'd better be."

"I will. In the meantime, let's get out some of those parenting books for the new line and try them on the kids. By the time Karol is ready to be their mom again, they'll be so well behaved she won't even recognize them."

Oh, great. More work. "Okay, but only if you promise that you won't go down the baby road again without me. It was hard enough to recover from my last attempt to stroll down baby lane."

Neal leaned in to kiss her, but she held out a hand in front of her. He shook it. "I promise. Now come here…"

For a second, Dyanne stiffened. Though the doctor assured

her that she wouldn't get pregnant, with Neal talking about babies she wasn't sure she wanted to take the risk of getting pregnant. At least not until she heard the song playing on the other side of the wall.

"That's one sharp intern you've got there, Dyanne."

Almost too stunned to answer, Dyanne managed a response. "Thank you, Mr. Chaise. It's both a pleasure and a surprise to hear from you."

He chuckled. "Oh, cut the act, Dyanne. You don't have to be so tight with me. Not that I don't appreciate it. People are so casual these days. Anyway, I called earlier and talked to Ryan. I was disappointed at first that you were tied up, but boy, that kid is something. Where'd you find him? I got more out of him than all the focus groups in the world."

Dyanne tried to breathe. Tied up? Earlier today she'd been right here…asleep. After finalizing Fallon's tour, rising early to transcribe another chapter of the book and making snacks for the kids, she'd sat down to show Ryan how to do a press release and woke up three hours later to the smell of dinner. Ryan had left a nice note, but made no mention of a call from the publisher himself. Now she didn't know how to tell her boss that the "intern" he was so enamored with was a ten-year-old neighbor boy whose publishing experience consisted of correcting his mother's unpublished manuscripts and reading. Lots of reading. She told him anyway. There were times for spin, but this wasn't one of them.

Her boss already knew. "I know! Ten years old. Isn't it amazing? The kid's a sponge. Your neighbor's boy, right? I wasn't so sure about you moving south but I have to say that like everything else you do, it was genius! You may have identified the next publishing giant. Did you know that he loves Tolstoy? Can you believe it? A kid that age…"

Dyanne could believe it. Now that she'd had the chance to

spend so much time with Ryan, his love of the classics didn't catch her so off guard, but even now sometimes when he quoted some rare text or spoke in Latin, her breath caught in her throat. What she couldn't believe was that one of the biggest men in publishing could be moved by it, too. Maybe too moved. Shouldn't a call to her actually have something to do with, well, her?

Still, the kid had covered for her. For that, she was thankful. "He's amazing, that's for sure. He has great insight into the Christian market—"

"About that. I think we're going about this all the wrong way."

"What do you mean?"

"When we established the African American line, we hired black staff. For educational products, we hire curriculum specialists. Why not get some pastors and everyday Christian folk on board with the line? Your father would be good. He's got a great sense of humor. I remember that book he did for us years ago. I'm thinking of bringing back into print if he's willing to work with us. What do you think?"

She groped for words, but found none. The silence stretched between them.

"Are you still there?" Mr. Chaise asked in a grim voice. He obviously wasn't used to his questions going unanswered.

Dyanne was still there, but she wasn't sure she wanted to be. Working with Fallon was one thing, but her father? "I'm here. Just a lot to take in. I doubt Dad would have the time, but I'll give him a call."

"Sounds crazy I know, but I've learned that I can teach a person about books, but I can't teach passion. That little boy today had passion. Your father has it, too. Get me more of that, Dyanne." His voice went down a little. "And take care of Fallon, okay. Take good care of her. I'm looking forward to this book. Personally, I mean. Call me when your father is on board. We'll see who else he suggests."

"Sure. I'm looking forward to Fallon's book—and I'm sure Dad will be honored that you thought of him. I don't know if he'll want to take the position, though—I'll see what I can do. Thanks for calling. We'll get right to work. Goodbye."

Dyanne put down the phone and took a deep breath. She'd been kidding when she sometimes referred to the Christian line as the great adventure, but it was turning out to be true to its name. And then some.

She walked out on the porch where Fallon and Neal were nodding off. Having had her own unplanned nap earlier, Dyanne didn't wake them. There was something about the heat down here and a full stomach that just lulled a person in. And they'd both been up early.

Instead she waved to Ryan and his mother, taking a walk around the edge of their property. They were laughing when they stopped to wave, but Karol's face looked troubled. Worried. Ryan, however, looked relieved.

Even at the age of ten, he'd mastered the contradiction of male-female relationships. If only she and Neal could do the same.

## *Mending Places*

Carved out of my best intentions
Piled high with the broken pieces
Of our best love. There is no
Address or knob for the door.
Green grass, sawdust promises
Wearing a mouth of stone.
A hole to heal the
Glue of all that once
Held, bone and sinew.
Nothing borrowed or blue,
No secondhand salve
Just honey and midnight.
Inky black and cold except
Where your bone is
My bone and your flesh
Kisses mine.
That hollow, life deep and
Day long is filled with
Needle and thread, marrow
And bed-buttons to close
The wounds of word and deed.


—Karol
Day 11, after Rob went to play golf

## Chapter Twelve

"We have to talk." Rob spoke softly, as if the children would hear, as if they weren't zooming through the yard next door.

Rob closed the window gently, tuning out the last and best of her distractions. Karol welcomed the silence, knowing that things had been leading to this all along.

She sat down on the floor with her back against the couch. Her legs crossed in front of her.

Rob took her hand and pulled her onto the couch, where they sat facing each other. "Everyone is praying for us, I hear. I even found out from some guys at church today that this is all a result of my 'problem' with pornography."

"Rob—"

"I do not have a problem with pornography, Karol. I struggled with it in college, but you knew that. I can't say that it's easy being on a computer all the time at work and never knowing where a naked woman is going to pop up, but I do everything I can to keep it out of my sight and trust God for the rest. The men I saw this morning, men who are supposedly 'praying for me' aren't men who know me. The men who really pray for me know that if I'm struggling, I'm not ashamed for anyone to know. But I should be the one who lets them know. Not you. Not Hope. Not anyone else."

Karol wrung her hands. "You're right. Hope made some calls and said some things that were totally out of line. It was my fault. She's my friend, but you are my husband. I should never put her in a position to be able to assassinate your character. Here you are doing all this to help me feel better and I'm kicking your feet from under you. We talked about it, Hope and I, a while ago. I thought you'd heard."

"I don't eavesdrop, Karol."

"Right. Well, I wanted to talk to you about this a million times in the past few days, especially before you left this morning..."

Rob looked away. Karol hadn't seen him this angry in a very long time. He was a good man, a Christian man, but a man all the same. She tried to steel herself for whatever he might say that he didn't mean. What she might say in return.

"I didn't lie to you when I told you that I was on that site to be someone's accountability." He looked as though he wanted to say more, but instead, he looked away.

Karol felt herself double over as though she'd been punched in the stomach. She found no words to respond, but the look on her face must have asked all her questions. Her husband's eyes answered them, though he spoke not a word. Singh. That's who Rob had been an accountability partner for. And Hope didn't know.

Everything made sense now; the way Rob and Singh seemed to drift farther apart even as Karol and Hope had become closer, the extra prayer sessions Rob and Singh had done with Brent Waverly. Hope had called Brent, but he probably knew the whole story. What a mess. And yet, it all could have been cleared up so easily if Rob had just told her what was going on. Suddenly, Karol felt a fierce but brief anger against both men. So much trouble. If only Singh had just gone to Hope about it in the first place... Even as she thought it, Karol realized how impossible that would have been. With Hope there was right and wrong, with little room left in between.

"I can't believe this," she said, trying to catch her breath.

"Believe what?"

"That it was Singh. All this time."

"I didn't say that."

"Maybe you should have. We've both been trying to be loyal to everyone but each other. I just can't believe that it was Singh, that he could let me think it was you. If it was him, I mean. I do find it hard to believe."

Tightness settled around Rob's jaw. "But it wasn't hard to believe that it was me, your husband."

Oops. "I didn't mean it like that."

Rob stood. "I think you did. It's easier for you to believe that I was doing something wrong than to believe that about Singh. I'm not perfect, Karol. I have my temptations just like any man. Mine however, aren't virtual. So call Hope and tell her that. At least people can get their prayers right."

Tears stung Karol's eyes. Everything had gone wrong. Horribly, horribly wrong. "So what are you saying? That there's someone else?"

He shook his head. "No, Karol. There isn't anyone else. I only want you. The enemy sure knows how to send women my way while I wait, though."

"Wait for what?"

"Wait for you to want me back. I'm going to get the children now."

When the door slammed shut, something inside Karol shattered. Her husband hadn't raised his voice or lifted his hand against her, but she knew that this afternoon's wounds would take a long time to heal.

This year seemed to be an endless losing.

\* \* \*

They were going to North Carolina, going to Hope and Singh's, to the girls' birthday party. Mia had waited months for it and she'd never celebrated a birthday without Eden. Maybe next year they'd stay home, but not yet. It was too soon, too raw. Everything was.

Karol hoped she wouldn't say anything to Hope she would regret. A part of her wanted to throw the truth in her friend's face, a truth she knew deep within herself even if her husband wouldn't substantiate it. In a way, that hurt worse than anything.

Ryan wasn't too keen on the trip, an entire day of balls and boats with Aaron and Anthony when all he wanted to do was sit in a tree and curl up with a book. He flipped pages frantically in the car, as if trying to fill himself with words before he saw his old friends, who always seemed to drain the words right out of Ryan, leaving him quiet and forgotten. Karol reminded herself to make sure that didn't happen. Her young man had come so far. She wouldn't let anyone, not even Hope, take away what he'd gained.

Still stinging from their argument, Rob had mixed feelings at first about visiting Hope and Singh. In the end, he admitted it had to be done. The trip to Charlotte took longer than they thought, eleven hours but the scenery made up for it.

As they closed in on their destination, Mia and Judah were ecstatic about seeing their old friends. Ryan didn't seem so excited. Karol couldn't blame him. Without meaning to, people always made comparisons among the boys and often Ryan came out on the short end, literally and figuratively. With Dyanne next door, he had someone who not only understood his love for books, but showed him the possibility of making a living in publishing someday. Unlike his mother with her box of poems under her bed, Dyanne and Fallon were the real deal.

With a stack of books from Neal's library and a new

moleskin notebook—an early birthday gift from Dyanne—he took in the ride in jots and tittles, steeling himself for the identity crisis ahead. Karol did the same. Singh had been quite happy to hear that they were coming, but Hope didn't seem as enthusiastic as she'd been on the phone the week before. It was as if she thought that Karol and her family were going to infect her children with their sinful ways.

*We just might,* Karol thought. We are sinners, all of us here. Only God's grace saves us from ourselves. That grace would have to be sufficient, both for Karol and for Hope.

As the mountains rose and fell along the road, Karol searched the scriptures and her own heart for the reality of her relationship with Hope. And her relationship, or lack thereof, with God. With time and prayer she began to see the pattern that had defined their days: Hope as the wise teacher and Karol as the forever student. In truth, Hope had taught her many things, but in a real friendship the love and learning should flow both ways. Things had gotten tense after the move because Karol had determined to follow God even if it led her to places she and Hope had never traveled.

"Nervous?" Rob pulled off at the exit for Charlotte.

"Yes." With the children in the car, it was all she felt comfortable saying. In truth, it was all that needed to be said.

"Me, too," Rob said.

From the backseat, between the pages of three-inch-thick fantasy novel came another response.

"Me, three."

Despite all the tension, the sight of her old friend sent Karol running across the driveway she'd seen only in pictures. The children clung to her sides as she embraced Hope.

Mia and Eden sprinted toward each other and collapsed in a hugging, crying heap. "Happy birthday," they both shouted. The other children released Hope and joined in.

Singh extended a hand toward Rob. Karol smiled when her husband pushed the hand away and hugged his old friend instead. The past few months had seemed like years. Long hard years.

Inside the house, there were gifts and cake, punch and cards. Karol looked for the new friends the children had made: neighbors or kids from the new church Hope spoke so little about. There weren't any. No other adults came, either, although there were houses close by on both sides. Karol thought it strange, but she didn't say anything. Singh's downcast eyes and nervous movements made her wonder what to say.

When she smiled at Rob, he didn't smile back. He, too, was watching Singh and Hope, who seemed like actors out of a movie who couldn't remember their lines. Something was wrong here. Very, very wrong.

Even the children thought so.

"We hate it here. It's so good that you came. Maybe now things can go back to normal. Everything is turned upside down." It was Anthony, who wasn't much of a talker. He cornered Karol by the punch bowl. Behind the usual mischief in his eyes, was something Karol had never seen there—fear.

Once all the gifts were opened, Singh sent the children out on the patio to play. Hope protested, but he said it would be all right. "We can see them from here. Besides, we need to talk."

*Tell me about it.*

As the glass door shut behind Ryan, he gave his mother a thumbs-up before pulling a handheld game from his pocket and heading for the largest tree. Karol smiled at the encouragement. She had a feeling she'd need it. They all would.

Singh wasted no time, calling them all together to pray. The prayer was short and powerful, a plea for cleansing and forgiveness, a call for truth and love. It sounded more like preparations for a judicial inquiry than a quiet conversation among friends.

"Rob, I apologize for the gossip and foolishness my family has stirred up against you. Of all people in the world, you are the last who deserves to be defamed or accused.

"Karol, Rob told you that he was on that site you saw to be an accountability partner for someone. He was telling the truth. Please, Rob, turn to your wife and tell her who that person was—"

"I don't think that's necessary, man—"

Singh shook his head. "Please. Tell your wife the truth. This is a day of reckoning."

Rob turned to Karol and told her for sure what she'd already known. "It was Singh. I was on the site for Singh."

Karol felt the tears coming and reached for her friend's hand, knowing that Hope was probably crying, too. They could get through this, all of them. Together.

Hope shot to her feet. "You're lying."

Maybe not.

Karol felt as though she'd been slapped. "Pardon me?"

Hope's face was red and flushed. "You heard me. Tell them, Singh. Tell her the truth. I can't say anymore. I know I shouldn't have made those calls. God dealt with me about it. But to ride all the way here to accuse my husband of the same thing? Oh, Rob. That's just too much."

Rob stared at Singh, who turned to his wife with tears in his eyes. "It's true, Hope. It was me. I am so, so sorry. I should have told you a long time ago. I just didn't want you to misunderstand, to think it was your fault in some way. It's my problem. All mine."

Something twisted inside of Karol as realization tore the mask off Hope's face. She looked at Karol in horror and stumbled away from them. Though things had been said and done that were hurtful, the moment washed all of that away. Karol reached for Hope, whispering all the best words they had shared over the years.

"This is a bad day. It is not your destiny. It is not the end. Jesus is the Alpha and the Omega. He wrote your beginnings. He knows your end. It will be well, in the end, all will be well."

Hope squeezed Karol's fingers with her own. "What a fool I've been. Worrying about you when my own house is on shifting sand. I knew something, but I didn't want to know."

"He loves you, Hope. You said yourself that most men struggle with this. Women, too. There is hope. There is help. Just give yourself some time."

"I don't know if I can. It's not just what he did but how he did it. Even worse is that he let me think it was Rob, let me tear Rob down…"

Singh took his wife's other hand. "You let yourself do that, sweetheart. I asked you, no begged you, not to say those things."

"You certainly did. It's all me. You didn't do a thing. It's all my fault!"

Karol and Rob startled at the sound they'd never heard before—Hope screaming at the top of her lungs. Outside, the roar of children went silent for a moment, but quickly resumed. Obviously, it was a sound they had heard before.

Singh crumpled against the wall, hands covering his face. "No, dearest. It was me. All me. I can lay no blame…"

More was said, but Karol couldn't hear, because Rob had her hand and was pulling her from the room. A quick survey of the kitchen served up the keys to their friends' van, which they'd driven many times before. Karol and Rob ushered the children quickly into it and asked the older children what park they usually went to.

"We don't go to the park really. Not since we moved here."

No park? That was strange. Rob wouldn't be deterred. "Okay, library then."

"We've been a few times, but I don't remember where it is," said one of the younger girls.

Whoa. Weird. If it was just their own family, Karol would have suggested a movie, but since their friends rarely watched movies or TV...

"If you take two lights down and a right, there's a dollar movie."

"And the mall!" someone said.

Rob and Karol glanced at each other uneasily at the prospect of movies and the mall. It would have been one of their first choices, but these were things Hope frowned upon. However, the situation was desperate. They started in that direction.

"Where's your church?" Ryan asked as they drove.

"We don't have one," one of the smallest children said. "Daddy is always on the computer and Mommy is always on the phone. We keep going different places. I wanna go home with you guys!"

With that, the car went quiet except for a sob or two. As they pulled into the movie theater parking lot, Karol reached for Rob's hand just as he was reaching for hers. Everyone in the van did the same without being told.

As he and Singh had prayed together so many times for other men, Rob now led his friend's family in prayer for their parents, their new life and their new home. His words were few but his voice was steady. When he and Karol lifted their heads there was something new and unexpected—a look of love from his wife.

## *To-Do*

Push Fallon on book deadline

Talk to doctor about headaches

Stay up with Neal on Bible Study

Call Dad until I reach him. Have to!

Go to church. Really this time.

—Dyanne, Day 13, missing the kids like crazy

## Chapter Thirteen

"To what do I owe the honor?"

Even though he drove her more than a little crazy, Dyanne had to admit that she always got a happy tickle in her stomach when she heard her father's voice. Then she'd remind herself that she wasn't a little girl anymore. She never really had been.

"You know me well, huh, Dad?" Though her father called their home often, he usually talked to Neal. Dyanne was most likely out of town, unavailable or simply not very interested. All their conversations ended the same way, with some religious or ethical debate and both of them even more entrenched in their opinions. Sometimes it just seemed easier to bypass it altogether. Now there could be no escape.

"Unfortunately, yes, I do know you well. If you were going for subtle, you pretty much struck out with the call. Start with an e-mail and work your way up. And calling me Dad instead of Father? What's with the big guns? It must be serious. Don't tell me. Are you pregnant?"

No matter what she did, that nonexistent baby remained the center of most of Dyanne's conversations. She couldn't imagine what it'd be like with a real child. Her life would be eaten alive. "No. I'm not pregnant. Nor do I plan to be anytime soon. Since your lie detector is on full power today, I'll cut to the chase. Or should I say Chaise."

"As in Steven J. Chaise? Your publisher?"

"The same."

"I met him once. Years ago. Seemed decent enough. Definitely loves books. That's hard to find anymore. Are you getting along well over there?"

*Maybe not, if you don't do what I'm asking,* Dyanne thought.

"Things are going well. In fact, starting a new imprint called GracePages. It's all Christian books."

A snort sounded on the line. "So I've heard."

All of a sudden Dyanne understood what her boss was talking about. Though her company knew marketing very well, some markets were best viewed with the eyes of those who live inside them. "That sound you just made is exactly why we need you, for legitimacy."

That made her father laugh. "You don't need me for legitimacy, sweetheart. You need Jesus for that. Tell Neal to call me soon. Do you still have company?"

"Wait. You know about that?"

"I do talk to Neal quite frequently. I think I've even talked to your guest a few times. I'd like to talk to you more, too, if you'd let me. I'm flying down that way for a conference soon—"

"Maybe, but can we talk more about this first? Mr. Chaise wants you to work with us—me. I'm not sure about the position. I know you're still preaching when people ask. Maybe we can work out a consultant position. The bottom line is that I need you, Daddy. Please. I know I can be less than kind but—"

"Okay."

She stared at the phone. "Okay? Just like that?"

"You asked. Nicely. I know what it's like to need something. Just pray that we won't regret it."

"You won't. I promise."

"Even you can't make those kinds of promises, Queen D. Talked to your mother lately?"

Dyanne took a deep breath. She talked to her mother even less than her father. Though she'd been an adult when her mother remarried, something about it just didn't seem right. Her times with her mother and her new husband were always polite, though. Painfully so. "No, I haven't talked to Mom. You?"

"I had lunch with her and Norman other day. They're doing well. They both asked about you. Give them a call."

Right, lunching with your ex-wife and her new husband. One big happy family. "Things are really busy, but I probably do need to call her. I'd better go. Thanks for agreeing to help me."

"Thank you, Dyanne. For calling I mean. I know that you needed something from me but it still means a lot. You mean a lot."

Wow. This was much further than she'd planned to go. "Ditto."

She pressed the button and put her head down on the desk, overcome with tears.

"I'm really proud of you," Dyanne said as she watched the final page of Fallon's daily pages curl out of the printer. She'd been more than skeptical about being able to finish the book in such a short amount of time, especially without the usual outline to go by, but somehow Fallon had managed to make things flow.

"Well, thank you. I'm trying. I struggled a bit when the children were away, but I wanted to get back in the groove so that Judah and I can try out some new recipes for Ryan's birthday party."

Dyanne tapped the stack of pages on the edge of the desk. She'd missed Ryan's company, too, but it'd forced her to think about her own life and make some connections of her own. She'd talked to both her parents in the past two days, something that rarely, if ever, happened. "So they are having a party for Ryan? I'm glad. I was hoping to do something for him."

"You still can. If you mean Karol and Rob, I don't think they're doing anything. At least not that they know of. Ryan would probably be the one to ask and since it's his birthday, he really can't. So Judah and I are planning a party!"

Blinking rapidly didn't help Fallon's words sink in. "While I'm glad that you're making progress, we're nowhere near ready to present this book to Steve Chaise. It's wonderful that you've been helping us with the Simon kids but the reality is work has to come first. We may have to let them know that we, you and I at least, won't be able to go on much longer."

"Dee Dee. It'll get done. Now relax. You're going to drive yourself—and me—crazy. What I want to know is if there's any news yet."

"Last I heard, sales were slowing but steady. About four or five hundred copies a week this past week. It'll pick back up once the tour starts."

Fallon's earrings jingled as she shook her head. "Oh, girl, you are so dense sometimes. I wasn't asking you about news on book sales. I'm asking you about news about you. You know, woman news?"

Dyanne pushed her glasses off her eyes and into her hair. Her mother had asked the same question a few hours before. "Do I have some kind of biological clock tied around my neck or what? Am I ticking that loud? There is no news, Fallon. I told you before, we've decided to wait."

"The question is, has God decided to wait?"

"What?"

"Nothing." Fallon's eyes narrowed as she peered out the window overlooking the front yard.

The look on her friend's face said it all. Someone or something in the front yard did not belong. Fallon didn't seem upset about it, whatever it was. Dyanne turned in time to see a

Mercury sedan pulling into the drive with Ohio tags. Forest-green. "What in the world?"

In her haste to get downstairs, Dyanne knocked a few pages off Fallon's stack. Fallon toppled the remaining pages when she tried to keep up, forgetting the sleeves of her caftan. She ran on, not slowing down a bit as she called out to Dyanne from behind.

"Who is that? He's gorgeous. And not young boy hot, either. Gray-headed Ed Bradley kind of fine. The kind of fine that I don't see often."

As she opened the door, Dyanne rolled her eyes at Fallon, and then smiled at the man on the other side of the door, which must have become revolving without her knowledge there were so many people coming and going. Still, she couldn't help but reach out and give her guest a hug.

"Hey, Daddy. Come on in."

Neal set a personal record for his four mile run. He'd seen the green Mercury from a long way off and though his iPod had quit a mile back and his legs felt like cement, the thought of seeing his father-in-law kicked something into overdrive. By the time he dashed to the porch and pushed the Stop button on his heart rate monitor, he'd made it home in record time. He hated to greet Reverend Kelvin Stokes in a sweaty running suit and muddy shoes, but he forgot all that when the faint scent of licorice and lime caught him in the doorway. Fallon and the reverend. He smiled at the former and ran toward the latter.

"Dad!" Neal said, running straight to the older man, who looked even better than the last time they'd seen each other. He held out a fist and his father-in-law did the same. They pounded hands in greeting but the reverend pulled him close.

"You'd better hug your old man, boy. You know you're as much my son as anything. I told your father that on the phone the other day."

Fallon's hand reached between them with a towel and a

cold bottle of water for Neal. Both men paused to look at her, and then look at each other. What he saw in his father-in-law's eyes made Neal shake his head: first, wonder and then, awe. That Fallon. There wasn't a man alive she didn't have some effect on, but this was a first.

"I see you've met our guest."

Dyanne's father, who was never without a ready word, failed to make a coherent response. "I—uh—yes, Dee introduced Dr. Gray and I—"

"Just call me Fallon. For now anyway. I have a feeling that you might be one of the few people who calls me by my real name. Do you like Ferris wheels?"

The reverend swallowed hard. "Yes, well. It'd be an honor to know you better and yes, I love Ferris wheels."

Just as it seemed Fallon would pounce on the man, she swept a sleeve in Neal's direction and headed toward the kitchen. "Well, you two have fun. I'm going off to start dinner. Again, nice to meet you."

"Likewise."

Dyanne, who sat on the couch, silent and stunned, paused to join the two men watch as Fallon walked into the kitchen with the grace of a much younger—and smaller—woman. Spinach, mangoes and Southern sun was a combination to be reckoned with, evidently. Dyanne looked as though she could use a cup of one of Fallon's juice drinks.

She held up her hands when Neal, still smiling, gave her the what's-going-on look. "He's here to work on the Christian line. Evidently Steve Chaise told him to come on down, too. This is the South's newest bed-and-breakfast, I guess. Not that I'm not glad to see you, Dad. I am."

"Obviously." Her father, who still hadn't quite recovered from Fallon, raked a hand through his almost-white hair. Though usually in control of any situation or conversation, the man couldn't seem to understand what had just happened.

Neal sipped the water he'd been given and peeled off his shirt and headed for the laundry room. His father-in-law had been single for a very long time and had totally lost touch with his effect on women. Neal's own mother had caught her breath the first time she'd seen Dyanne's dad. The gasp hadn't been lost on his father, who, though he laughed and joked with Reverend Stokes, wasn't as fond of him as he let on. Probably because Dyanne's father made it so obvious how fond he was of Neal. The feeling was mutual.

"Dad, I'm going to clean up. Then I'll be right down. We're glad to have you in any capacity, but I'm really excited about your working on the line. I've read several of the titles ready for the fall lineup and to be honest, I have questions. A lot of them."

That shook the man out of his confusion. "Questions? Wonderful. Take all the time you need. I'll go up and get settled into the guest room. That's where your guest—I mean Fallon—said to put my things."

A worried look passed between Neal and Dyanne, but she said nothing. She was definitely out of it, but Fallon seemed to have taken up her slack quite nicely.

Knowing how modest the reverend was and how, well, not-so-modest Fallon could be, Neal felt compelled to say something. "I think you'd be more than comfortable upstairs, Dad, but with so many ladies up there, you might like it better down here," Neal said, pointing out the larger downstairs bedroom.

Reverend Stokes forced a finger into the collar of his guayabera shirt, one Dyanne had bought him on her last trip to Miami. He seemed to be making room for his answer, which shocked everyone.

"Upstairs is fine. See you in a few minutes." With that, he turned and went upstairs, pausing only to take a whiff of the magical scents coming from the kitchen.

Neal pulled his wife against his bare chest and began to pray. He'd thought moving to Tallahassee would slow things down. He couldn't have been more wrong.

# *The Gift*

Long after the china breaks
Vows stretched, bent
Routine fits and starts
Of all-the-same days
There comes the gift
Ripe and shiny in
The corner of your eyes
A reflection of all the
Love I've ever known
Flung against all
You are. This morning
You smiled at me
And I was twenty again,
Stupid and breathless
For your kiss.
Tonight, I will unwrap
Our love with wiser fingers,
Knowing it is both fragile
And strong.


—Karol
Day 15 on the way home from Hope and Singh's

## Chapter Fourteen

"Are things any better?" Karol pressed her eyes shut for a moment, preparing for the response from her old friend. Things hadn't been going well for Hope and Singh.

"Not really."

"Did you visit the church Rob found? Did Singh go to the support group?"

"Yes and yes. The church is nice, actually. It was good to be back in fellowship. That much seems right. Everything else, well, it's just going to take time, I think. There's been a lot of damage done. The children, bless their hearts, don't know what to think of us."

"Nobody's perfect, Hope," Karol said with experience and conviction behind her.

"I know. Now. I can see that I tried to be perfect, tried to have heaven on this earth. This wretched, sinful earth. Oh, look at me, I'm doing it again. Being negative. It's just that, well, nothing makes sense. He says it's not because of me, but it has to be, doesn't it? If that's what he wanted, why would he let me believe—why would God let me believe—"

"We're human, Hope. We mess up. You are a beautiful woman, a wonderful wife. He doesn't want anyone else. It's the enemy trying to destroy your beautiful family. You all have touched so many lives, especially ours. You can get through this. You're coming for Ryan's birthday, right?"

"Yes."

"Okay. Let's just focus on making it until then, focus on today. There's grace enough for today. Pick one thing you want to do…today."

"Pick blueberries with the children."

"Okay. Do that. Have fun. Take pictures. Make pie. Smile. And trust God for tomorrow. Deal?"

"Deal."

"All right. Let's talk soon."

"Karol?"

"Yes?"

"I love you. So much. I'm so sorry. For everything."

"I know. Me, too."

"Don't stop writing. I was wrong before. You have a gift. It will make room for you."

The phone clicked softly in Karol's ear. Before they'd left North Carolina, Rob had sprung into action, finding a local pastor and support group that Singh felt comfortable with. Singh seemed to be glad to be tackling the problem with a group of strangers.

Hope had ups and downs, also, but by the time they'd left, things seemed to be off to a good start. Now it seemed things were unraveling again. Karol worried for her friends, but these days it was her own marriage that concerned her.

She'd been so ready to believe in Singh, but thought the worst of her own husband. Karol had allowed others to talk her out of the trust that had once been the foundation of her marriage. And yet, she was more afraid to trust now than ever. Though Rob wasn't the one struggling with pornography—at the moment—the realization that it could have easily been him, or any other Christian man she knew, was sobering.

The best way to explain it was to just say it, so she did. She walked outside to the shed, where Rob was putting away his tools.

"I'm afraid. If that happened to Hope and Singh, it could happen to us, too. I'm not the best wife in the world. My mothering skills won't win any awards. I think the reason I've felt discouraged about being a mother is because I don't feel secure as a wife. It's not your fault really. It's just that marriage seems so, so…"

"Disposable?" Rob kissed her forehead.

"Yes. That's a good word. Maybe I understand my mother a little better now. When I was younger, I thought that you'd always love me, that I didn't need to work hard at our relationship." She rubbed her husband's shoulders, knotted from carrying the younger kids to bed a few minutes earlier. They'd been working hard all day, making a tree house of their own.

He smiled at her touch, but not at her words. "I will always love you, Karol. And you do work hard at our relationship. Sometimes people are so busy 'working on their relationships' that they get sick of each other and mess the whole thing up. You are here and you believe in me. Thinking that you didn't for a while is what made things hard. I said some things I shouldn't have. I'm sorry if I made you feel insecure. You have no idea how much I'm into you."

*Likewise.*

Just before a tide of kisses carried them away, Karol spoke again. "You did get to me when you said that you're attracted to other women sometimes. I didn't recognize how much of a battleground marriage is. For me, it's my emotions, for you, maybe it's more physical."

Rob leaned against the shed before taking her hand and starting for the house. "I think it's both for both of us, just at different times. People try to make it seem as though women are all one thing and men are all the other, but the physical struggle came from me feeling like you thought less of me. You've always seemed so, I don't know, proud of me. That still gets to me even though I'm an everyday guy. I want to be better."

Karol fought back tears as they went inside, started up the stairs. Here she'd been blaming some Internet model for the problems in her marriage when she'd been the thorn in her own side. "I think that I felt like I wasn't enough for you anymore, like I needed to have a destiny outside of the family to keep you interested."

Rob laughed. "Oh, no, babe. I'm interested. I don't think there's anything wrong in having things you love to do. You're a great mom and wife. You're a great teacher and writer. There are lots of other things you haven't worked hard enough at yet to know whether you're good at them. I just want you to be happy when I get to you. Mia's getting older. You're about due for a dose of me-time."

"But what about you?"

"Karol, I get to do what I love everyday. Then I come home and hammer and build on things. And you don't bug me about it. You know I love these things—"

"It's just how you're wired, to build things. Whether it's a computer or a birdhouse, you just get how things work."

Rob pulled his wife to his chest. "Exactly. And you get how words work. I think that where we went wrong was trying to be Hope and Singh instead of being ourselves. We've got to find our own way."

She wiped her eyes. "Ryan said that."

"Smart kid."

"Yes. He is. What are we going to get him for his birthday?"

"A little brother?" Rob said in a mocking voice.

Karol punched him lightly. "Be serious."

"Okay, he's a deep kid for eleven, but he is going to middle school now. A tool set, maybe?"

"He's not you, Rob."

"Right. A book then. Some kind of rare and precious book. You'd know what better than I would. Unless…" He got up and turned on the light.

"What?" She watched in horror and amazement as her husband pulled the boxes of her poems and unfinished stories from under the bed. There were two huge boxes full. She held the sides of the mattress. "No way. Don't even think about it."

"Why not? He loves your writing. A rare and precious book. Your book. I could edit for you, do the cover, whatever you need."

"There's no way. It's impossible." Karol fell back on the bed. Talking about their marriage had been hard enough, but her sharing her writing with her husband, too? No way.

With a notebook in hand and a plea in his eyes, Rob sat down beside her. "Nothing is impossible with God, Karol. Nothing. You just told Hope that before we left. You've told me the same many times. It's still true. Besides, this stuff is amazing. I could kick myself for letting you shove it under the bed all these years."

"You pushed me, remember? We tried to publish that book of affirmations, remember? Nobody wanted it. Ryan did a great job on the edits but that's probably about the only thing that I'd be able to give Ryan to read." She nodded finally as Rob stared at the notebook. "Go ahead."

Rob turned a page. "I don't know. There's a lot of stuff here. That poem you wrote this morning was pretty good. I've been looking forward to tonight. Thought about buying some ribbon so that you could unwrap our love…."

Karol's mouth opened wide. She'd been half-asleep when she'd written that poem. Her notebook and pen had been closed and put away when she awoke. She hadn't considered that Rob might have read it. The thought of him reading that poem freaked her out, but she had to laugh as he pretended to tie a bow around his neck.

"Stop it."

"I will for now, but only because Ryan is still up. I really think you should do a book for Ryan's birthday. I'm going to read it all anyway so I can help you choose if you want—don't look at me like that. I am going to read it. All of it. Unless you don't want me to."

"It's not that. But sometimes the stories just come like they come, you know? I don't want you to know how strange I really am. I'm weird enough already."

"Strange but beautiful. I believe that's a quote from our first date."

She nodded. "I'm not sure how you got a second date with a line like that, but yes, that sounds about right."

He put down the notebook and took her hand. "You can do this, honey. Even the poems would be great. I know you still have that novel, too, the one you wrote in college."

At the mention of the novel she'd written but assumed Rob had forgotten about, Karol sat up straighter in the bed.

"Yes, I remember it. You read me some of it. Liked it, too. It was a good choice. I think your words, whichever ones you choose, will be a good choice."

"Are you sure?"

"Positive."

She settled back in his arms. "I love you."

He pretended to tie a ribbon around his neck again. "Prove it."

It was all there.

In the stacks of notebooks, bound together by rubber bands, were all Karol's words, her hopes, her dreams. Even in high school, she'd rambled on about love, even though she hadn't known for sure then what it really was. Her college work turned dark and unexpected in places, like a rush of English rain. There were other pieces that stole Karol's breath, like the novel she'd written as her senior thesis. A novel she'd written and forgotten.

At the first line, it all came rushing back:

When a person is born, there's supposed to be room; sometimes there isn't and the baby has to push, too, screaming into the world spent and aware that there will always be work to do.

Breath caught in Karol's throat. How had she forgotten this? It had taken her two years to write. At the suggestion of her professor, she'd spent another year editing it. She'd met Rob around the time she finished and never submitted it. And yet, as she turned the yellowed pages of her final handwritten draft, something bright and afraid leaped within her.

She read on, marking through words and changing them as she went:

That's how they say I was born, making my own way even then, pulling myself from death into life as Mama went away and I entered in. Some folks here are still scared of me for that, they say it ain't natural for a baby to come out alive with the mama dead like that. I don't remember any of it except for when it rains. When it storms hard, the thunder pushes through my sleep, squeezing me like contractions. Most nights like that, I wake up on the floor. Sometimes, like tonight, I wake up in places I don't recognize. This time, though, there is blood.

Karol stopped writing, again wondering what Rob—or anyone else—would think of her if and when they read this story. Like so many of the others in her secret box, it was a mystery, a tale that unwound between her fingers no matter how hard she tried to hold it still. It wasn't a bright book of

Christian affirmations or the mothering manual Hope might have penned, but it was what Karol had.

Who she was.

One of her afternoons had been spent cleaning out the attic, which was still hot and cramped, but without the scrapbooking supplies she'd never used—tried that on day three—the broken sewing machines Rob would never fix—gave them to Goodwill during week two—and makeup she would never sell—after she finished laughing, Karol just threw it away—there was room for her to think. The treadmill had been covered in clothes. It was here beneath the years and shadows that she'd found an old box, the one that contained her novel, the one that might change everything.

With the story hot upon her, pouring out and refusing to be quiet, Karol grabbed the notebooks—there were three, bound together with a purple hair scrunchie—and headed downstairs for the computer. Ryan passed her in the hall wearing an outfit she'd never seen and reeking of cologne that smelled a lot like his father's.

Karol didn't even break her stride.

She threw up a hand and kept moving, praying a quick prayer for the neighbors she'd so disliked just a few months ago. The computer blinked on and she rested the first notebook against something and began to type. The thought of writing had been so far away before, abstract and cloudy, a dream. But now, as the words tapped through her fingers, it seemed solid. Finite. And it held her to the chair as if it would never let go.

"You're a mother," Hope had once said. "You can't spend all your time scribbling in notebooks, daydreaming while your kids are running wild. There are other people to do that sort of thing." And maybe she'd been right. There would always be other writers, better writers. Karol sat down in the only chair and took a deep breath, thinking of all the affirmations and prayers she'd written down and shared with others over the years. A new one came, for her alone, whispered hurriedly at the computer screen.

"I am a writer. I give myself permission to create without guilt, to laugh when it's inappropriate, to dance when there's no music playing. I give my children permission to be who God has called them to be, even if I don't understand it. I am a word warrior: inspiring, powerful, vulnerable and honest. My battle is with myself. Jesus is my victory."

With that, Karol reached for her pen and set her timer. Her days were almost up, but she would make the most of the time that remained. After that, she wasn't sure how she'd find the time to continue writing, but she knew that somehow it would work. It had to.

She was a writer.

# *To-Do*

- Buy organic spinach

- Order mangoes—10

- Fax first chapter to Steve Chaise

- Send thank-you card to church for welcome basket

- Try new vitamins doctor recommended

- Pick up Neal's whey protein

- Read over Ryan's press releases

- Make dinner reservations for Dad, Fallon, Neal and I

- Spa Day!!!

—Dyanne

## Chapter Fifteen

"Morning, Dad." Though she'd been mortified when her father first arrived, Dyanne had to admit it was nice having him around. The two of them usually clashed like crazy, but for some reason things didn't seem as bad as usual. Or at least not yet. Usually by the end of three days, Neal started packing someone's bag—once he'd packed his own—and sending someone on his or her merry way.

"Morning yourself, sweetheart," her father said as he passed her on the stairs.

This morning, four days since her father's arrival, started with Dyanne and Neal running into the reverend at the bottom of the steps. It didn't take long for them to see what had stopped him cold—Fallon.

Her back was turned to them, but Dyanne knew the headphones in Fallon's ears led the MP3 player so often in the pocket of her friend's silk robe. The song must have been a good one because Fallon shimmied and shook from the stove to the sink and back again several times before she turned and saw that she had company. For the first time, Dyanne had a chance to see the illustrious Dr. Gray look shaken.

Fallon put a hand to her throat before slipping the headphones off of her ears. "Sorry," she said slowly. "I thought you all would be sleeping for a while yet." She looked at Dyanne's father with a pained expression. "Hope I didn't embarrass you, Reverend. Just trying to get my praise on this morning."

"And you did just that," Reverend Kelvin said with a big smile. "I was just wishing that you would have shared the song with the rest of us. We definitely need a big dose of whatever you're having for breakfast."

Neal shook his head as Fallon's eyes sparkled. She waved Dyanne's father over to the blender and retrieved another goblet from the cabinet. "I thought you'd never ask," she said, pouring the spinach-mango juice with precision. "Drink it right down and be ready to run to the bathroom, if you know what I mean…."

Dyanne's father looked a little worried, but he did as he was told. Another wide smile replaced his apprehension. "Oh, that's good! I feel that."

"You feel it, baby—I mean, Reverend?" Fallon looked horrified again. Dyanne started to think that maybe she should have stayed in bed a little longer. Watching the two of them was torture. Her dad had only dated a few times that she knew of in the years since the divorce, but it was obvious to everyone but her father that he was quite taken with Fallon. And she with him.

"Just call me Kelvin," he said, raising his glass again. "Tell me more about this stuff. Oh, and let me hear that song…"

Dyanne and Neal watched as the two of them retreated into the dining room.

"They're sickening," Dyanne said, scanning the fridge for an English muffin or bagel to settle her stomach.

Neal started a protein shake for himself and handed Dyanne a banana. "They're cute. I didn't think any man could have that kind of effect on Fallon except me."

"You're pitiful, you know that?"

"I do know that. And you're beautiful, even in the morning. Sorry I fell asleep before you came to bed. Did you and your dad get a lot done last night?"

"Tons." For the second night in a row, Dyanne and her father had reviewed the new line of Christian books from every aspect. He'd explained why a couple of the titles wouldn't work, given suggestions for the covers that Ryan had identified as "busy" and even given input on Fallon's book tour.

"She needs a nonprofit. A service arm of some kind. I read her book last night, the one that's out now. I watched her with those children yesterday. While she's been primarily doing relationships and women's issues speaking, she is the common sense grandmother that many churches are missing today. You can add to her brand by giving her passion another dimension. She's not a person only motivated by money. Give her something big enough to fit her life into. You're trying to brand pieces of her."

Dyanne had scribbled notes so fast that she'd broken a nail. She'd talked to Fallon about the suggestions the reverend had made a little bit before heading to bed.

The author shouted so loud that Dyanne worried for the neighbors. "It's just what I want to do!" Fallon had squealed. "I've been thinking this same thing for a while. I was going to wait until the tour was over to tell you. I know how you get all worried about these things, but I need to do this. I really do."

Eating a banana for breakfast was a bad idea. A really bad idea. Dyanne forced it down as she recounted everything from the night before.

"It makes perfect sense," Neal said as yet another blender whirred on their kitchen counter. "I understand exactly what Fallon means. We've done so much, you know? Been so blessed. And yet sometimes, in the day or two before the next goal is formed, the next plan set in motion, it feels sort of empty, like I need to do something bigger than myself. Like I need to be giving myself away."

*Give yourself away.* The pastor had said the same thing in his sermon on Sunday. Dyanne had been meaning to attend services—for market research if nothing else—but her father's appearance had pretty much forced her to go. If there was one rule her father had, it was that all able bodies were to be in the house of the Lord come Sunday morning. Even when they were out of town, he'd pull over at some church in the middle of nowhere and go right in. As a result, he knew pastors and parishioners in every denomination in near every city in the country.

Dyanne hadn't thought much of the small church Karol and Rob attended before her visit. A few days later, phrases and ideas from the simple sermon were still showing in every conversation she and Neal had. The really strange part had been at the end of service when they walked out the door and shook the pastor's hand. Though he'd given the people in front and in back of them a quick handshake and genuine smile, Pastor Newton had lingered over Neal and Dyanne, pulling them both into a hug. With the same simplicity and grace that he'd preached his sermon, he'd said only one thing to them as he let them go. "We want to see more of you."

From the firm nod that Neal had given in return to the pastor's request, Dyanne was sure that they would be back the next Sunday. She'd thought her father would gloat on the way home from service about his prayers being answered and how great it was that they'd gone to church, but he was too busy playing Name that Hymn with Fallon in the backseat.

Dyanne clutched her stomach at the memory. "Neal? I don't feel so good."

He put down his smoothie and lifted Dyanne into his arms. "What's the matter, babe? You don't look right. You've been working pretty hard. Let me take you up to bed. I'll work with

Fallon on the book this morning. I'm free except for a call at eleven."

She let herself relax in her husband's arms. "Can you stop at the bathroom, please?"

Neal picked up his pace. "Don't throw up on me, girl." He laughed but his voice sounded worried. No matter how hard Dyanne worked, she was rarely sick and when she did fall ill, it was usually with a cold.

He got her to the bathroom just in time and raced upstairs for her toothbrush and a washcloth. "Are you still having the headaches?"

She mopped her forehead with the washcloth. "Not anymore. I'm just sort of dizzy. The heat down here..."

"You don't think—"

"What?" Dyanne's voice was sharp as she jerked her head up out of the sink.

"I'm just saying. Could you be pregnant?"

"No." She pushed around him and out of the bathroom, but not before seeing the fear in her eyes as she looked in the mirror. The doctor did routine tests when she'd gone in for her headaches, including a pregnancy test. Hers had been negative, but the doctor had mentioned testing her again at the appointment and recommended that she start taking prenatal vitamins.

"Not to say that you'll get pregnant anytime soon. It's just best to have the nutrition levels high during the reproductive years. And the prenatals usually have the best quality nutrients. Good for the skin and nails. Don't worry."

She had worried. She was worried now.

Neal was, too. He didn't pick her up this time, but followed behind as Dyanne started back upstairs. "Do you want me to come with you?"

"Please."

Fallon and Dyanne's father came back into the kitchen.

"Dee Dee? Are you okay?" Fallon said, cutting off the funny story she'd been telling.

"Yes," Dyanne said, not waiting for Neal as she headed upstairs.

"No," Neal said, lifting his foot onto the next step. All of a sudden, he wasn't feeling so great, either.

Two lines. And not faint ones, either. Neal and Dyanne watched their home pregnancy test with wide eyes as the blue spread from end of the stick to the other in two fat grooves.

"We should have got the plus or minus one. I never pay attention to those commercials. What is that—an equal sign? Are you pregnant or not?" Neal was pacing the floor in circles. Dyanne was amazed he hadn't burned a hole in the rug from all the friction.

"The test is defective. I can't be pregnant. Go get another one."

Forty bucks and a lot of empty boxes later, Neal was sure of one thing—the tests were not defective.

Dyanne was just as sure of another thing—she was not pregnant.

It took the doctor that she'd visited a few weeks before to make her face the truth: two lines still mean what they've always meant.

"You're pregnant. Very early, but definitely pregnant."

Dyanne stared at the doctor and at the paper in his hand. "That's impossible. The prescription you gave me…I was taking them."

The doctor smiled. "So was my mother when she conceived me. I'm a little screwy, but I turned out okay. We will have to keep an eye out for the baby's development…"

Neal looked afraid to be happy but Dyanne could tell that he was. She was not happy. This wasn't how it was supposed to happen. This wasn't what she'd planned. She'd changed her mind, only her body hadn't come along for the ride.

*Trust Me.*

At the thought of trusting God, she became angry. Hadn't she been trying to trust Him? Hadn't she been trying to surrender? She'd wanted a baby more than anything, but she'd been willing to push it away to give it up. Work was really becoming interesting again. She had a new house. She was actually forming a relationship with her father. Fallon was blooming like a hothouse flower. And the tour… How would she make it around the country puking at every place they went to? The thought of an airplane ride made Dyanne want to head for the bathroom right now.

"I can't see much of anything on the ultrasound because it's too early, but the blood test is positive and your hormone level is sky-high. You are definitely pregnant."

"I just don't see how this could have happened. I came to you for a prescription. It didn't do what it was supposed to do. This never would have happened in New York."

The doctor smiled. "God is in New York, too, I'm afraid. We know a lot of things about the human body. We're learning more everyday. Sometimes, though, things just don't cooperate exactly. What you thought was your cycle was probably the baby implanting itself. It happens."

It wasn't supposed to happen. Not to her.

"Thanks, Doc. We appreciate you getting us in so quickly. I guess we'll be seeing a lot of you, huh?"

Dyanne shut out her husband's chitchat with the doctor and retreated into her own thoughts. She'd been so confident a month ago that she would be a good mother, so sure that having a baby was the right thing to do. Now, she wasn't sure about anything except that this was not at all the way she'd wanted to feel about finding out she was pregnant for the first time.

What's wrong with me? Dyanne wondered. How ungrateful and foolish she must seem. Women all over the world

were wanting babies at this very moment. Praying to have
them. She'd been one of them just a few weeks before. She'd
mourned the months when no one had proclaimed her
pregnant as the doctor had done today. She'd even envied
Karol Simon and thought her silly for struggling with motherhood. Now she wondered how her neighbor had ever
managed to get through all this three times and keep her sanity.

"Come on. Let's get you home," Neal said, helping Dyanne
up out of the chair.

"Oh, please. Don't talk to me in that tone. It's just morning
sickness, for goodness' sake. Nothing a little spinach and
mango can't cure."

"Did you really keep that down this morning?"

"It's the only thing I can keep down. Fallon finds it quite
amusing. Don't you dare laugh."

He dared. "I want you to know that I'm sorry for how I
handled all this. Going back and forth about it. I should have
just respected what you wanted in the beginning. That way,
this could have been a happy day for you."

Dyanne squeezed her husband's hand and leaned into his
shoulder, but she didn't respond to his remark. She wasn't sure
if there was anything Neal could have done that would have
made a difference. Like everything else on her life list,
Dyanne had gone after what she wanted—and gotten it. And
for once, she wasn't so sure that was a good thing.

"He hates it." Ryan announced Steve Chaise's opinion of
Fallon's book with a flat, bored voice. The verdict had forced
its way through the fax machine just sixteen minutes after the
first chapter had been sent.

> Good but not great. She's trying too hard. I need Fallon
> to be Fallon, but sharing her faith. Work on it and get
> back to me. Don't play it safe. Not this time.

Usually, Dyanne would have spent half the day trying to figure out how to break the news to Fallon. Now she had to get it out before she found herself head down in the toilet losing her lunch. Ryan, who'd read the pages as many times as she had, picked up the originals and scanned them again as though assessing them once more.

"What do you think?" she asked before biting the bullet and heading downstairs.

Ryan put the pages down. "I think he's right, based on that chapter. I've seen more of the book and things really do open up a lot later. Have you noticed that the pages since your Dad got here are a cut above the others? I mean really. She's in a good storytelling groove now. The faith seems more inherent instead of just tacked on like she remembered it was supposed to be a Christian book."

Dyanne nodded, pausing again to remind herself that this was the neighbor boy from next door and not some publishing mogul. Though in some ways everything in her life seemed out of control, she had to admit that God had been doing a great job in a lot of areas, too. She'd worried that helping out with Karol's kids would keep her from getting Fallon's book done, but the truth was she would never have been as far along as she was without Ryan's help. As for his comments about the book, she totally agreed.

"It's true. I really like the pages from the past four or five days. The story of how she became a raw foodist—"

"Except when she's not a raw foodist!" Ryan echoed one of Fallon's most famous quotes.

"Exactly. I was thinking last night that this second section is less of a self-help book and more of a memoir."

"Yes! That's what it is. A memoir. Wait. Give me a pen." Though Ryan could use the computer fairly well for a boy heading into middle school, when it came to book talk, he most often asked for a pen to scribble down something and pass it to Dyanne for her approval. This time, he seemed to be writing forever.

Dyanne's stomach had started its afternoon gymnastic session when Ryan finally passed her the notepad. There were several scratched-out phrases, circles, stars and arrows that Dyanne couldn't follow, but the final result was boxed at the bottom of the page with, "What do you think? New Title?" scratched beside it.

"The Green Grandma's Guide to God, Mangoes and other Miracles," Dyanne said slowly, already starting for the stairs. "I get where you're going, Ryan. I don't know if this will be the final, but I'm feeling it."

He smiled and started down the stairs behind her with his hands jammed into his front pockets in satisfaction. "I was thinking sort of Sweet Potato Queen vibe, but not, you know?"

She paused on the stairs. Until three weeks ago, the boy had only read classics, Christian novels and some fantasy here and there. Now he was doing market analysis like a professional. "I think you've spent too much time on our bookshelves. That one might be over your head."

He agreed. "Just scanned it."

Downstairs, they found Fallon, Judah and Dyanne's father cooking chicken and rice seasoned with the herbs from Fallon and Judah's latest project—a herb garden. She could tell from their expressions that they were about to ooh and ah her about being pregnant and insist she sit down and all that other foolishness, so she cut right to the point.

"Steve Chaise isn't too hot on the first chapter. Doesn't think it's genuine. Says it's forced and too safe. Doesn't sound like you. I think you should consider his—"

"He's right," Fallon said, stirring fresh lemon balm and garlic into the rice. "Kelvin and I have been talking about it this morning. He thinks my stories are my strength. I suppose I use them more in my speaking than my writing. What do you think?"

Dyanne smiled. Her father grew more useful every day. "I agree—"

Fallon waved her publicist away. "I was talking to Ryan. Speak up, child. You're the boss here, you know."

Though it was obvious he wanted to answer, Ryan's good manners won out. "I'll let Miss Dyanne answer that. We had a discussion before coming down." He took a step back.

Reverend Kelvin gave the boy a nod of approval.

"All right, Dee Dee. Hit me with it. I thought the kid would at least take it easy on me. You're a pistol when you're not pregnant. I know you're going to take me through it now."

Dyanne took the seat that her father held out for her. Protesting any longer would only make him insist more vehemently. "Sorry if I've been snarky, Fallon. I don't mean it. Bear with me. It's getting better."

"You're doing fine, sugar. Don't pay me any mind. That's my nerves talking."

They both laughed, Dyanne knew that Fallon had a point. Neal had been walking around on eggshells, too. She'd have to pray harder and get more sleep. Sleep and food were the big ticket items these days. "Ryan and I both like your latest pages the best. I think it starts heading to a good place in chapter three or so and just gets better from there. What do you think about a memoir instead of your usual type of work?"

Fallon stopped stirring. "A memoir? Oh, I don't know. Those always seem so…egotistical."

It wasn't easy, but Dyanne managed not to laugh in Fallon's face. "I'd say that you have a healthy ego, so that shouldn't be a problem. It doesn't have to be your whole life story. More like your take on life. A series of essays and stories. Your thoughts on God, vegetables and love."

Ryan whipped out his notebook and started scribbling again.

Reverend Kelvin smiled. "I think it's a wonderful concept. It could also fit with your nonprofit, once you figure out what it's going to be. God, vegetables and love is a good place to start. If someone could teach children just about those three things, the world would be a different place."

Dyanne wanted to hug her father as she watched Fallon's conflicted face become peaceful.

Judah, who'd been shucking peas intently into a bowl and taking in their every word, lifted his head only when he'd set the last one free from its pod. "Put some recipes in there, too. You're good with food."

Fallon let the spoon slide into the pot and put a hand on her hip. "That child done opened it all up for me now. If y'all need me, I'll be in the office. Kelvin, will you finish up this rice for me?"

The reverend had already picked up the spoon. "I've got this. You just cook up something good on that computer. Go on now. I'll bring you some food up later."

"Bring me some, too…" was all Dyanne could get out before she made a run toward the hall. As she banged through the bathroom door, she heard Fallon giggling on her way up the stairs.

While Fallon was great for comfort or a quick meal, there were many things about having babies that she just didn't know.

"Even if I'd had a child, everything has changed so much these days that it seems totally different from what I remember when my sisters and friends were having children," Fallon said after another round of Dyanne's anxious questions. She was going to recommend that Dyanne call Karol Simon next door, but Dyanne didn't want to be a bother.

Karol saved them both when she came over uninvited and smiling with a basket of hot muffins. "Look, I hate to barge in, but I know how it was when I was pregnant the first time. I'm no expert, but I just wanted to let you know that you can ask me anything and I'll find out if I don't know. We're up late so call anytime. If you need me to run errands for you when go in town, I can do that, too. Anything. Just let me know."

Dyanne bit into a muffin and started in on her questions: "Why does my belly itch? Should I keep working out? Can I really breastfeed for as long as they recommend? Are these colors right for the nursery?" On and on she went, until she stopped herself. "I sound like a bride, don't I? Planning her wedding."

Karol laughed. "A little. It's sort of like that in a way."

Fallon made tea and they sorted through paint chips and swapped wedding stories. Dyanne paused a little before sharing hers. "We got married at the courthouse. It was very romantic really. Neal had told me that he'd marry me after graduation, so we'd gotten some of the things we needed and were in the planning stages. Then he got accepted to grad school and I got my job and…we just got married."

"I love it!" Fallon clapped her hands together. "People do all that uptight planning and end up divorced before the wedding is paid off. We could use a little spontaneity now and then. Well, I can, anyway. You, Dee? I'm not so sure. If I'd known the Mango Man back then, I might have given him some different advice. I'm just glad that we've got you now."

Karol smiled. "Yes, I really am glad. I'm so excited for you, too. I know on the phone you sounded hesitant in giving me the news about the baby, but I really am happy for you. We all are. It'll be wonderful to have a baby around this place again. We'll try not to spoil your little one." She took another sip of tea.

Fallon crunched a biscotti she'd unearthed somewhere. "Speak for yourself. I'm going to spoil that kid rotten, right, Dee?"

The women's voices folded around her against the cold of her own expectations. She held their words tight and close, especially Karol's, who seemed so convinced that Dyanne

could and would make a good mother. Each day, Karol came
back, bringing a little something to smooth Dyanne's way—
sometimes it was as simple as a roll of paper towels to clean
up the last meal she'd lost, but she always made Dyanne feel
as if she wasn't alone, as if she'd crossed over into the sorority
of motherhood.

It was only after getting to know Karol better that she
realized this group wasn't as organized or well-outfitted as
she'd supposed. What they did have, these mothers, was
stronger than most anything else, a love different from what
a woman felt for her husband, her siblings or even her own
mother. It was a fierce and covering love, Dyanne knew, even
if she was only starting to feel the flow of it. It came more
slowly than she would have liked, but it came, often after
holding hands in prayer with Karol Simon.

# *Son Scribbles*

It seems like only yesterday you bounced past me, trucks in both pockets of your kindergarten coat. I thought you'd be short forever, following behind me.

What a fool I was.

I follow now, seeking the endless curiosity walking proud on forever legs. You are becoming defiantly handsome, strangely beautiful and eagle-eyed enough to see the strings to all my puppets. You know how I throw my voice, hide my soul.

My faith-paint peels away under your unflinching gaze, but love me

Anyway. I know I don't deserve it. I don't deserve you, the long, lean reflection of the best of me.

Just when I feel hopeless, you look up from dragging dreamy fingers

In the sand and tell me to go in peace, to rest in the grace that is you.

—Karol, day 19, for Ryan's birthday

## Chapter Sixteen

Karol's twenty-one days weren't quite up, but Rob agreed to let her be Mom for one day. Ryan's birthday. It had taken much more heart and hurt than she'd thought it would to rewrite the book that now rested in her hand. The cover was cool and hard, just as she'd always thought it would be. What she hadn't expected was the rush of emotion when Rob cracked the spine, read the first words.

"It's so good. Even after reading it so many times the past few days. I am so proud of you."

He'd seen everything in the past week, read through all the curling, pained papers beneath their bed. He'd seen all Karol's mistakes, all her fears, all the parts of her that only worked on paper, the pieces that even she could only see on the page. He'd seen it all and yet he loved her. If it were possible, she thought he might have loved her more. The quiet confidence of his feelings now felt fierce and proud.

That made Karol happy because it was what she'd felt for Rob all along, but been unable to express. In all those years, she thought she'd been trying to get published but her stories and poems had really just been one long love letter.

The breath caught in Rob's throat as he finished the dedication, a poem for Ryan. Ryan might not be able to appreciate the truth of the words until he was older and had children of his own, but that was okay, too. She liked to think that she was giving her son something that he could grow into but never grow out of.

"This is the best gift. Oh—" Rob swiped at his eyes but didn't actually cry "—he's just going to love it. And that cameo of him on the cover? Priceless."

A week before, Neal had taken a picture of Ryan fast asleep with his head in a book and a pen in his hand. The image had struck something deep in Karol and she'd decided to incorporate it into the cover of *Indigo Dawn,* the novel she had just completed. There was a young boy in the novel and Ryan fit his description.

"I enjoyed writing that poem, too. I think I'm going to do one for each of the children. Start a tradition. Poems for their birthdays. With gifts of course."

Rob closed the book and put it back in its nest of tissue paper inside the gilded box they'd chosen. He shut the lid carefully. "I think that's a wonderful idea. I don't want you to feel like you have to do that, though. You might be busy writing another novel. You have some really great stories—"

Karol put her thumb to his lips then brought it to her own. "Thank you for saying that. For believing in me. For so long, I was bound by those boxes under the bed. I didn't know it, but I'd put some expectation on myself and when I didn't achieve it—"

"Yet."

"Let me finish. When that first manuscript didn't get published, I think I felt like there was nothing else I could be good at. So I tried to be a good mother, but that's hard to do when you're living next door to Hope. So I tried to be the best wife—"

"And that's hard to do when you're married to a jerk."

Karol threw a wad of paper streamers at Rob. "You are not a jerk, but if you keep interrupting me you will be severely punished."

"Promise?" He grabbed her by the waist.

She laughed. "I guess this is God's way of shutting me up. Anyway, to make a long story short, I've decided to do what Pastor Newton spoke about last Sunday—give myself away."

"To us?" Rob asked hesitantly, no longer laughing.

With a nod, she confirmed his thoughts. "To you."

He held her face in both hands. "But what if you're meant for other people, too? What if we're—if I'm not enough?"

"You are more than enough," Karol said softly. "If God wants me to share my words with other people, He'll show me. He'll show us. Until then, you'll have to suffer through reading my stories," she said in a low voice.

They kissed slow and easy and held each other for what seemed like a very long time.

"How long before the kids are due back from Neal and Dee's?"

"An hour, I think, but I was going to get them early. She's hardly keeping food down, poor thing."

"Ryan is helping. Fallon begged me to let them come. They're all outside. Leave them for a few more minutes and follow me."

"I don't know—"

"Leave them. I think I've got a story for you. Or the beginnings of one at least..." Rob smiled and took his wife by the hand.

Ryan's party surprised everyone. Even Karol.

At the sight of her parents, who hadn't been talking to her much lately, her eyes went wide.

"Mom? I mean Faith? I had no idea you planned on coming. If I'd known, I would have—"

Her father's hug smothered her words. "Karol, you don't need to do anything special for us. And sorry for coming without any notice. I tried to call, but couldn't get you. Your mother just decided this morning to drive down. It's so good to see you. You all have to get up to Atlanta soon."

Faith ran her fingers through her new haircut—a shorter version of the old one—and pressed her lips to her daughter's cheek in something that resembled a kiss. "Yes, Pops—Eric—insisted that I call you, but you know how you all are about the phone. I just figured that you wouldn't be doing anything for the child with the way you were acting the last time I was here. I'm happy to see that I was wrong. Quite wrong, in fact."

That made Karol smile. Not only had she been surprised by the appearance of her parents, but Hope and Singh, who had called to cancel days before, had shown up, too, bringing the whole clan with them including Bone the dog. Mia had run so far and so fast and screamed so loud when they pulled up that Karol had thought a wasp had bit her. When she'd seen what, and who, had caused such a reaction in her little girl, Karol had run to join them, too.

Though their last meeting had been awkward and painful, the old friends fell into each other's arms with an easy grace that made both Karol and Rob smile. He and Singh headed off for the grill, while Karol and Hope cut cake and poured drinks.

That is, until her parents had arrived. Now she stood with them under the shade of the tallest tree in her yard with her sweaty hand enveloped in her father's cool ones. Rob had insisted that she give her parents one of the few books they'd printed. Karol didn't want to, but she did give them a copy. For once, Karol felt as though she had surpassed her mother's expectations and it should have felt good, but there was something in her mother's eyes that kept her from enjoying it—fear.

"Faith, are you all right?"

Judah wiggled between them to give his grandfather a hug.

Karol tried to wipe the icing off his face, but her dad shook his head and let the boy scramble up into his arms. Karol's mother normally would have had a fit, but she didn't notice. Faith's eyes were glued to the wraparound porch of the house next door.

"Who is that? That woman. Over there." Faith lifted her hand and almost extended her finger but so many years of manners training wouldn't allow her to fully point. Karol wished they'd included some other things in those charm classes her mother had taken as a girl. Many other things.

Judah swallowed and answered before his mother could figure out which person Faith was talking about. There were several people on the porch next door but somehow Judah knew exactly who his grandmother meant.

"That's Fay-Ray. My grandma. She rocks. Wanna meet her?" Already out of his grandfather's arms, he grabbed at Faith's slender hands with icing-covered fingers.

For the first time, she didn't pull away. Her purse, however, a slim suede bag from Italy, slipped off her other wrist and hit the ground. Karol and her father bumped heads trying to pick it up.

Faith crouched in a position from her daily yoga class and looked into Judah's eyes. "I'm your grandmother, sweetie. You know that."

The boy shook his head and took a deep breath, ensuring that he could get his words out all at once. "You're Number Two. Faith the Second. Mommy—I mean Karol's—mother. Grandmas make cookies and get dirty and dance in the kitchen. That's what me and Fay-Ray do. We have a garden, too. Wanna see? You come on, too, Pop Pop."

Karol held tight to her mother's purse and patted Judah's shoulder. "Her name is not Fay-Ray, honey. She's an author staying next door. Fallon Gray? Perhaps you've heard of her. They say she's quite famous. She's been a godsend—"

"Did you say Fallon Gray?" It was her father's turn to

squint across the balloons and streamers into the shade of the porch next door. "As in Fayette Renee Allen?"

"Well, I don't know about that..." Karol was in unfamiliar territory now, trying to understand what was happening. She remembered now that Fallon had mentioned knowing her father and made a comment about her mother, too. Both of them moved slowly across the yard, faces blank as though they'd seen a ghost.

Or worse yet, a skeleton.

Karol wrapped both hands around herself as Rob approached from the grill, where he'd left Singh.

"Is everything all right?" her husband asked. "I glanced over and you all looked like you'd gotten food poisoning from the potato salad or something. What's going on?"

She squeezed Rob's hand once and shrugged before setting off behind her parents. "I don't know, honey. And to be honest I'm not sure I want to know."

He followed close behind. "Do you want me to come?"

Karol shook her head. "Probably not."

"Do you need me to come?"

"Please," she whispered.

Though Karol and Rob had set off behind Karol's parents, they reached the edge of Dyanne's yard at the same time. Ryan was on the porch with Karol's book held high. Fallon's rich laughter peppered Ryan's recounting of all his mother had done to get it published. Dyanne's father took the book and had begun to flip through the pages when Karol's father, Eric, left them all and climbed the stairs of the house next door.

Fallon's laughter stopped abruptly. "Eric?"

"It's me. You look good, Faye. But then you always did."

There was an awkward silence as no one knew what to say or do to stop the conversation raging, one that required no words.

"I do what I can, Eric. I do what I can. That's a great girl you raised over there. Good grandkids, too. C'mon, Judah. It's okay. We're just old friends. Faith, you come on, too." She motioned to Dyanne's father, whose usual smile was absent. "This is Kelvin. He's Dyanne's daddy—she's my publicist—and a good friend. A very good friend."

At that, the reverend's smile returned. "Come on up here, y'all. Have a seat. There's room."

Eric took the seat next to Fallon, but not before stopping to shake the reverend's hand. Karol winced at the tightness of their grip. It was a wonder neither of them broke a finger. Both men kept smiling but Rob passed Faith on the stairs and extended his hand in greeting.

Ryan, unencumbered by the foreboding of his mother, pushed forward, shoving a copy of *Indigo Dawn* into Fallon's hands. "Did you see it? Mom finished her book. It's amazing. You've got to read it. Promise me."

"I promise. Congratulations." She tucked the book into her bag on the floor.

Judah plopped into Fallon's lap. She poured a glass of water on the table beside her and dipped a napkin into it and started to wipe his face. "I see somebody enjoyed the cake," she said softly, talking into Judah's curls. "Make sure you brush your teeth later. Now give me a hug and take Ryan back to his party. He just came to visit us old folks and tell us about his fabulous gifts. Go on now. We'll check on the garden later, when everybody is gone."

That was all Judah needed to hear. "Come on, Ryan. Let's go."

Ryan looked reluctant but he let his little brother take him by the hand. "Okay. I'll come back later and see how Miss Dyanne is doing."

Karol looked concerned. "I noticed she disappeared all of a sudden. I thought she might have just been tired. Is she okay?"

Fallon smiled. "It is well. She's resting. God knows. You just enjoy your family today. Your beautiful family. And congratulations on the book. I can't wait to read it. Faith, how have you been? You look stunning as usual. So well put together."

Karol watched in awe as her well-put-together mother crumbled before her eyes. "I'm doing all right, Faye. Thanks, um, for asking."

Rob looked at his wife with questions in his eyes, but Karol could offer no answers.

The reverend stood and smoothed the pleats in his pants. "Faye, I'm going to go on inside and see how Dee and Neal are making out, all right? If you need me, just holler. You know I'm here for you. I'll be praying." He turned to the rest of the group. "Nice to meet you, Eric and Faith. Rob and Karol, always good to see you. If nothing else, I'll see you at service in the morning."

Rob stood and shook the man's hand again. "Oh, yes. They say you'll be bringing the message tomorrow morning. I've heard about your teaching for years. I'm looking forward to it."

Dyanne's father laughed. "Yes, well, don't be too expectant. I've been praying and praying and the Lord hasn't given me a thing to teach yet. I may be learning the sermon right along with you. It won't be the first time. Goodbye now."

Silence descended on the porch again until Karol finally got up the courage to break it. "Faith? Dad? Is there something I should know? It's obvious that you all know each other. But it seems like there's more to it—"

"There is," her father said. He looked over at Faith and swallowed hard. "Faye—Fallon—was my first wife."

My name is Indigo and I was conceived of secrets. Even now, they are growing under my skin, things that humans aren't supposed to be able to do, things that no person is supposed to know. When it rains, I smell blood, I remember things done in the dark. Things still being done. I wonder now about my beginnings, if my mother really died when I was born or if her life was taken in payment for mine. Today is my birthday and though it isn't raining, I smell blood.

Karol sat on the edge of her porch, reading the words that had come to her so many years before. She'd thought then that she was making them up or that they'd made themselves and grown inside her, finally bursting inside her mind. Now, she wasn't so sure. Perhaps a piece of Indigo was her, a child born of secrets.

There were things children could never know about their parents, even grown children; hearing her father admit that he had been married to someone else before her mother, however, was more and less than Karol had ever expected. Seeing her mother dissolve into tears and beg Fallon for forgiveness sent Karol's mind into a whole different plane.

*This can't be happening,* she thought.

But it was.

Not only had her father been married to someone else and no one bothered to tell her, but obviously Karol's mother had done something wrong. Something terribly wrong from the look on Faith's face. The sound of her voice.

"I am so sorry, Faye. I was young and greedy. I didn't understand what marriage was, what I was doing. I didn't mean—"

"I know." Fallon's eyes were cold but somehow caring, too. With the same bearing she'd had for all these weeks of living next door to her ex-husband's daughter and playing with his grandchildren, Fallon comforted the woman who had obviously taken so much from her. The woman who had so often had nothing to give Karol.

Karol looked away for a moment, wondering if she needed to apologize, too.

*All that time Judah spent with her. So many afternoons. How painful it must have been....*

It was painful even now, Karol knew from the way her father looked at Fallon. And how she refused to look back.

"It was my fault," he said softly. "I should have been stronger. I should be stronger now. It seems as though both of us—Faith and I—were changed by what we did. For the worse. And somehow you were changed for the better."

Fallon stood up taller. She smiled. "God did that. The changing. It didn't come for a long time, though. A long time after you left me for that pretty little grad student. The one who could make babies, something I could never do. She was smarter, prettier, had more money. And she even had a plan for your life. Well, nothing worked out for me until I realized that Jesus had a plan for mine. Do you two know that yet? That Jesus has a plan—that He had a plan, even in all our mess?"

Rob started nodding, the same way he did in church. Karol hugged her knees. She'd hated her neighbors for being someone other than her friends Hope and Singh. She'd been angry with her friends for being less than perfect. And yet, here was Fallon-Faye-or-whoever-she-was sharing the gospel with the people who had turned Karol's life into something else with a few words, the people who had raised her and taught her about love.

Faith began to ramble. "I try to read the Bible. I try to pray. It seems like all I see is my sin. What I did to you, what I did to us. All these years later, it just seems like it was yesterday. Like we can't get past it. Eric—he's never forgiven himself. Forgiven me—"

"I have forgiven you. Both of you. Come here." She waved Eric over next to Faith and took both of their hands. "Father God, I release Faith and Eric from the sins of their past, even as You have forgiven me. I pray that You will bless their marriage from this moment forward and that they will walk before You in spirit and in truth. Bless Karol and Rob and their children for allowing me to come into their lives and see the good that came out of so much pain. Somehow mend the broken pieces of us and create what we all need—family."

"In Jesus' name, amen," Rob said first.

"Amen," Karol managed, only because her husband held her hand.

"Amen," Faith and Eric said together.

"We were planning to sleep in at the hotel tomorrow and head back to Atlanta, but I guess we should stick around and hear your friend preach in the morning. Though I doubt that anyone could preach a better sermon than you just did."

Faith agreed but her eyes were on Karol now. "I'm sorry," she said. "For everything. I should have told you, but when you were young it didn't seem right, and when you were old enough, I guess I was—"

"Ashamed?" It certainly summed up how Karol felt. Who wanted to be the vehicle used to break up someone's marriage? And yet, her father had never been anything but loving to her. Her mother, on the other hand, had sometimes made Karol feel unwanted. Now she knew why.

"Yes. Ashamed. I wanted you to be a good woman. A better woman than I had been. And you are…in spite of me. You're so much like Eric. I guess I never felt like you belonged to me. Maybe I thought God punished me or something."

"That isn't true—" Rob almost jumped out his chair on that one.

Faith smiled. "I know that. It just feels that way sometimes. I did everything I could to get your father, but it never seemed as though I could keep him. His heart was always—" she looked over to Fallon "—somewhere else."

Karol watched as tears welled in her father's eyes. He stood and helped Faith to her feet. "My heart is here now. With you. Faye has forgiven us. It's time we started forgiving ourselves. I suppose I thought that since I'd broken one good marriage, God would never let me have another. I don't know what to do, but we'll go to God ask Him to fix it. I know I can't."

*Me, either,* Karol thought, watching as Mia led a throng of girls chasing after Ryan with canned string. She couldn't fix her own life, much less her parents. This was a lot and in the days to come, she was sure there would be questions and confusion and hurt feelings, but right now, she just wanted to go home, even if that was just a few feet away.

She and Rob got up at the same time.

"Well, I guess Judah is smarter than us. He said you were his grandma and in a way I suppose you are. I don't know what I could have said or done if you'd told me before, but please know that I appreciate how you handled all of this. I don't know if I could have done the same. As always when I'm with you, you have taught me something.

"Right now, though. I think I need to get back to my own family before the kids overturn the tables. Our friends—the ones who used live in this house—have things in hand, but we'd better not stretch them too thin. It's always good to see you. All of you," Karol said before turning to walk away. She'd wanted to hug everyone but decided against it, knowing that she'd probably start bawling.

"It's been a pleasure knowing you, sugar. Your babies and that good man of yours, too. Whether you know it or not, being here has been a healing for my soul. I thought I was done with all this, that there was nothing left of it, but God always knows. Give Ryan another birthday hug and tell him not to spend all that money I gave him in one place. I'm going in to check on Dee Dee. See y'all at church in the morning."

Already on the stairs, Karol nodded. Her parents were still standing together, embracing. She waved to them and stepped onto the last step when the front door banged open and Neal ran past them, taking two stairs at a time, with Dyanne in his arms. Her nightgown fluttered in what seemed the only wind.

Dyanne's father followed with a grim look. He dragged Fallon toward the car.

Karol tried to ask what was wrong before they pulled away, but only one word echoed back as they drove off.

"Pray."

## To-Do

- Call Mommy

- Buy a tree

—Dyanne

## Chapter Seventeen

Dyanne knew when she woke up that something was wrong. Very wrong. She only had to call Neal's name once and he was there.

"I'm bleeding," she'd said softly. "I should have called the doctor. They warned me about spotting. It might be nothing."

Her heart wasn't in the words. She stood in the bathroom, looking in the mirror and saw the same face Dyanne had seen her mother make too many times. She was sorry now that Neal had to see it.

The heat outside had been surprising. Stifling. And then a little breeze had come, as if just for her, as her husband bounded down the stairs and gently laid her in the car. At the hospital, they'd confirmed what Dyanne already knew—she was losing the baby.

Now, a week later, she was still losing the baby. She'd decided against the procedure that would have scraped her womb and sent her home empty. The doctor didn't think it was a very good idea.

"You can pass it naturally, but I don't think you should. There could be infection. I'll have to have you come in each week and check your hormone levels to be sure that everything is gone."

Neal had fought with her about it, but in the end they were both glad that Dyanne had chosen to go home and let the losing go on. She realized now that what had happened to her mother—to her parents—hadn't just been the miscarriages, but this never-ending losing. On television, it looked so simple, the way women fell off horses and crashed their cars and "lost" their babies. In real life, it wasn't that simple.

All they had left now was the memory of the positive test, the memory of the doctor letting Neal put the stethoscope to Dyanne's stomach to hear the heart too young to be seen on the ultrasound. At the hospital, they'd asked to do a final scan, but Dyanne had declined that, too. She'd been waiting to see the beating heart, the forming limbs…. She couldn't take the finality of the empty sac the machine would reveal. What she'd seen and felt had been enough to tell her all she needed to know—her baby was gone.

Worse yet was the wardrobe of maternity clothes that Dyanne had bought the week before. Though her pregnancy had started quietly, growing beneath her flat stomach without her knowledge, her clothes were getting tight in places and she'd had a nightmare about showing up at one of Fallon's tour stops in Neal's T-shirt and shorts. A trip to Governor's Square Mall's only maternity store had fixed that. She'd even gotten a bathing suit.

Now she was folding it all and packing it up, the way widows did with the ironed, starched shirts of their husbands who had left for work some morning and never come home. Dyanne hadn't been happy about the baby at first, but she'd come to love her. In her mind, it had been a girl, with Mia's hair and Ryan's heart. Anya Christine. The name had come to her in a dream on the day of Ryan's party, minutes before she woke up to her worst nightmare.

Neal and Fallon had let up a little on hovering over her. She'd gone to church this morning to hear the sermon that her father had been supposed to preach the Sunday before. Neal had begged him to go and even tried to drive him to the church, but Dyanne's father wouldn't budge.

"I'm only leaving the room because she's your wife and the two of you deserve some privacy. There's no way I'm leaving this hospital. No way."

And he hadn't left. He and Fallon had been there, both at the hospital and now. They'd continued working on the book while she was at the hospital and had even faxed pages to Steve Chaise which had earned a hearty approval. Ryan had come each day with muffins, books, cards and finally this morning, another copy of the book his mother had given him for his birthday appeared.

Dyanne set aside the maternity jumper she'd been folding and picked up the book again. *Indigo Dawn.* She liked the title and knew Ryan had, too, though the boy liked his titles long and wordy.

The doorbell rang downstairs, disturbing her thoughts. The bell rang often now, bringing scores of strangers from the church and houses down the next road. It amazed Dyanne that people she barely knew could care so much about what happened to her family. Well, to her and Neal. It didn't seem like they really qualified to be called a family. Not anymore.

Still, she usually listened to see who it was and upon not recognizing the voice, shut the door to her room just loud enough for Neal to hear. He had a whole speech worked out now, smiles, apologies and all. This time, however, it was a familiar voice. Karol's voice. Dyanne stood and walked to the door, but she didn't close it.

Company was the last thing Dyanne wanted, but for some reason, she felt Karol had earned the right to come and sit between the stacks of unused maternity clothes. Though they'd started off on the wrong foot, she and Karol had a lot more in common now than they had at first: Ryan, for one thing. Motherhood, for another, however short-lived Dyanne's membership to the mommy club had been. Karol had brought her papaya for morning sickness and special wrist bands for vertigo. She'd answered all of the midnight questions that didn't warrant bothering the doctor. She'd been just happy enough when hearing the news to make Dyanne feel happy, too, instead of guilty. And now, she looked just sad enough to make Dyanne start crying. Again.

And Karol didn't try to stop her from crying. Instead, she walked inside with arms flung wide and tears streaming down her own face. There weren't any words spoken in that moment, yet Dyanne said everything she hadn't been able to say to her husband, her father, to Fallon.

The words came out in sobs instead of syllables, but Karol seemed to understand each one.

"I know."

Dyanne paused waiting for her to say "God knows" like Fallon had been saying every other minute since they'd come home from the hospital, but Karol didn't say it. Though Dyanne knew there was truth in the phrase, she was glad not to hear it again. Not today. Not now.

Karol held Dyanne tight and then let her go. She smoothed back Dyanne's tousled hair and kissed her forehead. She looked into Dyanne's eyes and said what no one else had dared to.

"It's not your fault. Really. It isn't. There's nothing you could have done to change it."

Dyanne buried her face in her hands. How had she known? Did it show that easily? She wiped her eyes and took a step back, supporting herself on the bed.

"What if it was my fault? I was ungrateful. I didn't want her. I wasn't happy. Maybe she knew that somehow, you know? Babies know things. At least I think they do. I tried to, you know, talk to her about it. To tell her I was sorry, but maybe she was already gone. I just wish—"

"Don't." Karol was on her again, in a crushing, yet gentle hug. "Honey, don't do this to yourself. Please. Believe me, motherhood has guilt enough on its own, don't go looking for more. You're a mother. It's just in you. Me? I have three kids and I'm still figuring it out. Ryan has learned so much from you. From Neal, too. I know this is hard, but don't let yourself slip into the pit. It's too hard to get out of. Ask me how I know."

Karol did know. Dyanne could see it in her eyes. She'd said things that needed to be said, too. Without meaning to, Dyanne had been blaming herself, questioning if she could ever be a mother. She'd even considered getting her tubes tied and forgetting the whole thing. She had an appointment. The only thing stopping her was the desperate look on Neal's face whenever he thought she wasn't looking. He wanted a child. Their child. Dyanne just didn't know whether her body or her heart could go through what it would take to give birth to one.

"I don't think I can do this, Karol. Keep losing and losing. I don't know how my mother did it. I thought that she was weak, but she wasn't. I am. I think I'm done. Just done with it all—"

"Don't try to figure it all out. Just deal with now. Today," Karol said, placing the stacked clothes into the plastic bin at the foot of the bed. With finality, she closed the lid.

"It's so hard not to," Dyanne said, dropping back onto the bed.

"I know, but you can't try and figure it all out. You'll drive yourself crazy. And you can't afford to be crazy. You have a handsome husband, a great job, a new house and lots of people who love you."

Her job. Dyanne hadn't given much thought to it in the past week except maybe to resent it. She'd put her work first so many times in her life, over Neal, and finally over her baby. During that first day in the hospital, she'd even considered quitting, only she had no idea what else she could do. She obviously wasn't very good at having babies. Instead, she'd just ignored it altogether, despite the deadlines looming just days away, like Fallon's book tour. Not even Neal had dared to mention it.

Karol had no such problems bringing it up. "Now that those clothes are put away, we can get you packed for the tour. Ryan has told me about your legendary lists. I'm sure you have one for packing. Hand it over and I'll get started. Do you want to do clothes or toiletries?"

Neither. "I'm not going, Karol. I have an appointment tomorrow and lots of grieving and groveling to do. Lots of ice cream to eat. I'm not coming out until winter."

Karol scanned the room and picked up a large binder labeled Master Planner. She flipped to the tab for travel. "Yes, you are going, Dee. You've spent months planning this and if Fallon didn't need you, they wouldn't be paying you. You are the director of your department. You're past the worst of it now and if you need the appointment you can go when you get back. You can do this. You have done this. You will do this." She started pulling out drawers in Dyanne's dresser.

Dyanne stared at her neighbor in shock. A scream rose to her mouth and thundered through her lips. She stomped her feet like a frustrated child. "Get out. Right now. You don't know me well enough to talk to me like this. I said I'm not going. You don't understand. Nobody does. I'm going to stay here, in this room and—"

"And what? Die, too? You can't. I won't let you. Look, I know you don't know me well, but you know that I just had a meltdown and have spent pretty much the past three weeks trying to be something other than what I am—a mother. You know that I've lost babies and had postpartum depression and all the other fun stuff that comes with the pink package. You are trying to be something other than what you are—a powerful, smart, businesswoman who has had a very bad thing happen to her.

"You watched my kids without even knowing me. Go on

his trip with Fallon and I'll do the same for you. I'll water your plants, feed your husband, check your mail and clean your house. Whatever. And when you get back, I'll do it a little longer while you climb in this bed in those pajamas and cry your eyes out. Because you're going to do that. A lot. But it doesn't have to be all you do. Okay?"

Dyanne was breathless, though it had been Karol doing the talking. All her excuses, all her pain had been ripped open, but cleansed, too. It hurt, but it felt good. She rolled over to her belly for the first time since she'd been home. It still wasn't flat, but it wasn't quite as round, either. That's what hurt more than anything, this limbo feeling of being somewhere between pregnant and not pregnant. Between a rock and a hard place.

"Okay. I'll go."

Karol dropped down on the bed beside Dyanne. "Good. That speech was the big guns. If you hadn't gone for that, I had nothing left."

The two women laughed so hard that Neal ran into the room to see if everything was okay. When he saw his wife laughing, he froze, looking both pleased and afraid.

Dyanne turned to her husband and smiled. For the first time in what seemed forever, everything was okay.

"We're fine, babe," she said. "Just fine. Come on in."

Her father knocked lightly at the door, but Dyanne wasn't sleeping. Nor was she still so upset that no one could talk to her.

"Come in, Daddy."

The doorknob turned slowly. Her father paused before coming in. "So the reports are true. Dee Dee is up and at 'em. Glad to hear it. You all packed?"

She nodded. "You?"

"I suppose. You know me. I pack pretty light. There's always a washing machine around. Or a Wal-Mart."

Dyanne frowned but this was no time for them to start a debate about shopping. And her father had a point, she'd stopped there a few times herself on the road. "Right. Well, we'll figure it out. Fallon seems pretty pleased that you're going."

"Weren't you going to ask Ryan to go, too? For his birthday?"

That had been the plan, but like everything else plans changed. "I was going to ask, but I heard Rob say something about their kids only going out of town with family members and I felt sort of stupid. We haven't lived here that long and we don't have kids of our own. No matter how much they like us, I doubt Karol and Rob would send their son off with me."

"I wouldn't be so sure. I guess you don't know since you were at the hospital and all, but it turns out that Karol and Fallon are related. Sort of."

Why couldn't things ever be simple? "Sort of? How can you be sort of related? Either you are or you aren't, right?"

Her father smiled. "What about you and Norman, your stepfather? Are you related?"

Oh…that kind of related. "Sort of. I get it now. Well, not really but I get what kind of not-so-related they might be. So was Karol's father Fallon's one love? If so, that's so tripped out."

The reverend cleared his throat. "I don't know if she'd still call him that now. I hope not."

Oh, boy. She'd been avoiding this discussion, the one about her father and Fallon. They were obviously a couple now and though she loved them both and they were far past the age of needing her consent or anyone else's, it was still, well, weird. Neal, of course, found it charming, but what else was new?

"Speaking of your mother. Have you called her yet?"

Huh? "Um, Dad. We weren't 'speaking of my mother.' We were talking about Fallon and some other dude and my neighbor, their almost love child. Obviously you are avoiding the Fallon conversation, too, so I'll go with the Mom thread

No, I haven't talked to Mom. I need to. I want to. She has
called several times. She even offered to come down."

"But you told her not to?"

"Basically."

"Which you didn't really mean and secretly hoped she'd
come anyway because of her undying love for you, but she
has no way of knowing that?"

She chuckled. "You know me pretty well, huh?"

Another smile. "Sort of."

The two shared a brief hug before Dyanne's father slipped
a copy of Karol's book into Dyanne's carry on bag.

"I have one already."

"Read it," he demanded.

"That good?"

"Better. Good enough to be published. It won't fit the new
line, but I think someone at Wallace should see it. Even Fallon
thinks so. God set you up good down this dirt road, sugar.
You're surrounded by writers."

Dyanne took a deep breath and lifted her curtain to look
down on the house next door. The children were planting
seedlings they'd gotten from Fallon. Karol waved up from
where she sat looking on. Ryan turned and blew her a kiss.
She held a hand to her cheek as if she'd caught it.

Her father was right. God had put her in just the right place
at just the right time. It was what happened from here that
worried her.

Behind her, Dyanne could hear her father dialing the
phone. She closed her eyes, knowing who would soon answer.
Her mother.

"Sorry, kiddo. Just giving things a push," her father said,
lifting the phone to his ear.

"Hello? Hey! Yes. I'm here with her now. She's getting
around. In fact, we're heading out of town if you can believe
it. No, I'll watch out for her. I'm going, too. Make her stay

home? Good luck with that. I'll let you tell her yourself." He handed the phone to Dyanne. "Be nice," he whispered.

He didn't have to worry. After experiencing once what his mother had gone through many, many times, Dyanne wouldn't dare be anything but nice. It was the other times, other things she'd said in the past that worried her now.

"Mom?"

"Yes, sweetheart. It's me. I've been so worried. I've called about tickets two or three times. Your father says you're going out of town? So soon? I don't think you should. I don't know, though. Maybe it's best to keep busy. At least at first…" Her voice faded, leaving nothing to fill the silence.

"I'm sorry, Mom," Dyanne said, biting the edge of her nail, long overdue for a fill.

"Sorry? For what? For not calling? Oh, I understand. You're so busy and now, well, sometimes you just don't feel like talking. It's not as simple as people make it out to be."

Dyanne nodded. "I know. And that's why I'm sorry. All those times, when I was younger, I thought you were weak. I wanted you to get up and get over it, to see that you still had me and that meant something. I thought that you all just wanted a boy and that I wasn't enough. Now, though, I see that things aren't as cut and dried as that. Marriage, trying to be a mother… It's hard."

"Yes." Her mother sniffed twice, but said nothing more.

"Pray for me while I'm gone, would you? I'll call along the road. Maybe we can get together in Chicago or Detroit. Oh, and in case we do meet up, I'll warn you that Dad is seeing someone."

"Really?"

"Yes. The author I'm touring with. Neither of them has said anything to me, but it's obvious that they are very close. She's a great person. I think you'll like her."

"I'm sure I will. Your father is a good man. I'm glad for

im. And for you. I was so worried, but it sounds like you must
ave some friends there who really care about you."

Dyanne looked toward her curtains again. "I do."

"Good. I won't hold you. Thanks so much for calling.
Well, thank your father, I guess. And thank you, for what you
aid. I'm so sorry that you felt that way. I guess I was too
aught up in my grief to really understand what you were
eeling. You are more than enough, my sweet. I think maybe
hoped that if I had a boy, he and I could be as close as you
nd your father are—were."

"Are."

"Yes."

"Well, goodbye."

Dyanne said her goodbyes and hung up the phone, glad that
er father had left the room. Though he'd seen her cry many
imes, there were some tears meant to be seen by God alone.

## *Reign Drops*

They spoke the words like
So much rain, soaking into
My dry soul like the
Best prayer.
Drops became sheets
Hail and hurt
What had quenched once
Now overflowed into
My neighbor's yard.
And yet, there is
No amen or selah
Fit to finish the
Grave and beautiful
Truth. To You,
There can be no
End, only another
Beginning.


—Karol
After deciding to let Ryan go on the book tour

## Chapter Eighteen

"So how does it feel to be Mom again?" Rob asked as Karol ran into the kitchen to officially reorganize everything.

"Wonderful, Dad. Just wonderful," Karol said, stopping long enough to kiss her husband on the cheek. "Or can't I call you that?"

"It depends. What do I get out of giving you the right? The little ones are still sleeping." He winked.

Karol hit Rob with a plastic spatula. "No, seriously. Do you mind? I see how I let all of this title stuff mess with my head, but I do realize that it is important to address one another with respect. If I haven't always done that for you, I'm sorry."

"This is getting too much like an afternoon TV show to me. I'll answer to most anything that you call me because I know you love me. It's usually what comes after the greeting that bothers me. So let's shelve that discussion for now. What I want to know is how you feel about all this stuff with your parents. You've hardly mentioned the whole thing—or them—since the party."

"Ryan and Fallon are gone now, so you don't have to worry about hurting either of their feelings. Just watch out for Judah. He's pretty protective about Fay-Ray."

*Don't I know it,* Karol thought. In the days since the Fallon

Gray entourage had headed off on down the road, Judah had been harder to deal with than when Hope and Singh moved away. Mia still had Neal and didn't have any qualms about reminding Judah of it, which didn't help.

Faith and Eric—Karol had no idea what to call her parents now—had stayed overnight and come to church. They'd hoped to see Dyanne's father as the guest minister, but they'd ended up hearing Pastor Newton instead. The sermon, entitled The Legacy of God's Love, was all about the family and the power of passing faith down through the generations. When different families stood at the request of the pastor, Faith cringed. There were people with several generations of strong Christian people, some who'd been instrumental in historical revivals, mission work and charities.

Karol's parents had always taught and been taught that education was first above everything, so to see so many people who had given their lives—and inspired their children to give their lives—to ministry must have been a shock. Even harder for them to swallow were the testimonies of doctors, lawyers, engineers and other professionals who had found ways to express their faith within their fields of expertise. At the end of the service, they'd scurried to their cars, probably half-terrified that giving their lives to Christ would land them in Africa as missionaries.

She'd done all she could to allay her parents' fears, but Rob was no help at all.

"I'd love to tell you that God would never require of you the things you heard recounted this morning, but I can't promise you that. No one can. What I can promise is that if you truly follow after Christ, His desires will become your own and wherever you end up, whether it's in your office in Atlanta or somewhere across the Atlantic, you will have peace. Not necessarily peacefulness, but peace."

That wasn't exactly what Karol's parents wanted to hear.

Fallon's love and forgiveness had obviously been more fun to listen to. Karol tried to get Rob to soften things a bit, but he wouldn't.

"People always try to make it seem like becoming a Christian is going to fix everything. In the spirit, it does. You are hooked up for eternity. In the real world, however, you're in a war, only now you're on the other side. Nobody told me that, so now I tell everybody that. Even your parents," Rob had said gravely.

He looked—and sounded—a lot gentler now, but Karol could understand her husband's desire to shoot straight with her parents about the Christian life. Though there were times when blessing abounded and everyone was in good health and finances were booming, there were also those times that people sometimes leave out of sermons. Hard times. And yet, even in the valleys, God had been there for Karol. Even when she hadn't been able to be there for herself.

And now as she sorted through all the conflicting feelings about her father's first marriage and her mother's role in it, God was still here. The problem was that something else was still around, too, the lingering feeling that Karol had always had, the feeling that her birth, her life had been a mistake. Now she knew a truth worse than her fears, that her life hadn't been a mistake, but the weapon her mother had used to wrest her father away from his wife.

Rob smoothed the hair back from his wife's face. "Are you all right?" he asked, though his eyes revealed that he already knew she wasn't.

To confirm it, Karol shook her head. Everything had exploded and run down the sides. There was nothing left to wait for, no pages left to turn in her story, but Karol still couldn't quite break through the last wall, the one behind her feelings about motherhood, marriage, even her parents. The last obstacle was how she perceived herself.

"Do you think she ever really loved me? Faith, I mean."

Rob pulled Karol onto his lap. "Of course she did. She does. She just has a strange way of showing it sometimes."

Her husband's answer didn't make her feel better, but she smiled at him for trying. "Dad used to be so apologetic. He would give me this look sometimes, like he was just so sorry. It was like grief and guilt all mixed together. It made me feel so sad, even though he was smiling. I guess we always shared that, he and I, a certain sadness."

"Maybe you shared sadness with your father when you were younger, but I see a wonderful joy in you. There is an expectancy about you, even with your mother. Sure, she doesn't always connect with you in the ways you hope for, but you never give up on her. You never give up on me. Don't give up on yourself, either."

Karol slid off Rob's lap and back onto the couch beside him. "What do you mean?"

He took a deep breath, as if gauging his words ahead of time. "This thing with your parents has a stranglehold on them. It has choked their marriage. Faith doesn't believe she deserves to be a mother, so she isn't one. Because of that, you have believed the same lie. Now that you know what happened, the enemy is trying to make you question your very existence. Your purpose.

"I don't care what Faith had in mind or what Eric wasn't thinking about the moment you were conceived, but I do know that neither of them had the power to give you life. Only God could do that. And He didn't do it so your mama could catch somebody else's husband. You are not the evil, darlin'. You are the good that came out of it. And I'm just foolish enough to believe that God wants to share that good with a lot of people."

Karol reached back and grabbed two fistfuls of her hair. She scratched her scalp. Massaged her temples. In a few sentences, her husband had summed up her battle. Her family's battle. In all that she'd been dealing with, she'd forgotten that somehow all of this was a fight to fulfill the purpose God had given her before the foundation of the earth. She might not think much of her mothering skills, but Karol knew there was only one way to win a fight in the spirit.

She slid off the couch and onto her knees. Rob's arm brushed hers as he slid in beside her. Karol waited to see if he would start praying first, but he kept quiet. As the hurts of the past few weeks passed before her closed eyes, Karol began to pray.

*"Father God, You said in the Word that the weapons of our warfare aren't carnal, but mighty, pulling down strongholds and vain imaginations. Release me from the thought patterns I've been trapped in concerning myself and my family. Help me to comprehend the truth that my husband has spoken over me today and walk in the fullness of who I am in Christ."*

*"Yes, Lord,"* Rob whispered in agreement.

*"I thank you God for making me a mother. Forgive me all the times I have forgotten the blessing of having children. Help me to make disciples of Mia, Judah and Ryan. May they go forth into the world and shine for Christ. Bless Ryan and keep him safe. Thank you for giving us the courage and faith to send him. May this trip and this summer set the foundation for his vocation and education."*

Rob put his arm around his wife, stilling her shaking shoulders. Karol's voice remained steady as she continued to pray, asking God to bless Fallon with spiritual children, increased influence and a deep abiding love that would overshadow the scar of her father's infidelity. She prayed for God to give her a closer relationship with Faith and that God would release her mother and father from the thoughts they'd had about themselves and their marriage as a result of their sin.

For Dyanne and Neal, who'd been such a large and unexpected part of God's work in her life this summer, Karol prayed a special blessing for fruit to come forth in every area of their lives and for God to bless them with a child according to His will.

After what seemed a stream of passionate words, Karol fell silent and collapsed in her husband's arms. Rob was usually the lead prayer warrior of the family, but as Karol fell into his arms, she was glad that he'd let her work through this one on her own. Still, it always felt good when he prayed for her.

Her husband didn't disappoint. He put his hand on Karol's head and closed his eyes.

*"Lord, I ask that you bless Karol's writing. Give her a new anointing to write for people in this same stronghold of not feeling good enough. Give her pure words. Honest, true words. Stories of grace and power. May her hurts be healing to others. Put her writing into the hands of the right people who can help her develop her talents for whatever purpose You have chosen. In Jesus' name, amen."*

Karol didn't know what to say. More and more lately, Rob had been pushing about her writing. She'd told him again and again that she was done trying to be published, but as her husband prayed, something flickered in her soul. She couldn't do anything after he finished but guard the small flame that had just been lit. Her first start was one word.

*"Amen."*

Every time the phone rang, Karol jumped. Their last call from Ryan had been three days before, though there had been a text and an e-mail from Fallon.

Karol clicked on the computer and read the e-mail again, still wondering what Fallon was talking about.

Hey, Mama!

Your boy fell asleep after a long day and he mentioned planning to call you, so I'd thought I drop a note to say that he's fine and keeping us all on our toes. Our publisher, Steve Chaise, surprised us by showing up at a signing today and he was very impressed with Ryan. Things have gone in a pleasant but unexpected direction in more ways than one, but we're all going with the flow. Lord willing, there will be good news to share very soon.

:::peace:::

Fay-Ray

When the phone finally did ring, it was Rob. Though she was happy to hear his voice, Karol couldn't help wanting to talk to Ryan. "I read that e-mail again. What do you think Fallon meant?"

Rob's fingers danced against a keyboard on the other end of the phone. "Who knows? This is Fallon we're talking about. I can't help wondering if she's talking about herself and the reverend. We've been doing some heavy praying the past few days. Maybe they're getting engaged or something."

"Wait, Mia. No, I'm not saying that you can't paint. You just need to put on a T-shirt over that top. No…Judah. No running inside. And put that puzzle away if you're going to get on the computer…anyway, yes. That makes sense. I guess Dyanne is all right. She didn't really mention her at all."

"Stop worrying. The boy is fine. You know how he thinks. No news is good news. He only tries to call because he knows you worry. They'll be back before you know it. Look on the bright side. Ryan met Steve Chaise, the publisher of a major corporation in the industry he wants to go into. Not bad for a rising sixth grader, I'd say."

Karol smiled. Not bad at all. "You always help me see good in things."

"Only because you see the good in me. Now go outside and run around with Judah before you go crazy pacing in front of that—is that a beep?"

"Yes! I'll call you later." Karol clicked away from her husband and over to the next line, preparing for either talking to Ryan or getting an engagement announcement from Fallon. What she was not prepared for was the call she received.

"Hello?"

"Hi. Is this Karol Simon?"

Her heart beat faster. "This is she. Is this about my son, Ryan? Is he all right?" Karol grabbed her purse, trying to remember where the group was touring today. If it was Atlanta like she thought, she could be there in five hours, maybe four…

The man on the phone laughed. "Ryan's just fine. I saw him yesterday, in fact. Let me introduce myself. My name is Steve Chaise. I'm your neighbor Dyanne's boss. I've been so intrigued by your son that when I found his mother had written a book for him I knew I had to read it—"

"What?" Karol balled the front of her blouse into her hand as she tried to comprehend what this man was saying? "You read the book? My book?"

"Yes. In fact, I have it right here. *Indigo Dawn,* correct? There would be some editing required and change in the book's format, but our company would like to publish your book."

Karol had always thought that if she got a call like this, she would drop the phone and scream or do some kind of silly dance. Instead she stared at her refrigerator trying to think of something, anything to say. Joy and fear were running neck and neck inside of her.

"Mrs. Simon? Are you there? Do you understand what I'm saying? I'm offering you a publishing contract. Now if you'd like some time to think about it, that's perfectly fine.

In fact, I recommend it. When Dyanne gets back, you can talk to her more, but we will need an answer by the end of the month. Do you have a literary agent?"

She managed a reply. "No, I don't. I tried to get one before, but didn't get any takers."

"No problem. You have an offer now, so you should have lots of interest. Again, talk to Dyanne. She'll know who to recommend. I have to go, but I enjoyed the book so much that I just had to give you a call. By the way, are the kids calling you Mom again yet? Dyanne told me how you two got to know each other and how Ryan ended up helping her out on Fallon's book."

How embarrassing. "Yes, they're calling me Mom again, but they were a little scared at first. I went a little crazy with that 'Mom's the Word' thing. I'm not proud of it."

"It worked, though. You wrote a book, made friends with your neighbors and got your son experience that a lot of college grads would kill for. I think the whole thing was pretty genius. In fact, if you decide to sign, what do you think about a two-book deal? One fiction and one nonfiction. The second book would be *Mom's the Word: 21 Days to Reclaiming your Name* or something cheesy like that. I'm no good with titles, but you get the idea, don't you?"

Karol slumped against her fridge. "Yes, I do. And I don't know what to say. I'm not really proud of how things happened, but I guess…"

"I understand. It's a whole lot at once. That's how it goes, you know. You go years with nothing and then bam, the flood. Anyway, I hope you come on board. Dyanne and editorial will take it from here. Nice talking to you."

"And you," Karol managed before sliding onto the kitchen floor. Meeting a bestselling author like Fallon had been as close as Karol ever thought she'd come to a book deal. This was too much.

Rob's prayer from that morning came to mind.

*"Lord, I ask that you do exceedingly, abundantly more than we can ask or think regarding Karol's writing. Give her favor with people who can help her fulfill her purpose. In Jesus' name, amen."*

She pressed the number for Rob at work and waited for him to pick up. When he did, the shout Karol had been waiting for finally came out of her mouth. Both the kids came running. Karol waved them off, mouthing that she was just okay. They stood still, but didn't leave.

"What is it?" Rob asked. "Are you okay?"

"I'm more than okay. You won't believe who just called me."

"You're right, I won't. Tell me."

"Dyanne's boss. He wants to buy *Indigo Dawn* and possibly a nonfiction book, about the Mom's the Word thing—"

There was a thud at the end of the line and lots of moving around.

"Rob? Are you there? What are you doing?"

He picked up the phone again. "I'm here. Just doing my victory dance is all. I've been waiting to bust that move for a long, long time."

"Well, I don't know. He said there would have to be changes and I need an agent and—"

"Stop it. God brought us this far. We'll get whatever you need. You just starting flexing your signing arm, Mrs. Author."

Karol called the children to her, thankful for once that they hadn't listened to her. She hugged them close and handed them the phone.

"Here. Talk to Daddy."

As the children held their ears close to the phone to hear Rob's version of the story, Karol sat up on her knees and lifted her hands.

*"Thank you,"* she whispered. *"Thank you."*

## *To-Do*

- Detour from Baltimore to NY to see Dr. Ross

- Continue taking prenatal vitamins—just makes me feel better

- Talk to Dad about him and Fallon

- Make sure Ryan is getting enough rest

- Check sales

- Follow up with thank-you notes for first leg

- Buy ticket for Neal to meet us in NY

—Dyanne

## Chapter Nineteen

"Do you feel any better?" Fallon asked as she rubbed Dyanne's back.

With a plastered-on smile, Dyanne whispered through her teeth. "Don't worry about me. This is all about you. These people are here for you— Yes, I am her publicist. Radio interview? How about two o'clock. Yes, I remember where it is. We'll be there. Thanks."

Fallon scrawled her name across the next book that Ryan held open for her. "Thank you," she said, holding the reader's hand sincerely. "Thank you so much for coming out."

There'd been a rush of people at the table, thirty or more, and everyone had questions. By now they had things down to a science. When things calmed down, the reverend walked through the store and passed out flyers directing people to Fallon's signing. Ryan stacked the books, held them open and slid in a bookmark after Fallon signed them. And Fallon, well, she was just herself. No putting on there.

She waved to Dyanne's father, who was on his feet with a stack of flyers in his hand. Fallon shook her head. "No, baby. We need to get Dee Dee back to the room to lie down. She don't look right to me, you know? All around her eyes and everything."

Dyanne watched her father's eyes narrow with concern. He'd told her not to come on the trip, and now she wondered if he hadn't been right. Everything had been fine at first, better than fine when they heard the great news about Karol's book. Ryan had burst into the hotel room waving Fallon's cell phone over his head.

"The book! The book! Wallace Shelton wants to publish the book!"

This would have sent most people into a frenzy, but for a book publicist, a well-known author and a preacher who'd published quite a few books in his time, there wasn't much of an initial reaction.

That quickly changed.

"What are you talking about?" Dyanne had been deep in a blissful sleep, the kind she hadn't experienced in quite a while. Ryan had seemed like a figment of her imagination until he bumped into her bed.

Still not quite able to articulate the news, Ryan had turned in circles until he saw his mother's book on the nightstand. He snatched it up and held it over his head. "Mama's book! Mr. Chaise is going to publish it. He wants another book from her, too. A two-book deal!"

The party was on then. Dyanne was up on her feet and heading for the phone in Ryan's hand. She had to get the administrative details. Fallon and the reverend were dancing in a circle to an impromptu rendition of "Ease on Down the Road" from The Wiz.

As Karol explained the details of Mr. Chaise's call, Dyanne calmed her fears and referred her to several good literary agents. She had to cut the call short, though, and run to the bathroom to throw up. Everyone else in the room stopped singing.

That was two days ago and it'd been pretty quiet in their little group ever since.

Dyanne's father put down the flyers and pulled out his

phone, dialing wildly but keeping his eyes on his daughter. She knew who he was calling—her husband. And for once, she was angry about either of them trying to take care of her.

"I've called Neal. He's going to go ahead and get an earlier flight. I hate to ask this, but are you bleeding? He says if you're bleeding I'm to take you to the hospital. Right now."

*Keep it together. You're working. You can't break down here.*

"No, Dad. I'm not bleeding. I am going to get a cab back to the hotel, though—"

"I'll take you!" Both Fallon and Dyanne's father said at the same time.

The reverend shook his head. "No. You need to stay here. There's still another hour in the signing and some of these people are coming from a long way to see you. I'd love to leave Ryan to help, but I can take him with me, that way you don't have to keep an eye on him…."

They went back and forth about who would do what while Dyanne watched the room swim around her. She almost wished that she'd been able to recount the telltale symptoms that her father and Neal were looking for. Instead, Dyanne felt what she'd been feeling since before the "event" was even over—pregnant. It wasn't her body that worried her so much now, despite the morning sickness, nausea, vomiting and other symptoms that were playing a trick on her somehow, but rather Dyanne's mind that worried her.

She didn't want to go to another examination room only to be told the opposite of what her body was saying. When Dyanne thought she couldn't be pregnant, there was a doctor to bluntly tell her the error of her ways of thinking. When she thought that things were going great and envisioned herself as a beached whale on some Floridian shore, a doctor had given another pronouncement: you're not pregnant anymore. Whatever the next doctor might have to say,

Dyanne was sure that she didn't want to hear it. She was also sure that she had to get out of this bookstore and out of this mall now… Right now.

"Oh, goodness, Kelvin. Where is she going? Look at her swaying like that. Come on, Ryan. We're all going. I'll run and tell the manager that I'll have to reschedule. I don't think there are many books left anyway."

Dyanne would have normally insisted that Fallon stay until the last second of the signing and until every book was signed. This time, she couldn't do anything but hold on to her father and put one foot in front of the other.

As they headed for the entrance, the manager flagged down and thanked them for such a great signing.

"We sold out," he said. "Best signing we've had in years. Please come back anytime."

Dyanne managed a smile and nod before staggering out of the store and into a flood of strangers. There were people moving from every direction, most of them families with young children. In each little face it seemed that Dyanne saw the little girl from her dream. Anya Christine. And yet none of them were her. They couldn't be. Dyanne's baby was dead. And if she didn't get a grip on that fact, she wondered if she might not lose her mind. In a glimpse, she finally felt the full weight of what her mother had gone through again and again.

The air outside was hot but nowhere near as thick and humid as in Florida. Dyanne stopped on the way to the parking lot and held on to a pillar to catch her breath.

Her father's forehead knit together. "I think we might need to go to the hospital, Dee. Just to be safe. How long has it been since you had your hormone levels checked?"

Dyanne tried to think. "Two weeks? I missed that last appointment when we left but we'll be home Friday."

"No. We'll find a lab here. I'll call your doctor. We need to make sure that the hormones are dropping and that everything is clear. If anything is left then there can be an infection. It could be bad."

As they piled into the car, Fallon held a hand to Dyanne's forehead. "No fever but the chile looks as ripe as a melon. If I didn't know what I know, I'd say she was still—"

"Shhh…" Ryan finally said. He'd been quiet through most anything, reading between lines. "Just let her go to sleep."

Dyanne closed her eyes and curled up in the last row of Fallon's hybrid SUV. She didn't want to go to the hospital, but at this point anywhere they could take her would be better than how she felt now. She closed her eyes and offered up a short, but effective prayer.

*"Lord, help me."*

When Dyanne woke up, Neal was there. She blinked a few times to be sure, but it was actually him.

"Either I slept a very long time or you got on a very fast plane. I think Dad overreacted. I just got a little green. I guess it's to be expected."

Neal rested his hand on her shoulder when she tried to sit up. "Not really. You shouldn't be throwing up or near passing out. Yes, your dad told me everything. I had the doctor in Tallahassee fax a lab request up here. We'll go out as soon as you feel up to it and have the test done at a walk-in lab."

Technology. There was no way to get away from this. "I don't think that's necessary." What she thought wasn't something Dyanne wanted to say out loud. She didn't have to. Neal said it for her.

"So what, you think you're going crazy? That it's all in your head?"

She was all out of defenses. "Yes. That's exactly what I think."

The room, which Dyanne now realized had contained her father, Fallon and Ryan, emptied out quickly, leaving the two of them alone.

"You aren't going crazy, Dee. You just lost a baby. Things happen. We'll get it sorted out."

Dyanne tried not to panic. She tried and failed. "I'm so tired, Neal. So tired of everything. Who knew that this would be so hard?"

Her husband, always there to support her, lowered his voice. "I'm tired, too. Trust me. We've got to figure this all out. All I care about now is you."

What did that mean? She thought back to the concerns the doctor had when she decided against the surgery he'd suggested. One of the doctor's biggest fears had been infection. He'd said that a surgery then could prevent a surgery after, one that might ensure that Dyane never have children. And this, Neal's hands on hers, his lips on her cheek, was her husband saying that when it came down to it, she was all that he wanted.

If only she felt the same.

"They're publishing Karol's book."

Neal smiled. "Yeah. I heard. You did well with that one."

"Me? I didn't—"

"Sure you didn't. Come on. Let's get over to the lab. They're going to fax results to Dr. Ross in New York, also. He's coming in tomorrow morning."

"He's coming in? For me? How—Neal I think you're totally overreacting. Like I said, it's probably all in my head…." Dyanne said as she got up and ran toward the bathroom.

A few minutes later, Dyanne leaned against the sink washing her hands. In the next room, she heard something she'd never heard before.

The sound of her husband's grief, heaving from his chest.

## *To-Do*

Nothing. There is nothing I can do.

Pray. Maybe God can do something.

—Dyanne

## Chapter Twenty

Having her blood drawn didn't hurt. The waiting did.

Neal was back in his protector role and all Dyanne could do was watch. "Please. Can you tell us something about the test?"

"We've faxed the results to your doctors. I'm sure they'll be in touch with you soon."

To their surprise, both doctors called not long after the appointment. Both seemed concerned.

"Take her to the hospital, just to be sure. Her numbers are way up. It could be retained tissue. It could be something else."

Neal was tired of something else. "Like what?"

The doctor paused, probably thinking of his malpractice premiums. "There's no way for me to be sure. I can't make a diagnosis without seeing her. There are a number of possibilities. Ectopic pregnancy among them—"

"What?" Dyanne didn't know which word hit her hardest: ectopic or pregnancy. "There is no pregnancy. You looked at everything. My hormones went down—"

"I'm sorry this happened while you're away. Go to the hospital. Perhaps I can recommend someone where you are once a diagnosis has been made."

While Neal drove, Dyanne looked up "ectopic" on her

BlackBerry, which had finally come back from being repaired just in time for the trip. A friend in college had had one of those tubal pregnancies, but Dyanne couldn't remember exactly what they'd done to treat it. What she really couldn't deal with was the possibility that there was still a pregnancy at all.

The other doctor, Dr. Lee from New York, had been Dyanne's gynecologist for all the years she'd been married. He was an old-school doctor, the type that younger physicians rolled their eyes at when he lectured them. The type that the hospital called for to deliver the babies that no one had been taught to deal with. He knew things that weren't in books, things that could only be learned by living. He'd also been telling Dyanne for five years that she ought to go ahead and have a baby. His accent, a motley brogue from around the world, fell heavy on her ears after every annual appointment.

"You work too hard, Dyanne. You're getting angular, bony around the neck. Don't let this city get to you. It'll make you all pointy and sad if you let it. Make the time. Move to the island. A girl like you likes to win and won't let up until she does. You would have made a great doctor, you know. But since you aren't one, have a baby. The world has too many books as it is."

Dr. Lee's words and the frequency with which he'd said them, came back to Dyanne now as the man's voice echoed out of Neal's closed phone.

"Got yourself a babe there did you, Dyanne? I'm so proud of you. The both of you."

A sob choked in Dyanne's throat but she choked it back down. She loved that old man, but sometimes he could be cruel, so cruel. The look on Neal's face said that he thought so, too.

"We had a baby, Doc. Lost it. We don't know what's going on now. Dee's got some tissue or something in her tubes. I don't know."

"Hmm…I don't know. That's not what the labs say to me. Is she bleeding?"

Dyanne spoke up. "No."

"When you get to the emergency room have them do a scan, both inside and out. I'm a bit off my game these days and older than even I think I am, but I'd wager that you two have a surprise waiting for you at the hospital. I'll ring the driver and we'll start heading your way."

"Please don't. I don't know why Neal called you. I know you're heading toward retirement now. I had planned to come up for a check, just for my own peace of mind, but there's no reason—"

"You, dear, are reason enough. Those gifts you get me every Christmas give an old man something to look forward to. The fruit of the month just arrived—organic cherries. They're like candy. I'll bring some. Now drive safe and don't worry."

For some reason, Dyanne really wasn't worried. If there was one thing that all of this was teaching her, it was that she was not in control. Neither were doctors, husbands or book publishers.

A text appeared on her phone.

KSimon: Praying 4 u !!!

Dyanne.Thorn: Thnx

She'd also learned that friends didn't always come from the places you expected. And that home is where the heart is. And right now, her heart was back in Tallahassee in Fallon and Judah's herb garden waiting for some summer rain.

*Rain on me, God. Give me something. You said to trust You, so I will. I just need You to come with me. To show me what You want me to see.*

When they arrived at the hospital, Dyanne's father, Fallon and Ryan were already at the emergency room. Neal had probably called them somewhere in all of this, but Dyanne had missed it. Either way, she was very glad that he had.

"Daddy." She buried her face in her father's shirt before being called back to a triage room. Neal seemed upbeat and cocky again and assured everyone—meaning Fallon—that everything would work out.

"Doesn't it always?" he asked.

Dyanne couldn't argue with that. It was just what it took for things to work out that worried her. She didn't really want to be the vessel God used to make things okay.

*And why don't you?*

Hmm...good question. Fear. There was no other way around it. Dyanne was deathly afraid. Of what she wasn't quite sure, since she'd already tried to get pregnant, gotten pregnant when she wasn't trying and lost a baby all within a few weeks. She wondered if it wasn't the fear of not being able to have any children. That would have been reasonable, but she'd almost eliminated that possibility herself before coming on this trip. If she was honest, she'd probably have had the surgery already if she'd stayed at home instead of coming with Fallon.

So if she wasn't scared of losing the baby or not having any more, there was just one more thing to deal with: Dyanne was afraid of God.

*I just don't always know what You're going to do. I know Daddy says I'll understand it when I get to heaven, but I guess I want to understand it now.*

After getting her vital signs and asking several questions, the nurse sent Dyanne back out to the waiting room. When she walked out, Ryan grabbed her hand first. He hadn't said much in all of this, but now his eyes were filled with purpose and determination.

" '*Faith is the substance of things hoped for. The evidence of things unseen.*' " He let out a breath and released Dyanne's hand. "I was supposed to tell you that. I think I was supposed to tell me that, too."

Before she could respond, the nurse called Dyanne back one last time and gave her the shock of her life.

"All done. You can sit up now," the nurse said, patting Dyanne on the shoulder.

The ultrasound that Dr. Lee had recommended had sounded harmless, but it had turned out to be quite the adventure. Neal laced his fingers in hers as the nurse stepped into the hall.

"It looks like your doctor has arrived," she said. "I'll let him go over the scans with you. Good luck!"

Good luck? Sometimes people said the dumbest things. Dyanne made a mental note not to use that phrase in these types of situations. She'd take one of Fallon's "God knows" over that any day.

Dr. Lee walked in with his usual pep. Only his eyes, set back deeper in his face since they'd seen him last, and his hair, a much brighter white than Dyanne remembered, gave away his age.

"Ah. The newlyweds. Come, come. Let's see what we have. Cherries?" He patted his pocket.

Neal looked as if he wanted to throw up. He had a thing about not eating in hospitals. Fruit from an old guy's pockets was probably out of bounds, too. Dyanne shrugged and opened her hands. It was too late to escape the contaminants of the hospital, she figured.

Dr. Lee chuckled. "Good girl." He looked the screen over and nodded. A technician entered the room and helped him zoom in on what he was looking at so that the two of them could see.

Neal saw it first. He dropped Dyanne's hand.

Dyanne covered her mouth.

On the screen and inside Dyanne was a heart.

A beating heart.

"But how?" Dyanne's fingers trembled as she asked the question. Neal held her shoulders gently as he stared, mouth open, at the monitor.

The doctor popped a cherry into his mouth. "A twin, I believe. I had a case like this back in 1972. She'd had no X-ray and went home to carry on naturally. A month later, she was back in my office asking when she'd be thin again. It took a while for me to give her an answer. Later that year, she had a healthy boy. He still keeps in touch."

She fell back against the bed. "Did you say twin?"

"Yes. You lost one, but the other thrived. The hormones went down but now they're back up again. I can definitely see why there was an ectopic concern. But now you know for sure. You're having a baby, pet. You're finally having a baby."

The words rushed over Dyanne like a blanket of water, a sheet of rain after a long drought. Neal was kissing her eyes, her ears, but she couldn't see him, couldn't hear what he was saying.

She was somewhere else, some place still and quiet, the cave where all her monsters lived. In her heart, Dyanne stepped over the threshold and went in, knowing that God was with her.


Airport goodbyes had never been Dyanne's thing. After so many times of leaving Neal behind or being the one left behind, she'd learned how to turn off her emotions and do what had to be done.

Her baby, however, had not quite mastered goodbyes. Rising hormone levels and miraculous news make for messy goodbyes. Thus, the crying…

"Don't cry, honey. Everything is going to be just fine. Your daddy is going to take good care of me," Fallon said, looking a little too convinced. Her hair had grown a little and her earrings had gone from fist-size down to fifty-cent pieces. Dyanne wasn't sure what that meant, but for once, she didn't let it worry her.

"I know it's going to be okay. Daddy knows what to do. It's just that, I'm going to miss you. Who is going to make Green Mama smoothies for me?"

"I am!" Ryan's hand shot up.

They all laughed. Neal put the boy's hand down. "We'll handle that together, sport."

Dyanne shook her head and gave everyone one last hug before starting for the front of the plane. Ryan seemed pretty happy about his first plane ride. His parents hadn't been quite so excited, but they all agreed that Ryan should come home with Neal and Dyanne instead of staying on the road with Fallon and Reverend Kelvin. The two of them had tried to act disappointed when it was decided that they'd go on alone, but Dyanne knew better.

"I know what you're thinking, Dee. Don't worry. I'm a grown woman who can hold her mustard. True enough, your daddy is fine, but the Lord will watch over between you and me. I can't put a hand on the man without feeling bad. Real bad. Believe me, I've tried."

"Hush, Faye. Let's get these kids on the plane," the reverend said, trying not to laugh. "Don't pay her any mind, daughter. You know you don't have to worry about us old folks. You just go home, put your feet up and take care of that baby."

Baby. There it was again. It was on everyone's lips now, but Dyanne still had to force herself to say it. It still seemed so bright and shiny of a word, too big of a dream. The fear that she'd faced at the hospital, the fear that God would somehow pull the rug from beneath her when she least expected it hadn't gone away. Dyanne wasn't convinced that the pregnancy would go to term, but she'd decided that maybe it wasn't just about that—the outcome.

Maybe it was about making a peaceful place for one of God's souls to live inside of her for however long he or she was going to live. Maybe it wasn't about Dyanne and Neal at all, but about something eternal and breathless that she couldn't hold in her hands.

Though she had yet to give birth and wasn't sure that she ever would, Dyanne had learned quite a bit about motherhood.

She'd always wondered how people like Karol had more and more children and somehow managed to love them all. She realized now that every bit of love made more love. She hoped, no prayed, that this love would be enough to get her through whatever came next.

So far it had seen her through thousands of miles of uncertainty. Now it would carry her home.

## *For You*

For you, dancers sway dipping
Moonlight into dark. One heard
Heaven's call, slipped away.
Mother pulse music born, you
Kept her song inside.
And so, in palm shade, high
Tide, we will sing of your
Shadow. We will dance the
Duet made one, clapping
Thankful thunder that
Your smile sings
For us in cloudy hollows.
We will sing of your shadow,
Knowing both given, one
Taken, but none lost.

—Karol
Upon learning about Dyanne's baby

## Chapter Twenty-One

The agent that Dyanne recommended was good. Perhaps too good. While Karol and Rob had braced themselves for a few days or weeks of excitement about Karol's possible publication, the agent had something else in mind altogether.

"So you're telling me that Steve Chaise called and offered you a contract? Over the phone?" the man asked Karol for the second time.

"Yes," she said, hoping they could finally get past this part of the story and move on to what she needed help with, which was basically everything else. With the gentleman quiet for the first time in the conversation, Karol dived in and recounted the rest of the call.

"He offered for one book first and then another. Said a two-book deal would probably be best. Are you still there?"

"I am. Forgive me, but I just find all this a little hard to believe. I've heard that Chaise has had some sort of great awakening, but I truly had no idea. And this book of yours, well these two books, you say that they are for the new faith line?"

It took all Karol had to try and explain. Writing a book was one thing, talking about what she'd written was something else altogether. She had a newfound respect for

Fallon, who kept her words—written or spoken—so read on her tongue.

The man made grunts and pauses throughout her explana tion, stopping occasionally to ask another question. Or two

Already Karol was exhausted and had a feeling tha although he'd come the highest of all Dyanne's recommen dations, this agent might not be for her. In fact, she wondere if she'd take the deal at all. As much as she loved to write this other side, the business side was hard to handle. Sh could see why Dyanne and Fallon were so tough. So resilient Maybe if she were like them, she could tell this man what sh needed and discern whether or not he was the one to help he Ten years ago or maybe even five years ago, she definitel could have done it. Now? She wasn't sure that she wanted to

"Sir? You know what? Thank you for your time. This i really all quite overwhelming. I probably should have though about this a little more before I called you…."

Rob was shaking his head and waving his arms, but Karo didn't care. He wasn't the one standing in the middle of th dusty lane with the crystal slipper, the shoe everyone want but that fits only Cinderella. It looks good in the movies, bu it doesn't feel so great to have someone staring at your toe and trying to assess how exactly they managed to squeeze i where they obviously didn't belong.

"Mrs. Simon, wait. Please. Forgive me. I was caught off guard by your story and hadn't been able to reach Dyanne fo the backstory. Please, send me a copy of your book and an e-mai outlining everything proposed in the call. I will honestly le you know my recommendations whether we agree to worl together or not. Agreed?"

Rob was nodding frantically, but Karol wasn't so sure As Dyanne had pointed out, it takes a team to get to the top of any mountain—or past the cover of any good book Whether she got published now or not, surely the mar would be able to teach her something about the publishing industry. If nothing else, it might be something Ryan could use in the future.

Ryan. He'd completed the front leg of his first flight by now and Karol hadn't been there to offer him gum so his ears wouldn't pop during takeoff or explain how the bathroom works thousands of feet in the air. And yet, it had all happened, regardless of her location. Her son was growing up all at once it seemed.

Rob handed her their last copy of *Indigo Dawn*. She slipped it into a Tyvek envelope while Rob looked up the agent's contact information on the Internet.

Karol gripped the envelope with both hands. "This book. It's for Ryan. Just for him. I'm glad that people like it, but I don't know if that matters. I'm most excited that he liked it—"

"Stop it, will you? It's okay to be scared. This is a big deal. But don't think for a minute that you're fooling me with that humble pie routine. I read everything in that box under the bed. You weren't writing those things for yourself. Maybe you convinced yourself of that, but it isn't true. Somewhere in the back of your mind, even then, you wanted someone to pick up your words and see something of themselves in it.

"Well, that has happened. There's really no way to stuff Jack back into the box. So let's not try. Let's just do what the man said and see where that leads us, okay? It's what you would tell me. What you did tell Dyanne."

Karol shuddered. "Don't remind me. Every time I think of that, I could just cry. Being a busybody like that and forcing the poor girl out of bed onto a road trip? What on earth was I thinking?"

Rob typed up the label and watched it ease through the printer. He accepted the sheet from the feed tray and applied the label to the envelope. Then, he kissed his wife's fingers, one by one.

"You were thinking about what might have happened i[f] someone had come and pushed you out of bed when we los[t] a baby. Or maybe what might have happened if Hope hadn'[t] been here after you had Mia. As much as I envied the close-ness you had sometimes, that was one time I was thanking God for Hope several times a day. You had no way of knowing Dyanne would get sick. And maybe if she'd been at home they might not have known about baby B."

Too many ifs in a sentence were always dangerous, he[r] mother had once said. Though not the most nurturing person, she was right on many counts. "Baby B?"

"You know, twins? Baby A and baby B? I don't know why, but I keep thinking this one we're getting is B?"

Karol had to laugh. "The one we're getting? Do you hea[r] yourself? Don't tell me you've gone baby hungry on me. Mi[a] is finally about to start kindergarten."

"Nope! Helping Dyanne and Neal out will be baby enough for me. Besides, you're going to be a bestselling author, I've got enough kids around here to take care of."

A timer sounded in the kitchen and the two younge[r] children emerged as though they knew they'd been mentioned.

"Are you guys done on the phone, Daddy?" Mia whispered.

"All done," Rob said, waving Mia and Judah into the room. "Now it's all about the two of you. What do you want to d[o] first—library or park?"

Judah turned slowly as though he'd heard something. Karo[l] had thought she'd heard someone pull up or drive away many times in the days since Neal had left, but it was often just he[r] imagination. This time, though, it might her neighbors, bring-ing her son back home.

"Is that Ryan?" she asked following Judah to the window.

"Nope," he said. "It's Number Two and Pops. I guess we're going back to the museum. I wish Fay-Ray were here."

Karol pinched her eyes shut. "Me, too, Judah. Me, too."

* * *

"You're going to have to build us a mother-in-law suite as often as we're coming down here," Faith said with a voice that made Karol wonder if she was kidding.

"If you're serious, Mom, let me know and we'll start building. There's another two acres still to be cleared in the back lot," Rob said in his best project-starting voice. He meant it, too.

*I love that man.*

Before Faith could talk her way out of it, Eric reached out and shook his son-in-law's hand. "Are you serious, son? Because if you are, maybe we should talk about it."

Rob embraced his wife's father. "Let's pray about it, too."

Eric nodded in understanding. "Most definitely. Since our last visit to your church, I have to say that God has been turning our lives upside down. One of the reasons I'm asking about a cottage or something here is that we're really considering selling our place in Buckhead and doing some traveling—"

"We haven't decided anything yet, Eric. Let's not get ahead of ourselves. Anyway, we didn't come for that. We came to celebrate…again."

Mia walked into the center of everyone and twirled her skirt. "You came for me, Number Two? For my recital?" She'd started praise dance classes at the church and her first performance was in a few days.

Faith shook her head. "No, not yet. We'll be back for your birthday, though, don't worry. We came to celebrate Mommy. Fay-Ray called us and told us that Dyanne's boss is going to publish your book—"

Oh, brother. "It's not exactly like that, Mom." Karol paused a moment to see if her mother would let her greeting slide by as easily as Rob's had. Faith's smile tightened, but she made no other move to correct her daughter. Faith didn't sound as though she was ready to go on a mission trip quite yet but something was definitely going on.

Eric looked disappointed. "Oh, no? Faye made it sound as though it were a done deal. Said the president—"

"Publisher," Karol corrected.

"Whatever. The head of the company called up and offered you a deal. What's the problem, Karol? You've been writing books since you were four years old. Words are what you love. When you were fourteen and keeping that rat's nest of paper under your bed and you refused to throw it away, I believe your argument was that you made sense on paper. Has all that changed?"

For a man who didn't talk much, Karol's father suddenly had a lot to say. Maybe too much. Judah and Mia looked quite amused at the little scolding Karol's father was giving her. Even Rob had some kind of goofy I-totally-agree look on his face.

"That hasn't changed, Dad. I still make sense on paper. I've just learned how to make sense other places, too. I'm not saying I won't take the deal or anything. I'm just saying that I won't get all caught up in it and drive myself crazy like I did last time."

Ouch. She'd said it. Until now, even Karol had missed it. When the possibility of publication came before, Karol had thrown herself into it with everything she had—and some things she didn't have—only to have her hopes dashed when the company went out of business six months before her release date.

The differences between that small publishing house and what Karol was being offered now was huge, but underneath it all she knew better than to truly trust anything or anyone in the publishing game. She'd been down this road before.

*Trust Me.*

Rob smoothed over the silences. "Well, whatever you're here for, come on in."

Once inside, Karol sent the children off with her father and invited Faith to the kitchen table to talk.

"So you talked to Faye, huh? Have you all been keeping in touch?"

Faith picked imaginary lint off her summer sweater. This was going to be a long morning.

"They're fine. In fact, we just talked to them today."

"Great. Where are they headed next?"

Faith frowned. "They didn't tell you?"

"Tell me what? I talked to them at the airport this morning. They were seeing off Dyanne and Neal. Ryan is with them, too. Where did you talk to them?"

"They're getting married. On a Ferris wheel or something crazy. I'm sure Faye will have mangoes in her bouquet, too. They're something else. I don't know if I'd do it again at this age, but they definitely are happy. I say more power to them."

Karol threw her head back and laughed. "Me, too, Mom. Me, too."

The first time Karol had seen Dyanne arrive next door, she'd been very unhappy about it. When the rental car drove up this time and Dyanne got out, Karol had very different feelings.

Ryan ran to his parents and clutched them around the waist. He had a big smile, but the red streaks in his eyes told the rest of the story. Sending him along may not have been the best idea, but they'd all learned something.

"Thank you for letting me go. I learned so much. When you go on tour, Mom, I'll know how everything is supposed to go—"

"We're just glad you're safe," Karol said, holding her son close. Her eyes, however, were on her neighbor, gingerly exiting the car.

Rob took Ryan by the shoulder and hugged him to his side. "Go on, Kay. Talk to her."

She swallowed hard and stepped across the grass, no longer noticing the line that marked their two properties. The manicured grass had settled back into its natural pattern and the wildflowers the landscapers had so diligently pulled up were starting to bloom. From the look on Dyanne's face, she was starting to bloom, too.

Neal waved to Karol and started over to Rob and Ryan. The younger children had been occupied inside with their grandparents, but at the sight of Neal, Mia came squealing out of the house and bounding into his arms.

"There you are!" she screamed, making everyone laugh.

Karol and Dyanne stared at each other for a long time, both with satisfied, yet sad smiles.

"I'm sorry I pushed you to go. I'm sorry about everything. I got it wrong, but I meant the best."

Dyanne shook her head. "No, I'm glad I went. I got to see my old doctor and some of the things at the start of the tour really did require my presence. Now that Dad sees how things work, I think he'll be able to handle Fallon from here on out."

*I'll say,* Karol thought.

"About those two. You might want to give them a call once you're settled."

"Any reason? Is something wrong?"

"I wouldn't say that. Just give them a call."

Dyanne raised an eyebrow. She rested back against the car.

Neal stopped midsentence and kissed Mia's cheek. "Miss Dyanne is going to be a mommy. I have to take her inside so that she can rest. Do you understand?"

Mia nodded furiously. When Neal walked off, the little girl began to clap her hands. "They're starting a new tree, Daddy!"

Rob swallowed and waved for Karol to come home. "Yes, baby. A new tree. Isn't that wonderful?"

Karol held up a hand to Rob to signal she was coming, but she stayed right where she was. "I just want you to know that I'm sorry for how I treated you at the beginning, when you first moved in. You know, sometimes the grass always looks greener on the other side, but we've all got something to deal with. I'm so thankful that you looked past my actions and became my friend. Now go and rest. I'll leave you goodies on the porch whenever I go out. I'll e-mail you funny pictures. On Sundays, we'll sit on the porch—"

"Don't. You're acting like me now, making lists. Let's just be, Karol. Whatever time you make for me will be a blessing. Now, I've got to go. Big Daddy is waiting." She nodded toward Neal, who was tapping his foot on the porch.

The two women, who had seemed so different when summer began, now looked more like sisters than neighbors. Karol had slimmed down. Dyanne had filled out. Karol had straightened her hair a little. Dyanne's refused to do anything but curl. More than anything, though, it was the peace on their faces that bore the most resemblance. The peace of knowing that sometimes there aren't any answers, sometimes there aren't even questions. Sometimes there is only the enduring truth that Fallon stated so often and so simply—"God knows."

# *Reflections*

I'm not the fairest of them all
No stilettos hold my promise
Between eyes, plain and brown
Rest the diadem, undeserved
Beauty upon my brow.
Perhaps when I am old
And once again young, the
Reflection of You will
Greet me in the panes
Of unwelcome windows.
Until then, when I look
Up and see a queen
Staring back, I
Will blow her my best kiss.

—Karol L. Simon
After the books arrived

# Epilogue

*One year later*

There was a fence now, but it went around two yards instead of one. It kept the puppies out of the road and the rabbits out of the garden. Behind both houses were two smaller homes: one crisp and contemporary and the other rustic and natural. The children had their run of the place, especially the baby. When anybody put her down, that is.

"It's my turn to hold Anya!" Mia smoothed a wayward curl and crossed her arms, pointing a demanding finger at her oldest brother, Ryan.

He wasn't impressed. "Look, I'm watching the baby, okay? And you, too. Just try and keep your clothes clean. As soon as *People* magazine is done interviewing Fallon, the ceremony is going to begin. And nobody wants a dirty flower girl."

"Except me," Neal said, walking up behind them and taking the baby from Ryan's arms. "I like my flower girls any way I can get 'em. Right, baby girl? But you do look really pretty, Mia. I'd hate it if everybody else didn't get to see your new dress. So I guess you'd better do what Ryan says and keep clean. Later on, we'll come out here and play baseball."

Her eyes widened. "Promise? With the real bat?"

He nodded. "And the real ball, too."

A wind kicked up, sending the scent of jasmine and cherries rushing past them. Even the baby leaned forward and reached out her hand, as if trying to catch some of the aroma.

It was a great day for a wedding or at least their version of one. Dyanne had been crushed at first that her dad and Fallon had gotten married without them, but her father reminded her of his own heartache when she and Neal had eloped to the Leon County courthouse in Tallahassee after their college graduation. Dyanne calmed down a bit then, expressing some regret of her own about her shotgun wedding.

After today's vow renewal for Kelvin and Fallon, Neal would probably have to plan a real wedding of his own. He doubted that his parents would come. They'd never been close with Dyanne. Not even now, after the baby. It hurt sometimes to think of it, but Neal didn't think of it much. He was too busy spending time with people who loved him, the new family God had given him, the new friends.

Dyanne and Karol were inseparable now, off to the gym most mornings for Latin dance, lunch and brainstorming about books several times a week. They all ate dinner together most Sundays depending on who was in town, and Neal had started going to church early to clean windows with Rob and the boys. Hope and Singh came to visit often, too, each time teaching Neal and Dyanne some new little thing about their house, which was quickly turning into a home. It was a good life, one Neal hadn't imagined could exist, though sometimes, like today, it was stretched too taut with things to do.

Mia got a mischievous look and started off, with Neal and Ryan running behind.

"Don't do it, Mia. Your dress!"

The little girl—who wasn't so little anymore—had a lead on them and had already grasped a handful of what everyone had feared most when dressing Mia in her pink satin dress.

The cherries.

Dyanne had them planted while she was pregnant and had eaten so many of them the summer before that Anya was nicknamed Cherry before she was even born. Still, the sweet fruit was responsible for many messes, most of them including Mia.

And today wasn't a day for messes. There'd been enough of those.

Just as Mia was about to put the cherries in her mouth, Grandma Faith rounded the corner. With a deft stroke, she pulled the silk handkerchief from the pocket of her suit and confiscated the cherries.

Mia wailed. "Number Two, please... I was gonna eat those!"

"That's Grandma to you and no, you were not going to eat those. You're a flower girl, but I don't see why you can't spread a little fruity love, too. I'll put these cherries in your basket and later, you can eat your fill of them. But for now, you have to stay pretty, so that all the rainbows in your basket will want to come out. They're shy, you know."

"Like me?" Mia asked.

Neal rolled his eyes. If that child was shy, so was Fallon. "Are they almost done, Faith? Is it time yet?"

Though nearly twice Neal's age, Faith had a timeless grace about her. He couldn't help but smile as she smoothed back her hair before checking her watch.

"The interview is far from over, dear. In fact, they want to talk to you next."

"Me?"

Faith nodded as Neal handed his little cherry off to Ryan. She shook her head. "Yes, dear. They want the baby, too."

Already sweating in his tuxedo, Neal tried not to groan. In the months since Anya had been born, there had been numerous stories about the twin who survived and was discovered during Fallon Gray's famous "Legacy of Love" book tour.

Fallon had not only gotten married right after the baby was discovered but written the bestselling memoir, *The Best*

*Daughters I'll Never Have,* in a record nine days and on her honeymoon at that. The memoir of Fallon's failed marriage, infertility and late-in-life love mingled with her love of gardens, children and family had launched the GracePages line and skyrocketed to the top of every bestseller list, which was a great thing for everyone. The downside? Two of the main figures in the book were Karol and Dyanne and little Anya, too. Neal was now known to millions as the Mango Man and sometimes, like today, he just wasn't up for it. Still, he sucked it up and entered the flowerbed that was Fallon's home, wearing his best smile.

When he entered the house, the front room was empty. He should have known something then. He headed into the kitchen anyway, noting that he'd have to get Dyanne if she was a part of this. She knew how much he hated surprises—

"Surprise!"

Neal froze. It wasn't a room full of voices, but one. One he hadn't heard in person for a very long time. He turned slowly. Anya burped as he did.

"Mom?"

His mother kissed him quickly before wrenching the baby from his arms. "It's me," she said before letting loose a mouthful of baby talk so incomprehensible that even the baby turned back to Neal with a funny look.

He shrugged. "They can't help themselves. Be kind," he whispered to his only daughter. He watched the two women, older and younger, in amazement. The shock of seeing his mother hadn't quite worn off.

"How did you get here? What about the interview? Where is everyone?"

"Your dad brought me. He's in the backyard. The folks from *People* are back there. I saw one of them gnawing on a rib. I think Fallon has changed her mind about the attire for the vow renewal."

Great. Neal had figured that Fallon would change her mind about something, which was why he'd tried to just run everything through before the unexpected arrived. When the interviewer pulled up thirty minutes before the family wedding ceremony Fallon and Kelvin had missed out on the year before, Neal had started to worry. Now he started to laugh.

"It is what it is," he said, loosening his tie and stepping into the backyard. What he saw there took his breath away.

All of his brothers, his father, his cousins, friends that Neal hadn't seen since undergrad—they were all there, smiling and waiting. Dyanne was there, too, next to Fallon's pool holding a bouquet of purple hydrangeas. Fallon's bouquet.

"I don't understand," Neal said after withstanding the crush of hugs and handshakes from his family and friends.

Fallon, barefoot and wearing a caftan and a wreath of roses on her head, danced over and gave him a kiss. "You wanted so much for Kelvin and I to have a ceremony. You planned everything so nice, but, baby, we had all the fanfare we needed back on that Ferris wheel in Las Vegas. Then I remembered Dee Dee telling me how you both had to pack up and move right after college and all you had time for was a justice of the peace wedding."

Neal frowned. It hadn't been as bad as Fallon made it sound. "It was complicated. I got a graduate teaching position at the last minute and had to report to campus. Dyanne got her job at Wallace. We had to find a place in New York quickly, which is hard to do. It was okay. We've been so many places since—"

Neal's father cleared his throat. "Don't try to cover for us, son. Your mother and I didn't handle things very well. We thought you were too young and to be honest, we weren't sure that Dyanne was the right woman for you. I'm delighted to say that you both proved us utterly and completely wrong. We're here because we should have been here a long time ago. We're here to celebrate your marriage with you and your friends."

"Thank you, Dad." It was all Neal could think to say. His head was sweating and his suit was sticking to him, but in that moment he didn't feel any of that. He could only feel a weight he hadn't known was there slide off his shoulders and crash into Fallon's pool.

"So this is just for us then?"

Fallon shook her head. "Nope. You know me better than that. You just got the best gifts. Come on out everybody!"

And so they came: Karol and Rob, Eric and Faith, Hope and Singh, Pastor Newton and his wife, half the church and most of the neighborhood poured into Fallon's backyard. Husbands and wives all of them, some still in their work clothes, others in flowing gowns and rented suits. All smiling and holding hands. Ryan filtered through the crowd passing out candles.

When he got to Neal, he apologized for not filling him in. "The ladies made me promise. You understand."

He did understand. All too well.

Pastor Newton's voice filled the spaces between them. "Thank you everyone for coming. We've come out today to celebrate family and the way God made the family— marriage. We thank each of you for coming out to renew your commitments. We commit to you as a church, as a community and as family that we will pray for your marriages and stand as witness today to the love you all share. Light the candles please."

Hope and Singh lit the first candle. They passed it to Rob and Karol. Dyanne and Neal took the flame next and the light continued on, guarded by cupped hands against the evening wind. When Kelvin and Fallon passed the final flame to Pastor Newton and his wife the sun had set and the flickering candles, each held tight by a pair of hands, seemed to dance across the yard. Floating candles were lit in remembrance of spouses who had passed on. They wafted lazily across the pool giving even more light.

Neal looked down at Dyanne, who was holding the baby

while he held the candle. It was all he could do to keep from carrying her home right now.

"I know this is getting pretty romantic, so I'm going to keep it short. Some of you all look pretty renewed already. Let's pray.

*"Father God, we thank you for creating marriage. Please bless each union here. Renew the commitment to love, honor and cherish one another. Where there are strangleholds, bring freedom. Where there is contention, bring peace. Most of all, Lord, bring You. We have so many problems, but You are the answer to them all.*

*"Bless our children. Help us to raise them to love You and to love people. Help us to be vulnerable with one another and accountable to each other. Give us a vision of what You want our families, our church and our community to be. Give us the victory in every area of sin that besets us. Thank you for being the third party in all of our marriages. Pass between our broken pieces now and make us one. Make us whole. In Jesus' mighty name…"*

*"Amen!"* The shout echoed off the water as well as the lingering breath when everyone blew out their candles. All around people were hugging and crying. It was hard to hear what they were saying, but you didn't have to hear, really. Neal didn't have to hear. He knew. He was about to say it, too.

He kissed Dyanne's cheek. "I'm sorry."

She tugged at his chin and returned the favor—on his lips. "You need to work on your aim. And your apologies. Save them for when they're needed. There's nothing for you to be sorry for."

Neal took Dyanne's hand and started toward Rob and Karol, who'd left Hope and Singh and were moving toward them, too. People held out their hands to take the baby, but Dyanne shook her head.

"I'm sorry because tonight I realized that our not having a wedding was a big deal. I've always acted as though I was the one who's done all the sacrificing, but you've given up a lot, too. You might have had another job if I hadn't packed us up

for Columbia so fast. I made you stop going to church, push
away your friends…. Now those are all the things I need, th
things I love. Your things."

Dyanne wiped away a tear. "Our things. God brought then
all back to me. To us."

In the center of the yard at the edge of the pool, the tw
couples met up. Ryan wriggled under someone's arm an
reached out to take the baby. This time, Dyanne consented
probably because of the way Anya kicked up her heels an
cooed at the sight of Ryan. It didn't hurt that Fallon an
Kelvin were right behind him waving.

"We'll take her back and put her to bed," Dyanne's fathe
said, disappearing into the crowd before she could object.

Now empty-handed, she took Neal's hand in hers an
turned to the couple who had become more than friends, mor
than neighbors over the past year. The four of them touche
foreheads as they came together in a group hug.

"We love you guys," Karol said, winking at Dyanne an
slipping off her shoes.

"Us, too," Neal said, fumbling with his toes to get hi
shoes off. Rob was already out of his jacket and trying to hea
for the pool.

Karol, who had just completed her first book tour an
joined Fallon on the bestseller's lists, gave her husband
playful shove backward and took Dyanne's hand.

The two women ran toward the pool hand in hand, laughin
all the way. The husbands followed, but slowed down to watc
as their wives tumbled over the edge.

"Mom's the word!" Karol shouted as they jumped in.

Neal braced himself as the splash rose from the pool an
washed over him in a cleansing wave. He looked up at the sk
and raised a thumb as Ryan had earlier.

*Mom's the word, indeed.*

* * * * *

# QUESTIONS FOR DISCUSSION

1. As the book opens, Karol Simon has lost a best friend, but gained a new neighbor. Her reaction to the new people next door is less than hospitable. Have you ever had a close friend or coworker move away? Were you surprised by the emotions left after they were gone? Did you transfer any of those emotions to the new people who took their place?

2. Rob and Singh are close friends, too, but they deal with their friendship a bit differently than their wives do. How do you feel about the way these two men deal with their concerns about their two families becoming too close?

3. The young mothers in Karol's church are looking for a mentor, but she doesn't feel qualified to give them the answers they need. Yet later, Karol feels compelled to do some of these same things for someone else. What do you think made the difference?

4. Karol's children seem out of control when Dyanne and Neal move in, but they've been fairly well behaved until the neighbors move away. Has your family ever gone through a "phase" where things just seem off-key for a while? How did you deal with it?

5. One of Karol's poems is "Jesus Be a Fence." Have you ever had problems with your neighbors or wished you had more privacy? Do you like fences in general or do you think they are barriers? Explain your answer.

6. Karol's mother refuses to be called Mom, but she calls her husband Pops. What do you think about spouses referring

to each other this way? How does Faith the Second use her name to shield herself from being shelved into a particular role? Does she feel the same way at the end of the book?

7. When Karol realizes what her husband and Singh have done, she is very angry. Do you think she handles the situation well? What might you have done differently given the same circumstances?

8. Fallon Gray is Dyanne's biggest author. She comes to Tallahassee to write a book and instead she finds God writing on her own heart. Is Fallon someone you'd want to meet in real life? Did she say something in the story that spoke to your heart? If so, what was it?

9. When she meets Karol and her children, Fallon has a sense that they are "always people," the kind of folks God gives you who always understand who you are. Do you have these types of people in your life? Did you hit it off with them immediately when you first met them or was it a gradual process?

10. In her fervor to be prepared for the baby she wants to have, Dyanne makes a very expensive impulse buy that causes an uproar in her marriage. Have you ever bought something that you regretted later? Did you return it or keep it? Has anyone ever bought something with part of your money without telling you about it? How did you feel?

11. Karol's oldest son, Ryan, starts to bloom when the neighbors move away. How does his emerging adolescence affect his perception of the loss of the neighbors? What do we learn about Karol through Ryan?

12. Rob is a patient and kind husband, but as he tells Karol often, he is also a man. In all their ups and downs, what does Rob seem to want most from Karol? How does he differ from Singh? Could you imagine any man you know giving his wife twenty-one days off from motherhood?

13. Though she wants more than anything to have some time to herself, when Karol gets that time, she's unsure at first what to do with it. What would you do with twenty-one days off from your responsibilities? Is there a passion you've set aside for someday?

14. Karol once thought her friends Hope and Singh were perfect. In the end, she realizes that only God is perfect. Have you ever set someone up higher than he or she could live up to? Did you still love them when they failed to meet your expectations? Have you ever been the person who had a fall in someone's eyes? What is your relationship with that person like now?

15. Both Karol and Dyanne think the grass must be greener on the other side. Do you think that both women come to respect one another in the end? How does Dyanne help Karol find her old self again? How does Karol help Dyanne discover the person she wants to be? Which of the books in the story would you want to read first—Karol's or Fallon's?

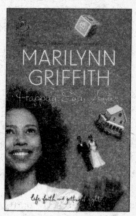

*Love Inspired*

With an orphaned niece and nephew depending on him, commitment-shy Clay Adams calls upon nanny Cate Shepard to save them all. With God's help, Cate's kind, nurturing ways may be able to ease the children into their new lives. And her love could give lone-wolf Clay the forever family he deserves.

Look for

# Apprentice Father
by
# Irene Hannon

Steeple Hill®

*Available February 2009
wherever books are sold.*

LI87515

# REQUEST YOUR FREE BOOKS!

## 2 FREE INSPIRATIONAL NOVELS
## PLUS 2
## FREE
## MYSTERY GIFTS

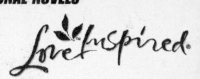

**YES!** Please send me 2 FREE Love Inspired® novels and my 2 FREE mystery gifts (gifts are worth about $10). After receiving them, if I don't wish to receive any more books, I can return the shipping statement marked "cancel". If I don't cancel, I will receive 4 brand-new novels every month and be billed just $4.24 per book in the U.S. or $4.74 per book in Canada, plus 25¢ shipping and handling per book and applicable taxes, if any*. That's a savings of over 20% off the cover price! I understand that accepting the 2 free books and gifts places me under no obligation to buy anything. I can always return a shipment and cancel at any time. Even if I never buy another book, the two free books and gifts are mine to keep forever.

113 IDN ERXA    313 IDN ERWX

| | | |
|---|---|---|
| Name | (PLEASE PRINT) | |
| Address | | Apt. # |
| City | State/Prov. | Zip/Postal Code |

Signature (if under 18, a parent or guardian must sign)

### Order online at www.LoveInspiredBooks.com

### Or mail to Steeple Hill Reader Service:

**IN U.S.A.:** P.O. Box 1867, Buffalo, NY  14240-1867
**IN CANADA:** P.O. Box 609, Fort Erie, Ontario  L2A 5X3

Not valid to current subscribers of Love Inspired books.

**Want to try two free books from another series?**
**Call 1-800-873-8635 or visit www.morefreebooks.com**

* Terms and prices subject to change without notice. N.Y. residents add applicable sales tax. Canadian residents will be charged applicable provincial taxes and GST. Offer not valid in Quebec. This offer is limited to one order per household. All orders subject to approval. Credit or debit balances in a customer's account(s) may be offset by any other outstanding balance owed by or to the customer. Please allow 4 to 6 weeks for delivery. Offer available while quantities last.

**Your Privacy:** Steeple Hill Books is committed to protecting your privacy. Our Privacy Policy is available online at www.SteepleHill.com or upon request from the Reader Service. From time to time we make our lists of customers available to reputable third parties who may have a product or service of interest to you. If you would prefer we not share your name and address, please check here.

LIREG08R